Salivation

Phoenix Mendoza

Copyright © 2024 by Phoenix Mendoza

All rights reserved. No part of this book may be reproduced or used in any manner without written permission of the copyright owner except as permitted by U.S. copyright law.

The names, characters, places, and incidents depicted in this work are fictitious. Any resemblance to actual persons, living or dead, events, or locales is coincidental.

First edition January 2024

Table of Contents

Preface	*i*
The Rockstar	1
Salivation	37
Jonah's Joyworld	59
Blackbird	87
Feeze!	115
The Place	141
Prodigal Son	151
The King of Hearts	173
Absolute Zero	183
Acknowledgments	271

Preface

When I first set out to finish some stories from my past and assemble them into a collection, I did not anticipate that they'd align so neatly upon a theme. I thought the mere fact they were each resuscitated from states of partial decomposition and infused with new electricity so they might live again would be the element that held them together as a unit. Frankenstein's monster, cohesive only because, it contained stories that had at some point been left for dead.

But as I dug through the charnel houses of tattered notebooks and old laptops and hard drives, I was surprised (and delighted) to discover the same obsessive motifs and insistent synchronicity threaded through my best work. I soon realized that any story from my past *worth* being finished, edited, and included in this collection was about the same two things: hunger, loneliness. Hunger born from loneliness, loneliness born from hunger. An ouroboros of wanting and devouring, of consuming one's own tail down to blood-slick bone. A yawning desperation for something—anything —to fill the void of one's own gnashing teeth. Even something hollow. Even something dangerous. The pursuit of connection and the starvation fueling that pursuit were the themes my younger self lived in, breathed in, put pen to paper and wrote about over and over again. I was a lonely, hungry girl, thus, the creation of this collection had been mortifying.

Let's think about that word for a moment, mortify. From the Latin word *mortificare* and the old French *mortifier*, both meaning to kill, deaden, put to death, all of which feed into its contemporary meaning, to humiliate or embarrass. Mortification, ultimately, is a shame so severe that it makes us want to die. This felt like a fitting word for my process—months of delving back into my oldest and rawest work to find pieces worth revisiting. Like digging for truffles, there was a lot of dirt, and a lot of shit. Much of what I forced myself to reread was painful, juvenile, confessional, and ultimately unsalvageable. But where I found loneliness and hunger, I also found rich soil. Black fertile earth to plant seeds in, all of which grew into works I ended up including in *Salivation*.

I am not ashamed of these stories, they do not embarrass me, but this collection is a series of small mortifications, if you will. An anthology of executions: stories I have written and rewritten and carried around with me for so long finally being laid to rest. Shared with the world, imperfect and sewn together from exhumed parts, half-rotten. I've put enormous amounts of care into them, but due to their nature, I have relinquished the expectation of them being perfect.

The truth is, I am no longer a purveyor of hunger and loneliness. I'm older now, married and abundant and living the life I would have eaten my own tail to live back when I first dreamed up these stories. There is not much I want that I don't already have now, so I am ready to let these tales go. Bury them, release them unfettered into the world so that you, my readers, can become the force that carries them into the afterlife.

At the beginning of each story, I chose to include a brief description of its history and origins, since no two were arrived at by the same means. Some have been left nearly untouched, some have been heavily edited, and some have been entirely rewritten, where not a single word of the original incarnation is included in the version you'll find in this anthology. However, each has been embalmed with love. These are characters and concepts I've spent, in some cases, over a decade with, and though they are meeting their deaths with me, I know they will find new life with you.

Speaking of new life: in a literary landscape saturated with saccharine, commodified "queer" romance and cowardly pigeon-toed horror, I am honored to offer you a collection of stories that is utterly lacking in shame. *Salivation* is neither horror nor romance, but instead the corruptible place these two entities compost together to form something else. The stories and characters in this anthology are strange and filthy, profane and tragic, grotesque and ridiculous, unsettling and honest. But most of all, they are fiercely hungry, desperately lonely. They do not apologize for themselves, and I refuse to apologize on their behalf—as an artist, I do not believe in content or trigger warnings. I don't want my readers to feel safe when they pick up this book, I don't want them to know what shadowed corridors or funhouse mirrors they might encounter upon embarking. My sole intention, always, is to make my readers *feel*. Feel hungry, feel lonely, feel revolted, feel shocked. Feel dread upon meandering through this graveyard, leaving roses at the foots of the headstones you grow to love most. For those of you this appeals to, welcome to *Salivation*. Bring a fork.

The Rockstar

I developed the concept for this story back in college. My earliest memories of it are of walking through the empty and snow-flocked streets of Florence, Massachusetts, with the woman who would eventually become my wife, telling her the barest bones of this story. I knew I wanted to write something about an unusual friendship between a man who lost his girlfriend to suicide and the frontman of the band she loved most, though the characters and circumstances changed significantly over the years. I attempted to write it three times and abandoned every version in the early stages. For a decade, I imagined this story was meant to be tonally quite heavy, but when I sat down with it this year and freed it from that weight, it flourished into this version I meant to tell. Here it is–it's come a long way since those winter walks in Florence.

The Rockstar

The Rockstar wasn't hard to find. In the months after Charlotte killed herself (pills, too many for it to be an accident, swallowed with a 7-Eleven Slurpee that came up blue when she vomited one last time on the bathroom tiles), you were insane with grief. You couldn't eat, you couldn't sleep. All you could do was stalk him online.

Zoom in on old pap shots to find out which Starbucks he went to (Belmont Shore), which bars he left plastered on Saturdays (the Bamboo Club, Port City), which park he walked his two fat, blue-eyed husky dogs (Kaisa and Whitney) at (Bixby Park). You learned his haunts, his digs. There was a house, too, that he was photographed in front of all the time (a big stucco monstrosity on the Rivo Alto Canal with floor-to-ceiling windows on the water-facing side).

You memorized the way he smiled for the cameras, how pinched his bloated, washed-up body looked in his stupid leather pants and scrappy fishnet tank-tops, figured out how to spot his ridiculous bottle-black Tommy Lee hair in any crowd. But he wasn't Tommy Lee—he wasn't *that* famous. His band had a smaller, cultier, crazier following. They referred to themselves as Pill Poppers or Poppies because the band was called Percocet Pitch, PP for short, and you always thought that was stupid as hell. A stupid name for a mediocre, milquetoast, mall-goth band that was only popular because the singer was pretty and sang songs about death, and there's a certain sort of devoted sad-girl to whom that shit *really* appealed. You would know. Charlotte *loved* Percocet Pitch.

Charlotte loved Percocet Pitch so much that you never told her you thought the name was stupid or that their music, *yeah,* even their supposedly genius debut record, was overrated and derivative at best. You never complained about the posters papering her dorm room walls or how creepy it felt to lie there in bed with a million tiny versions of the Rockstar glowering down at you with his moody raccoon eyes. You weren't that sort of boyfriend—the kind who insulted the stuff Charlotte liked. All you ever did was roll your eyes a little or turn the music down if she was blasting PP in the car.

Percocet Pitch made her happy, and it made you happy to see her happy. Everyone was happy.

Or so you thought. But then, Charlotte went and killed herself seven months before you were supposed to get married. When you found her, Percocet Pitch's supposedly genius debut record was playing from her old turntable she'd set up on the closed lid of the toilet. She was cold, her fingers already bruised and stiff, and there was a suicide note stained in 7-Eleven Slurpee blue vomit under her flattened cheek.

That suicide note was not addressed to you, or to Charlotte's mother, or to god. That suicide note was addressed to the Rockstar.

———

You lose your job at the real estate office, you lose the house. You move back into your childhood room, and for months, you sit hunched over your old Dell desktop computer, scrolling through sale records of the mansions on the Rivo Alto Canal, comparing every old listing with the collage you've cobbled together from tabloids until you come up with his address. Stacks of unopened boxes tower around you like a castle's fortress wall, some containing neat, cardstock wedding invitations that you never sent, some with samples of table centerpieces you and Charlotte were supposed to choose from. You still have a tab open on your laptop with the Ikea and Pottery Barn gift registration, so you simply don't open your laptop. Each memory is like a gravestone, each gravestone like a finger jutting out from the soil, dirt crusted under the broken, unfiled nail. You're living in a cemetery. You're a rat, chewing on hair, chewing on bones.

You imagine killing the Rockstar, sometimes. Buying a gun from a gun store, walking right up to that eyesore on the Rivo Alto, and shooting him point-blank between the plucked eyebrows when he leaves to go drinking, or get Starbucks, or mosey around the park signing autographs. Other times, you just imagine damaging his property. Throwing a brick through that enormous wall of windows, dousing the whole thing in gasoline before dropping a match. Two husky dogs and so many pairs of leather pants, going up in flames. Maybe you'd get lucky, and the Rockstar would be sleeping in there when you did it. A hundred million Pill Popper girls just like Charlotte waking up to the tragic news, strapping on their Demonia boots and little lace dresses and tiny hats with mourning veils, congregating like flies on a corpse in Bixby Park to cry their mascara right off. Blasting that supposedly genius debut record from their phones.

You decide not to kill him, because of those girls. Those girls are just like Charlotte, they'd kill themselves if the Rockstar was killed. Suicide is contagious, you've heard that before, it's why the police sometimes keep celebrity causes of death a secret even after they know. To minimize the ripple effect spreading out from that single, selfish act. If they won't take mercy on those girls, it's gotta be you. Someone has to care for the Charlottes of the world. You couldn't save Charlotte, but you can maybe save the rest of them.

———

You also decide not to kill him because part of you wants to *talk* to him. Not just make him pay for what he did but make him *listen* to what he did *before* he pays for it. The Rockstar has no idea who Charlotte was, he's too busy partying at the Bamboo Club or Port City to give a shit about his psycho fans, he's too busy living his fat-cat life in his fat-cat house. Too busy profiting off of all the songs he wrote about theoretical death to care about *actual* death.

The Rockstar sings constantly about killing himself. He never did it, though. He just made a religion out of it instead, a religion that spoke to those girls. That's how Charlotte talked about it, anyway. She talked about the Rockstar the way Christians talk about Jesus. She *evangelized.* He saved her, he understood her, he loved her. She could tell because of his music, apparently—it spoke to her rotten, black little soul in a way that no one else could.

That's what her suicide note said, anyway: *no one has ever understood me the way you do, Ritchie (*Ritchie Riot, that was his freaking stage name, unbelievable), *and no one ever will. I suppose that's why I'm doing this. I see no end to the loneliness, unless I was able to be with you, somehow. But I'm not with you.*

She was not with the Rockstar. She was with you. That wasn't enough, apparently.

Thirty pills later, an end to the loneliness. Boxes of wedding invitations. Enough to pave over a parking lot, enough to make an entire fleet of paper airplanes, enough to stick one to every headstone on every grave in some small town cemetery.

You write his address down on one of those unsent invitations, on the front where it says in looping script, *Save the Date!* You don't bring a gun or gasoline or a book of matches. You don't bring anything but yourself, your phone, your bone to pick.

It's wild, how there's no security. You half-expected armed guards, like the Rockstar is the Queen of England, like his hideous house is Buckingham Palace. But there's no one here at all, besides him. You know he's there because a light is on downstairs, and you can see the shape of him moving around through the enormous window as he makes himself a cocktail. You wonder why he doesn't have servants to do that for him, some butler named Jeeves, and hope it's because he's running out of money.

There's a keypad, an automated gate, and cameras. But you don't care about any of that—you're wearing business casual, and you have a clipboard, you look professional. The thing is, you are the sort of guy who can sneak in anywhere, you are so unremarkable and normal that everybody trusts you. White, 5'9", brown hair, brown eyes, handsome but not too handsome. You're not a pretty girl in eyeliner, he's not gonna be worried about you sneaking in to steal his eyeballs and eat them, like Charlotte might have. He's gonna think you're delivering a package. So that's what you say. You dial him using the keypad, and he, not some butler named Jeeves, answers, because the Rockstar is running out of money.

"Hello?" he says, in that voice. Raspy, used. Back in the day, he had a smooth, sexy croon perfect for melancholy death ballads and psycho-sexual wails, but he drank and smoked so hard for so many years that he ruined it. That's why Percocet Pitch hasn't released an album in so long—his voice is shot. You read a bunch of headlines about it, about how he got this thing called "kissing nodes," where swellings developed on his vocal cords and he had to get surgery to cut them off.

He couldn't sing right, not after that. Career down the drain, he has to live on cult movie cameo appearances and car insurance commercials now. "Who's this?"

"Mr. Richard Smith? I'm delivering a package," you say. Richard Smith, that's his real name. So normal, so basic, so pedestrian. Serves his ass right. "I could leave it here outside the gate, but it's heavy. I'd worry someone would steal it."

"Jesus Christ," he gripes, a loud sigh registering as a statically crackle that hurts your ears. "Don't leave it outside the gate. I'll let you in, just a minute."

And as easy as that, you've penetrated the perimeter. His yard is astroturf instead of real grass, and there are tons of dog turds all over it, like he hadn't cleaned up or paid someone to clean up his dogs' shit in ages. Some of the piles are old, fossilized, but you can still smell them, and so can the flies. You swat fruitlessly at them as they buzz around your face, waltzing right up to the concrete porch, like you belong there. Like this is your house. Your delivery route. Your friend. Your girlfriend.

You drop the package, which is just a box of unopened wedding invitations. They land with a resounding *smack*. Inside, the dogs go crazy, barking and flinging themselves at the gigantic window, probably leaving streaks of drool. "Jesus Christ," he says again. You can hear him, his fucked up voice, his kissing nodes. The Rockstar is right there, on the other side of the door.

You stand expectantly on the concrete, knowing somehow that he would come get the package instead of leaving it to fester in the sea-salt and dog-shit air. He's an Amazon guy, you can tell, the sort of miserable dude who orders stupid trivial stuff for himself online every time he's sad. K-cup machines and Encyclopedia Britannica sets and Skin Energy Jet Peel Hydrafacial Machine 8-in-1s for his in-home spa. It's probably how he tricks himself into believing he isn't actually running out of money.

Whatever he thinks is in this package, you're counting on him wanting it *now*. His special treat to fill the void, the Jet Peel Hydrafacial he's been dreaming of.

Sure enough, the door opens. There stands the Rockstar, holding a gin and tonic with a fat slice of lime, his mundane brown roots growing in beneath the artificial black, his skin sagging, his eyes tired. It's irritating because he's actually *not* ugly in person like you wanted him to be. He's perfectly handsome. Perfectly tortured, the perfectly flawed picture of the perfectly flawed ex-frontman of a cult goth band. Exotic, sad, sensitive, great in bed. The sort of man girls leave guys like you for every damn day.

You stare at each other, his frenzied huskies lurking behind him and barking in a shrill, ear-splitting chorus. "What, do I need to sign or something?" he rasps. Then he reaches for your clipboard, chipped black enamel on his blunt nails, cliche leather wristband on his stringy beef-jerky arm.

"You killed my fiancé," you blurt.

He looks at you, blinks. "What?" he says.

An inhalation, easier this time, an almost-euphoria spreading through your body like a drug injected right into the junkie vein. "You killed my fiancé," you repeat calmly. "Or, she killed herself because of you. And she cheated on me with you. She was in love with you."

The Rockstar, who is probably a sadist, actually *laughs.* Throws his head back and cracks up, the wheezes turning into coughs as he takes the clipboard from you and signs the wedding invitation clipped there without looking down at it. "Look, man, you've got the wrong guy. I promise, I didn't sleep with your girlfriend. Sorry she's dead, but it wasn't me. Scout's honor." He moves his hand across himself, something between the sign of the cross and a pinky promise. Then he hands the clipboard back. "Have a nice life."

"I am not going to have a nice life because Charlotte is *dead*. Do you even fucking care?" you spit out, annoyed that he's not taking you seriously. In all the times you've imagined this, it's gone differently. You read him his crimes, he begins backing away, guilty. You chase him into his house. You scream at him. You read him the memorized suicide note. He cries. There's a jury of animated cats, and they yowl and yowl, pointing at him with their claws, singing, "Guilty! Guilty!" Then the grand finale: the Rockstar kills himself, just like he always sings that he will. End scene, curtain drop.

But in reality, it's not going down like that. He's just looking at you with watery dark eyes, sipping his cocktail while his dogs do backflips behind him on the marble floor.

"Hey," he says. "I'm sorry your girlfriend—"

"*Fiancé*—"

"The *girl* you were gonna marry—Charlotte, you said? I'm sorry about her. But I didn't know her, okay? And I sure as hell didn't fuck her or kill her."

"She loved you," you say, jamming yourself into the door as he tries to close it in your face. One of the dogs lunges for you, flings slobber all over your face before the Rockstar's sinewy arm shoots out and catches it by the collar. "Kaisa. No," he says firmly, shaking the dog a little before dropping it to the ground. It skitters off, the other following close behind. It's weird, to be standing in silence now, stuck half-in, half-out of the Rockstar's echoey foyer. "She loved you," you repeat, breathless. "More than she loved me, anyway."

He looks at you like you're something insanely pitiful. A baby bird that's fallen out of its nest already half-eaten by ants. Roadkill. Gum on the bottom of his winklepicker. The Rockstar sighs, kneading at the bridge of his nose. "Are you gonna try to hurt me?" he asks.

"No," you lie. Or maybe half-lie. You don't intend to hurt him, you intend to make him hurt himself. It's different.

"Okay," he says, gravely voice softer, sorrier. "Come in. I'll make you a drink."

He lets go of the door, and you slither to the marble floor, which is splattered in dog spit. On your hands and knees, you crawl after the Rockstar. Your face is all wet.

———

He makes you a gin and tonic that is mostly gin. You sit at his chrome and granite bar, looking out that enormous wall of windows to the water. Little kids are playing, making sandcastles in the sand along the peninsula, screaming and chasing each other in the pinky-orange, lava-lamp glow of the sunset. You wonder if he's a pervert, if he sits here to spy on toddlers, if you could get him arrested for possession of child pornography. What a scandal, Perez Hilton would shit himself. TMZ would make you a millionaire.

"I'm sorry about Charlotte," he says, handing you the drink. "I hate it, every time. I know I'm not responsible, but I feel like I am."

You are responsible, you want to say. *It's fucked up to write so many songs about suicide and love and how love is suicide when you know your fanbase consists entirely of unstable, unmedicated goth girls.* But instead you say, "Every time?"

"Yeah, you think she's the first?" He shakes his head, downs his drink, makes himself another. "There's been a few Pill Poppers who offed themselves because of the music, the lyrics. It's terrible."

You crunch your ice, suck your lime. You haven't eaten all day, so the gin goes right to your head. "And you *don't* feel responsible? Maybe I'm crazy. Maybe *I'm* the crazy one, but I think if my music made *multiple* people take thirty sleeping pills, I would feel like it was my fault. I would maybe, uh, *stop writing songs.* Maybe take up a new hobby. Paint-by-numbers. Underwater basket weaving. Yoga."

The Rockstar sets his drink down on the counter and clambers into a very clumsy downward dog. You don't know if he's showing off, stretching out, or what. You shoot daggers from your eyes into his ass—it's not in leather tonight, he's wearing sweatpants like a normal person. Heather-gray, no briefs underneath. His dick is just swinging around in there, freeballing. "I didn't *write* those songs," he says, voice strained as he heaves himself back up to his feet. "You think that's *my* art? I'm just a singer. A pretty face. Those songs were written in a writing room. Take up your girlfriend's—"

"Fiancé's—"

"*Charlotte's* suicide with Manny Briggins and Chase Caulman at Spotlight Records if you want someone to blame," he says. "Hell, before Percocet

Pitch, I was in a Devo cover band. When I wrote songs, they were rip-off Devo songs. Nonsense lyrics, fun lyrics, feel-good lyrics."

You stare at him, try to imagine him in a red plastic hat. You can't, not really. "You know what my favorite band is?" he asks then, without waiting for you to guess. "The Village People. I love the Village People. *Young man, there's no need to feel down!*" he sings in the fucked up, degraded version of his famous voice. It gives you chills. A private concert. "Now *that's* a good lyric. Timeless. The doom-and-gloom stuff—that was just marketing."

You look the Rockstar up and down as he swims in your gin-addled vision. There are traces of make-up in the crinkled skin around his eyes, his nails are painted, he has loads of tattoos. In addition to the sweatpants, he's wearing a beat-up Motley Crue t-shirt with a hole in it, through which you can see his pierced nipple. "It doesn't seem like just marketing," you say, gesturing to him and nearly toppling off your barstool. "You're alone in your house on a Friday night, and you've got *mascara* on."

He shrugs. "Yeah, well. I wear black on the outside now because black is how I feel on the inside. Finding out some fifteen-year-old overdosed in your name every few months will do that to a guy. They wanted me to be some prince of darkness, so I became him. I can't just leave him behind, not now. This," he says, gesturing to his skinny legs and his beer belly and the inked spiders and snakes and skulls on his skin. "This is atonement."

You slide your glass across the bar. He refills it. You drink.

The Rockstar

The Rockstar puts you up in one of his many guest bedrooms. You're too drunk to drive, and he doesn't want to call a cab to his home address. "Don't you have, like– a private chauffeur?" you ask him, slurring your words and stumbling down his endless hall because you're wasted. "Or are you running out of money?"

He doesn't say anything. He pushes you into the four-poster bed draped in black velvet atonement. He pulls off your tennis shoes and nudges them into the closet. He brings you the wastepaper basket from the bathroom in case you need to throw up. And once you've collapsed onto the midnight-dark sheets with the room and its Tim Burton art careening around you, he tucks you in, like you're a child.

You blubber, like you're a child. "It was blue," you tell him between sobs, past caring what he thinks, even past hating him. "She drank a 7-Eleven Slurpee, so it was blue. She talked about you, in the note. She said she loved you. That you understood her. Maybe—maybe you can tell me about her," you hiccup, snotting all over the black pillow. "Maybe you can tell me why she did it. I thought she was happy, dude. I thought we were happy. Everyone was happy."

"I don't know why she did it," the Rockstar tells you, taking a wad of toilet paper in his fist and mopping up your dripping nose. "I didn't know her. She didn't love me, she loved the idea of me. The prince of darkness, the schtick. They never love *me*, you gotta understand that."

But you don't, you can't. The Rockstar is lovable, is the thing. He's handsome and he smells good and his house is nice inside, even if it isn't on the outside. He lays his hand on your head like he's testing for fever, he brings a chubby, sweating bottle of Fiji water in from the kitchen and sets it on your bedside table. When you wake up in the middle of the night with cottonmouth and a throbbing head, wondering where the hell you are, he's even left you a sticky note and two Advils.

I took your keys, don't try to drive, it says. His handwriting is looping, cursive, almost girly. *Save the Date!* you think.

———

You sleep in exquisitely late. Well into the afternoon, all those months of teeth-gnashing insomnia finally catching up to you, laying waste to you here in the Rockstar's guest bedroom. When you finally get up, you're groggy, you're hungover, and you're ravenous. You could eat a horse. You could hunt the Rockstar down in his own game room or sex dungeon or movie theater or whatever it is that lies in cool, dark, subterranean silence in his basement and roast him on a spit. He seems like the sort of person who would have a spit in his backyard, for star-studded celebrity BBQs overlooking the water. He would play the Village People. Everyone would sing along.

All this time, you've been imagining the Rockstar's parties looking different. You pictured dark nightclubs, mountains of cocaine, blood in goblets, vampire cosplays. A bass-thudding cathedral festooned in black-clad girls and their glittery silver jewelry, glinting like decomposer beetles all over him. A hundred Charlotte carbon copies crawling on his skin, droves and droves of simpering fans pouring out the stained glass windows, the Rockstar at the center of it all. The prince of darkness loving it, eating it up.

But now, as you lie blinking and nauseated on his guest bed, staring at the *Corpse Bride* poster that looks like it came from Spencer's Gifts, you realize the Rockstar isn't who you thought he was. He isn't who *Charlotte* thought he was. He's not god—he's just some guy. A little cheesy, a little sad. You're not sure what to make of this realization. You don't know who you are, without hating the Rockstar.

You drag yourself out of bed, stumble around the room looking for your shoes. You can't find them, so eventually you give up and start zigzagging barefoot down the hall, trying to remember the way to the Rockstar's kitchen. You can barely remember anything after that downward dog last night—maybe he drugged you. Maybe he robbed you, took your keys and found your car and drove it away to some shady sale lot so he could make a quick buck because he's running out of money.

But then, there he is. The Rockstar, in the hallway in front of you, like a ghost, like the monster from a monster movie. You open your mouth to scream but nothing comes out. "Don't throw up on the carpet," he says. "I just had it steam-cleaned."

"Did you roofie me?" you snarl.

He snorts. His hair is combed back, tucked into a black baseball cap with some band name you've never heard of embroidered on it, and you're not sure you've ever seen his forehead like that. It looks weird, pale, vulnerable. "Hey, buddy," he says, holding his hands up. "I didn't do shit. You're just a lightweight."

You don't know what to say. You stand, barefoot, stomach growling. "Do you have anything I could eat before I go?" you finally ask, because you're not sure you'll make it to where you're parked without passing out if you don't put *something* inside you. "It can be small, like, one of those mini boxes of cornflakes or a banana or a poptart or something."

He waves you over, then claps your shoulder and steers you down a massive, sprawling marble staircase. You feel like the heroine in a gothic horror novel. "Come have eggs," he says. "I make a mean scrambled egg."

"You don't have, like, a live-in cook or something?" you ask.

"Nah. But don't get me wrong, I'm not some master chef. I order takeout, mostly. It's California, so you can find anything you want. Sushi for lunch, Indian for dinner, Ethiopian midnight snack, boba any goddamned time of the day because boba is the elixir of life. But breakfast—it's the most important meal of the day, so you gotta take it seriously. I make it myself, every morning, I wake up and *bam*—scrambled eggs. Or steel-cut oats. These killer smoothies, with wheatgrass. That shit cleans you *right* out, let me tell you. You want some? A wheatgrass smoothie with the *huevos*?"

You've stopped, you're standing there doubled over at the foot of the Rockstar's staircase, mouth flooded with saliva. You're trying not to throw up. Bam, all over his floor. Blue like Slurpee, except, no, it would be translucent, like gin. Like tears. Like water.

He slaps you on the shoulder again. "It'll be good for you."

You swallow.

———

The almost-puke passes, and you recover enough to sit at the bar again, a reflection of last night. Only this time, the windowed room is flooded in sun, the water outside too bright and reflective to even look at without burning your retinas. The dogs pace around you in a circle, curious enough to sniff at your stool when you're not looking at them, uncertain enough to growl when you offer your hand. "They're not used to visitors," the Rockstar says, throwing stuff into his magic bullet blender that he probably bought off Amazon when he was sad. Oranges, peel and all. Ice. Soymilk. Kale. Strawberries, with their tops. Yogurt. You watch him, this wizard at his cauldron, this fruit sorcerer committing blasphemous acts of forbidden and arcane fruit alchemy. He hits the puree button, turns everything into a green slop.

It is very surreal, for you to watch the Rockstar make smoothies in a sunlit kitchen. It is very surreal to see him doing anything normal. You've grown so accustomed to him over the years— his smoldering eyes staring back at you from Charlotte's desktop background, his voice coming in through her beat-up car stereo. He's been everywhere, he's haunted your home, haunted your sex life, haunted the pipes and the sewers and the refrigerator and the graveyard. Everywhere Charlotte was, he followed. Maybe you built him up into something inhuman in your head just as much as Charlotte did.

The Rockstar sets a smoothie down in front of you. "Cheers," he says.

It's surprisingly good. A little weed clipping adjacent, a touch of soccer field, but sweet enough that you don't feel like a grazing horse. While the Rockstar beats eggs, you finish the whole thing, and remarkably, it makes you feel slightly less like dying.

―――――

Because you woke up so late, afternoon comes and goes before you even realize it. Pretty soon, the sun is setting again, and you're still there, at the Rockstar's house on the Rivo Alto Canal. Someone on the peninsula side sets off fireworks, and it makes his dogs howl. He gets down on the floor with them, throws his head back and starts to howl, too.

Your mom texts you: *are you ok? You didn't come home last night, we were worried. Not that you're still a child! Just let us know everything is alright. xx kisses. ps dad made chili*

She's been like this ever since you moved back in. Volleying awkwardly between overprotective concern and gentle nudges toward the door. She doesn't expect you to get over what happened with Charlotte, but she *hopes* you will, and sooner rather than later. No one likes to have their crazy adult son living back at home, freeloading. Plus, it's an awkward story to tell the neighbors or her friends from the book club. *He was all set to get married, but then the girl killed herself. She was in love with some rockstar she'd never met, it turns out. Yes, em-*

barrassing, all of it so embarrassing. We're so embarrassed.

I'm fine mom, you text back. *I'm staying with a friend.*

You don't know why you lie.

———

The Rockstar doesn't ask you to leave. He gives you a tour of the house, shows you the room with the platinum records on the wall, posters from Percocet Pitch concerts in New York, Milan, Hamburg, Tokyo. There's other memorabilia, too, but he sees your face go pale when you think of Charlotte and cuts the explanations short. "She would have liked it?" he asks hopefully as you leave, and you nod stiffly, heart aching.

"She would have lost her shit."

He nods to himself, like hearing that makes him feel better.

The basement isn't a game room or a dungeon or a home movie theater, it's a gym. It smells like sweat and rubber down there, and the Rockstar strips his hat and shirt, lies down on a bench, and straight up starts pumping iron. "I never have anyone to spot me," he says. "This is cool."

He looks reedy, tired, old but strong. This grandpa who is both skinny and bloated at the same time, chicken-skin gathering around his armpits as he lifts, counting, groaning, muscles flexing in a sheen of perspiration. You don't see what she saw in him—except you do. You see it, see *something* as you watch sweat glisten and collect in the hollow of his throat. You must, otherwise you would have killed him already. Crushed him under his barbell, stuck his hand in the bender. He's making it easy for you. You've had a hundred opportunities to do the deed, but you keep not taking them. Instead, you follow him around, like one of his dogs, thinking *why am I doing this? Why am I doing this?*

You ask, "Why are you doing this?"

He sets the bar down. "Working out? So I don't get flabby. Keeps you young. You wouldn't understand because you're already young."

You shake your head. "No, I mean...letting me stick around instead of calling the cops. I came here last night under false pretenses. I tricked you. You're a rockstar, and I snuck into your house, you should, like. Have someone arrest me."

He sits up, wipes sweat from his brow with an inked forearm. "I feel bad," he says.

"For me?"

"Yeah, for you, for your girl...for all of them. Everyone who lost someone because of me. You know, I wish I could go up to them, the parents, the husbands, the kids, whatever, and say I'm sorry. Give them flowers, make them a drink, beat them some eggs. Give them a hug, you know. Tiny stuff, human stuff. But I figured none of them ever want to hear from me ever again, they hate me. But you show up—I dunno. It helps."

"I hated you," you tell him. "I might still hate you."

He stands up, opens his arms wide, turns his head to the side like a Christian in a movie. "I get that," he says. "You can hit me, if you want. Get a nice punch in."

The Rockstar

You stare at him. His handsome jaw, the dark stubble, the swift, nervous bob of his Adam's apple as he swallows. "Go ahead. It's only fair."

You have never punched someone in your life. Once, at a party in college when you first started dating, a guy grabbed Charlotte's ass. You stared, shell-shocked, too horrified and angry to do anything about it. *Hey, guy,* you'd said to him. *That's my girlfriend.* It had been embarrassing, honestly. Hey, guy. Who says that?

Charlotte hadn't needed defending, though. She'd grabbed the guy's hand and bent his fingers back so hard that he'd screamed. Then she'd kicked him in the balls with her gigantic stompy goth boot. Charlotte had punched people before—why can't you? Why can't you punch the Rockstar? He deserves it, he's asking for it.

You curl your fingers toward your fist, stand there with your teeth clenched tight, wind back like you're gonna pitch in a baseball game, but nothing happens.

"C'mon," he says, pointing to his cheekbone. "Right there. Crack it, gimme a black eye." Then the Rockstar gets down on his knees in front of you. There's a sweat mark around the neck of his shirt from lifting weights, his black tank-top blacker there, against his pulse. "Punch my lights out, baby."

You sit down on the floor instead, suddenly shaky, static around the edges of your vision as you blink. Then your eyes spill over, and you're crying again. Only this time you're sober, so it's worse. The Rockstar sits down next to you, legs folded underneath him like a grade schooler. Criss-cross applesauce. He loops his arm around your shoulders, and you can smell his cologne. "I'm sorry," he says. "I didn't mean to freak you out. I just thought it might be therapeutic, you know. To deck me in the face."

"She wouldn't have wanted me to hit you," you admit. "She loved you. She loved you more than anything in the world. You were all she talked about, all she drew. All her poems sounded like your poems, or—well, the lyrics she *thought* you wrote. She could relate, like, literally anything back to you. I think if I gave you a black eye, she'd haunt me. In a bad way."

"What would Charlotte do, if she were here?" he asks.

You snort. "Kick me out and jump your bones, probably."

The Rockstar nods. He reaches out, takes your face in his hands, swipes his thumb under your nose again to collect the snot, which he wipes on his shirt. Then, in slow motion so that you have plenty of time to think *there's no way the Rockstar is going to kiss me,* the Rockstar kisses you. On the mouth. With tongue. Like you're a girl. Like you're Charlotte.

Thinking of her, you kiss him back. One last kiss for your dead fiancé, one last kiss for Charlotte. Channeled through the Rockstar like he's a medium or a Ouija board, like he can carry a message to her in a little tiny ship in a little tiny bottle, sailing on his spit.

He tastes like smoothie. There's the scrape of his stubble on your chin, the click of your teeth together as he pushes you against the gym wall, palms down your neck, to your chest, squeezing you there like you have a tit to squeeze. You grab at his hair because Charlotte loved his hair, you push a little whimpering sound into his mouth because she would have. You make out with the Rockstar like you're the groupie Charlotte wished she got to be. You make out with the Rockstar like you're Charlotte. You make out with the Rockstar like *he's* Charlotte. You cry the whole goddamned time, so everything smells like salt.

He pulls away, eyes glinting and scary like two black holes you could fall into. The same black holes that watched you from the walls of the dorm room you fucked Charlotte in for the first time. Black holes that have seen your white pimply ass, thrusting. "You could still hit me, if you wanted to," he says.

"Maybe later," you tell him, wiping your lips on the back of your hand, feeling black and white and numb all over.

―――――

Once it's dark, the Rockstar suggests a walk with the dogs. You think of the park, of Bixby, of the autographs you've seen him give there, but instead, you end up on the sand. He wears a hoodie and reflective aviators, black skinny jeans that hide his tattoos. So regular. He looks like a different person, not the Rockstar at all. He could just be any older guy, he blends in with the hippy surfer and sunburnt vacation home types, he says things like *Hi, Marv!* and *Gooday, brother!* as he waves, the dogs streaking ahead in comet white, barking with high pitched siren sounds. Random men wave back to him, their rich neighbor, their guy. You're the only odd one out.

"I thought you were *always* Ritchie Riot," you tell him eventually. "That you never took the mask off. That you liked the attention from the fans."

He stumbles, tripping over a mini dune and kicking up a rooster tail of sand as he rights himself. "Nah. I try to be normal sometimes. Most of the time. If I want to be seen, or my agent wants me to be seen, *then* I put on the costume."

You realize in all your months of careful stalking that you only saw him when you were meant to. When he was performing. It makes you feel like being here wasn't your plan at all, that you never hunted the Rockstar down, the Rockstar lured *you* in. Cast a fly like a fisherman and reeled you into his house like he wanted you there.

He takes off his shoes, finds a piece of driftwood, and tosses it for the dogs, whooping and hollering. Whitney squats to shit in the sand, and the rockstar doesn't pick it up. You walk side by side but not together, heading deeper and deeper into the darkness on this narrow little stretch of beach near the canal. It smells like summer and burning charcoal and roasting carne asada, mostly, but every once in a while, you catch a fishy overtone, like something's died.

Sure enough, eventually you come upon the pale, bloated corpse of a sea lion that washed up onto the shore. It's buzzing with gnats. You cover your ears until you have to cover your nose, eyes streaming at the stench. The dogs roll in it, and the Rockstar yells, grabs their collars, and drags them into the water. He wades right in, the sea-foam climbing up his legs, battering his body. When he returns, he's wild-eyed, wet, his hood has fallen off, his hair is everywhere, and the dogs are zooming in circles around him, pink tongues lolling. He looks almost boyish, right now. Not an old, crispy man but a kid, a vampire, the sea god Poseidon. He looks like he did when Percocet Pitch released that supposedly genius debut record and a million sad girls fell in love with him.

He hands you one of two dripping rocks he must have fished out of the foam. "Make a wish," he says.

You chuck yours back into the waves. *I wish Charlotte wasn't dead,* you think.

It's a stupid wish.

―――――

Back at his house, he makes you a drink, then another. You try to pace yourself but can't. "You'll always be a lightweight if you don't build a tolerance," the Rockstar tells you as he hands you the third.

Your head spins, your stomach turns. The house is a blur again, of black and chrome and loneliness. You try to walk up the stairs to the guest room, but he grabs your arm, steers you further down the hall, to the master bed. "Ta-dah," he says, throwing open the saloon-type doors.

You stand there blinking, trying to make sense of it. The rockstar's room is like a kid's room—toys everywhere. Shelves upon shelves of little action figures, tabletop game dioramas, and replica spaceships from a sci-fi show you don't recognize. There's a gaming console and an enormous flat-screen TV, there are movie posters, '80s slasher stuff, and anime. Most impressive of all is a giant, hyper-realistic fiberglass velociraptor statue in the corner, killing claw elevated and yellow eyes narrowed. The Rockstar stumbles to it, drapes his arms around its neck, and starts to tongue-kiss its open mouth. "My clever girlfriend," he slurs. "The only woman I've ever loved."

Dizzy, you tip backward onto his huge black bed. It undulates grossly beneath you with shocking fluidity—a waterbed, you realize. You're gonna be seasick. But the second you try to propel yourself off it, the Rockstar catapults in beside you, and there's no hope for ever getting up ever again. You sink into the swaying motion, bouncing and bobbing and lost in the rubbery velvet-clad folds.

You realize there's a mirror hammered into the ceiling, and as you gaze up at it, you almost laugh. You and the Rockstar—you look so stupid together. You, the average joe, the everyman, the tech support. Brown hair, brown eyes, not-skinny-not-fat, toned but not muscular. A void of mediocrity and then, beside you, the washed-up Rockstar, Richie Riot, the prince of darkness. You don't know what Charlotte ever saw in you, compared to that.

"I'm not the guy I played onstage," he says, like he doesn't know what Charlotte ever saw in him, either. "The fans, the interviewers, the critics…they all got it wrong. They thought I could be a heartthrob. A dark Casanova, you know. A panther, a predator, *rwaow,*" he explains, holding up his hands like kitty paws and making a kitty sound. "They told me it would come naturally if I just started *being* him. So I was that guy, for a while. Or I *tried* to be that guy—I slept with girls and sang about death, even though I wasn't really into either."

The Rockstar

That hits you in the gut, makes a warning siren go off in your head. The animated cat chorus singing, *Danger! Danger! Guilty! Guilty!* You try to roll away from him, put some space between the Rockstar's fever-hot bod and your own, but all you do is send the waterbed rippling again.

He keeps talking, kneading at his throat. "The thing I learned is that you can't make yourself into that guy if you're not that guy, you're stuck being you. But it took me a long time to figure it all out—I thought my life was over when my vocal surgery didn't go right. I didn't know who I was without the voice, without the mask. But it was just starting. I'm only just figuring it out, who I am, without the jerks in the suits telling me who I ought to be to sell more records. I still don't know, really."

It feels like a confession, like you are a priest. "Oh," you say.

The Rockstar reaches out and takes your hand, squeezes it. Your heart races, your mouth goes diatomaceous earth dry. It was okay to kiss him when you decided not to hit him. It made sense, it was like choosing a rose over a grenade. It was a ritual, a seance. You were kissing Charlotte, and Charlotte was kissing you, the Rockstar was just *there.* Acting as a conduit, giving you closure.

But Charlotte is gone, your wish did not come true. The Rockstar is not a murderer, he's just a man. You are, too. You are two men lying on a waterbed, staring up at your reflections in a sex mirror, holding hands like Titanic survivors about to freeze to death. You're drunk, he's drunk. You feel like you're supposed to say something, but you don't know what to say.

You bob there, out at sea, and eventually you drift off. The lights are still on, and the velociraptor watches you like when you fall asleep, she'll go in for the kill.

———

In the middle of the night, your eyes fly open. You try to get up, but the bed sucks you back in, like dinosaur bones in the La Brea tar pits. You're still drunk, and the room is pitch-black, so at some point, the Rockstar must have gotten up and flicked the lights off. You reach for him, and your hand collides with his skin—the skin of his hip, skidding down to his hairy thigh. The Rockstar is naked. You can feel his bare calf crossed over your shin like a sword.

You think of what it was like to share a bed with Charlotte, how she always ran warm so that if you tried to cuddle her, loop an arm around her plush waist, she would groan and wriggle away. But the Rockstar doesn't wriggle away. He pushes back into you, lets you hold on tight. "Charlotte," you say, because you wish he was her. "Charlotte."

He rolls over. His breath in your mouth, his hair tickling your face. Then you're kissing, kissing like his nodes. "Pretend I'm her," he says. "I'll make you feel good."

But it's impossible to pretend he's Charlotte—there's the sandpaper jaw, the cologne, the waterbed beneath you, the mirror above you. Pointless, hopeless. So you pretend that *you're* her, instead. Charlotte, in the Rockstar's bed. He took you home from a concert, he's about to make love to you here, on the artificial ebb and flow of his fluid-filled mattress. You're cheating on yourself, on your loser real-estate wannabe fiancé back home. You've waited your whole life for this, this exact moment.

He starts to mouth his way down your body, so you shove him off. You don't want him to blow you because it would break the illusion—Charlotte didn't have a dick to suck. "I want to do it," you tell him, pushing him onto his back where he swells and surges with the waterbed, legs apart, big dick (of course he has a big dick) diamond hard against his stomach and dripping wet at the tip, like he's been lying here leaking for ages.

You've never done this before, but it can't be that hard. Charlotte was great at it, an artist. You'll be an artist, too, a cocksucking maestro. Up and down, closer to the heat of him until he's bobbing in your mouth, amniotic, fetal, wet and quiet and salty. He lays his hand on the back of your head.

You do it like a pornstar. Slide deep and gag on him, let the ugly red mushroom head hit the back of your throat again and again, like a battering ram. You drool into his pubes and make eyes up at the Rockstar just like Charlotte always made eyes up at you whenever she gave you head. But you make them harder because this isn't *you* with your lame-ass dick, this is the Rockstar. This is her Poseidon. So you worship that rod, tongue his joystick like it's your job, like you wanna make him fall in love with you. Your eyes overflow, your lips overflow. Spit and tears everywhere, a slutty retching sound on each downstroke. Charlotte would have been so sexy about it, so you act so sexy. Choke on him, moan at the taste of his sweat, cram his meat as far down your throat as you can, like a python unhinging its jaw.

The Rockstar comes crazy fast, like, way faster than you were counting on, *just* when you started to get the rhythm of blowing him, humping the bobble-heave of the waterbed in time with your hungry sucks. But you're not done, Charlotte wouldn't be done. You swallow the first spurt like a good groupie and gag up the next in a flood of your own thick spit, take it in your hands, rub it all over your face like lotion. You coat his balls in wet kisses, you lick down into the salty, bitter ditch of his perineum, crank one of his old man legs back to his stomach to expose his hairy asshole, and make out with it. You think about eating him alive—taking chunks of flesh and chewing them up, swallowing them, ripping him apart. Lying there in the ruins of his ribcage, sailing off in the bloody, soupy mess of his organs because you think she would have wanted that. She would have wanted to consume him, take him into her, become one with his essence forever.

So you bite the Rockstar, harder and harder. His thigh, his stomach, his ribcage, his pierced nipples, his shoulders. You're a rat, chewing on hair, chewing on bones. But your jaw gets tired before you draw blood, and the drunkenness hits you like a Mack truck, t-bones you right there in the side. You're too tired to yell at him, to get off, to cry.

He knows, somehow, knows like god, so he packs you up into his arms and rocks you like a little baby. You fall asleep with his jizz crusting on your face, your own personal Jet Peel Hydrafacial 8-in-1. You dream about showing the Rockstar Charlotte's first communion dress. Its tiny puff sleeves, its bitty lace hem.

In the morning, he makes you another smoothie, this time with frozen blueberries, vanilla ice cream, spinach, mango, egg whites, and bee pollen. "I'm gonna order some spirulina off the internet," the Rockstar tells you, bite marks all over his arms. "It makes stuff blue, bright-ass blue. You'll love it."

You don't tell him blue foods make you think of 7-Eleven Slurpees. You just drink your smoothie down, pick little bits of crispy semen off your face, from your sideburns. He sings "Stayin' Alive," just the chorus, over and over again, lifting Whitney's front paws off the ground and dancing with her.

In broad daylight, you go walking on the beach again. He takes your hand in his, bounces the joined fist on his thigh, then swings it back and forth. No one stares at you, which feels weird. You think the whole world should be staring, taking pictures, texting gossip rags. Ritchie Riot and some guy, standing barefoot in the sea.

"This is the life," he says, looking out onto the glittering water. "After all those years of singing sad songs and boinking sad girls, this is the life, man. You got the sand between your toes, the sunshine on your face."

Suddenly, it's too much. You jerk away from him, hand sweaty, heart puked up into your throat in a slick of his soldiers. You must move too fast because Kaisa snaps at the air, lunges and bites you, right on the ass. Just a little nip, but it tears your pants anyway, and there's two punctures welling up with blood. It stings.

"Bad girl," the Rockstar says, stomping toward her, pointing at her face. She goes limp, lies down, puts her paws up in the air to show off her fluffy white underbelly. And you get it. You feel like that—like you're going limp, lying down, putting your paws up in the air, showing off your fluffy white underbelly.

Back at the house, you brain the Rockstar with his eight-pound hand weight. You chop off his arm with one of his stupid ninja katana swords and BBQ it on the spit. You mince him up in little tiny pieces, swallow half, feed the others to his dogs. You shrink him down and put his whole body in the magic bullet smoothie maker and blend him into a puree. You knock over the Clever Girl statue and trap him in his room, let him starve to death up there, grow mummy-thin and flaky. You run him over with your car. You drown him in high tide. You drop to your knees in front of him like he dropped to his knees in front of you, and you beg him to hit you. Beg him to shish-kebab your head on his giant Rockstar cock.

You don't do any of these things, actually, but you think about how Charlotte might have wanted to do them—crush him up, absorb him, possess him, break his bones, wear his skin. How loving someone doesn't feel that different from wanting to kill someone for killing someone you love. How being obsessed with a rockstar is sort of like fantasizing about murder. How forgiveness is sort of like giving up a grudge, going belly up like a dead fish.

The Rockstar orders blue spirulina powder off the internet. You text your mom: *I'm gonna be staying with that friend for a while.*

Then you and Kaisa go on a little potty walk out to the water while you bleed from her teeth into your pants. You forgive her, you have given up the grudge, you have gone belly up.

As the sun sinks below the horizon, you chuck your phone right into the surf.

Salivation

When I was in college, I obsessively drew this creature in my school notes. It was heavily featured in all my planners, all my diaries, all my worksheets. This not-horse haunted my every margin, followed me from class to class, city to city. It is the embodiment of hunger and loneliness. Eventually, I stopped drawing it on things, I stopped thinking about it, and in time, it stopped stalking me. But as soon as I began the process of selecting stories for this collection, part of me knew this story, this creature, would be at the center of it. Before my thesis even developed into a thesis, this beast returned to watch me with its luminescent green eyes, its swiveling, barnacle-encrusted ears above the surface of my memory. It waited, silently reminding me, always, that it is immortal.

Salivation

It helps to imagine that I'm bringing them somewhere beautiful.

Not because it makes death easier—years upon years of brackish water in young lungs, young blood on brackish lips have already sanded thorns down to routine—but because it provides me with the comforting myth of my *own* death. After centuries of factory towns with their ash and smoke-tinted sewers, of the swampy bayou sludge where mosquitos hum over the puddles so lonely even the alligators stay away, of melted snow streams and the polluted Hudson River and the sloppy blue-warm Pacific and the oily Long Island Sound, I'd like to believe that there's somewhere beautiful for me in the end, too. Some sweet hereafter populated by millions of drowned children I've brought to salvation.

A long time ago, I noticed the similarity between the words *salivate* and *salvation*.

I eat. Suck bones clean and spit them out where they tumble through icy darkness in slow motion and eventually settle on the silt at the bottom of a river. I eat, imagine this place where I'm hungry for a different meal, where everyone thanks me for what I've done for them, for delivering them from evil, from loneliness, from boredom. Water runs clear in this place, and everyone dies when they choose to.

I tread the water of real life, head above the surface like a piece of black driftwood, ears swiveling, eyes searching. I watch great huffs of air leave my nostrils and crowd the black of the sky like the ghosts of things that shouldn't have been said and think of this heaven of me among grateful children.

He's there, of course. Moon-pale in the center of them all, solid even when the rest muddy and fade. He's there, and he takes my muzzle between cool palms and says, *It's alright.* And then he smiles.

―――――

It's been a long time since there was someone I thought about. I know I'm not even thinking about him like a person, only an idea, the idea of youth and promise and warmth and love, the things that are for mortals and humans, not immortals and monsters.

Still, as I slide beneath the surface of the water and sink to my floor of lakeweed and clean bones, I think of him, and I think of him.

―――――

I don't know much about him. His name is Moor. He is sixteen years old, and he goes to the vocational school down the street, though often, he doesn't actually go. He's tall and willowy, with fine, tousled hair sun bleached to a white-gold. He doesn't know how to swim.

His eyes are gray, which is the color of everything in this town, the color of everything in every town, but it seems like a different gray, somehow, not the gray of steam and smoke and cracked pavement but the expansive, reflective gray of skies and of storming oceans. He lives on the river, in a mobile home with two ghosts, since his mom is dead and his dad is a drunk. He tells me these things, stretched out on his mattress while I lie on the floor, everything coming out of him like it's a secret. His story isn't unique, it isn't different or more beautiful than the stories of any other children I've spoken to, seduced, drowned, eaten.

The difference is that Moor thinks he loves me.

He doesn't actually love me; he only loves what he *thinks* is me, the mask I've made to lure him in, the character I've become. The glamour I've donned to hook his guts and pull him to the water to drown. He doesn't know *me*, not my name, not what I am.

I don't doubt he loves the fiction I've created for him, though. I'm not one to say whether or not Moor knows what love is. He's only a child, but I am ancient, and I know nothing of love, so I stay silent and pretend he's different even though I know he's not.

That is how I kill: I become what they want. An old, never-forgotten lover who appears naked on the beach some night when they think they've let go, with wet hair and sorry eyes and a voice that's all wrong but begs anyway. A child's mother, the old apron, the comforting perfume, a comb in her hair and her arms extended, heels sinking in sucking shore mud.

Often, I'm some beauty of my own creation, what I imagine them to imagine when they're alone and wondering if they'll die that way, fingers creeping toward heat between thighs. Most frequently, I don't even have to try that hard. People are predictable; they're all lonely, and they all want the same thing. They all pretend to not believe in love, but then they all go tripping after it without a second thought, all the way into the water, all the way onto my back.

Most frequently, I choose children. Children get lost, children wander with tears on their cheeks and their hands outstretched for anyone, any adult, even one dripping and strange. I used to think it made me a monster that I picked children more often than adults, but now I don't think anything *made* me a monster, I was just born one. Anyway, if the myths humans tell about children are true, that they're pure and innocent and more deserving of life than the things life will turn them into, then denying them salvation and free rein in my heaven would be doing them a disservice.

I don't actually believe this. But an endless life of guilt will make you write things you don't believe.

I never come as myself. Sometimes it's close, like when some little girl in breeches canters past with a switch in her hand and horses in her heart, and I'll become a white stallion with a long, braidable mane. Or Black Beauty, or Flicka, or Seabiscuit. A trusty steed nickering for sugar cubes, offering an everlasting friendship that will gallop into the sunset. It's never a real horse, just the Platonic ideal of a horse, a fictional horse. A perfect horse.

And they'll approach, enraptured. A bright, thrumming bliss on their round faces, tiny fingers trembling as they lift to stroke a warm nose, fearless to touch and be consumed by exactly what they wanted. I am not irresistible, but I know how to look like I am.

I make sure their eyes are closed when I finally drag them under. I want the image of perfection etched onto their eyelids, I want them to die believing that they found their long lost lover, their mother, the ideal beauty, a noble mount. They'll lean in for a kiss, they'll wipe tears with a fist, and in that split second, I'll change into myself and take them.

―――――

For Moor, I'm a young boy like him. Slightly older, darker, but just a boy. When I chose this form, I didn't yet know Moor, didn't know he had a creased up Calvin Klein underwear catalog under his mattress, didn't know he turned around to watch his shop assistant walk away, eyes fixed on the lines of his back as they disappeared into his Levis. I didn't know he was lonely, that he had his father's pistol loaded and on his desk between the dusty school books and dustier catcher's mitt. I didn't know he was looking for salvation, while I salivated.

I did know *I* was looking for salvation, but I also knew I wouldn't find it. Centuries of towns like this, no reason for here to be different. He probably wouldn't find it, either, especially not if I killed him before he turned seventeen.

That was my plan, to kill him. I do always try to pick beautiful ones to drown, and he lived nearby, was alone most of the time, and didn't seem like he would be missed. He was a dreamer, the hopeless kind who dreams to escape the present, because he doesn't think he can escape in the future. I'd already heard him say, while tossing rocks into my river, *I'll never get out of this town.* I imagined him saying this to a friend, while they shared a cigarette, but when I surfaced a few feet away from him, disguised as water and more water, I saw that he was by himself, sitting on the river bank with his arms around his knees and eyes the color of slate.

I decided then that he was mine. I would show up older, wiser, the promise of a friend. I'd take him to the bend of the river that surged the fiercest one evening to show him something wonderful, and as he peered into the water with his back toward me, I'd become myself, nudge my nose into the lovely curve of his lower back, and take him into the water to consume.

But then everything changed, because Moor fell in love with the boy I became, and I had never been loved, and I was salivating for salvation. Hunger of any kind makes even monsters foolish.

I wrote rules years ago to prevent this, but it never happened before, so I never had a reason to break them. I told myself I shouldn't think of people as anything more than a meal, that I shouldn't stay in one body of water for too long, that I shouldn't speak to prey, just find it, become what it wanted, drown it, and eat it. This seemed easy, because most people were easy. They were predictable, they fell for me, they saw the thing I created and wanted it badly enough to drown for.

Moor was no different. I only *wanted* him to be, because he caught me off guard, and it's hard to surprise something immortal.

Before him, I always knew when to expect love. When I appeared as someone's dream of beauty, their high school sweetheart, their war casualty husband. I'd see the glistening in the eyes, the glistening of love for the skin I was wearing. When I became the boy I became for Moor, I wasn't expecting that glisten. Maybe the shine of admiration, the flame of pride. But not the love. Moor surprised me, old me, *ancient* me, and it felt like he was falling in love with the monster hiding in the mask, not the mask itself.

He wasn't, of course, but I still haven't killed him, I still haven't shown him something beautiful by the river. Instead, I meet him as he walks home from school on the days he goes, and we walk together, elbows brushing and voices raised in elation as we teach each other things. I lie on his floor and help him with his homework; I study the curve of his nose and the silk-white dust of his eyebrows as they knit in concentration. He shares things with me, stories about his sister who died when she was a baby, about his father who never recovered, about the scar on his own throat where he cut himself with a skillsaw replacement blade. The life I invent to tell him about in exchange for these tales is a lie, constructed of small fragments and shards of the stories I'd collected from people I'd consumed, lives I'd shattered, interrupted, ended.

I want to tell my real story, but there is not much to tell. *I've been alive forever. I've slept for years sometimes, but I keep waking up. I swim in my spare time, and eat, and discover what it is that people want so I can give it to them. I salivate. I am salvation. I seek salvation. I found you. You're not salvation, but here you are.*

―――――

It happens so fast that most don't even cry out. Kissing lips suck in water, sobs are silenced with ocean, and then it's over. It's easy to believe I'm taking them somewhere better. This world is pockmarked in sorrow, anyway.

The children in the story of the Pied Piper—what if they *wanted* to be enchanted? What if they were brought from the misery of routine, the bleakness of life, to a fantasy world in that cave with the dancing rats and the panpipes? Isn't that what everyone longs for, some kind of magic to change them, make them matter? Deliver them from despair?

———

I choose a stretch of desolate land behind Moor's trailer. It's littered with broken reeds, silver and sad in their solitude along the bank of the nameless river that runs through town. There is caution tape draped across the twisted gray branches of stripped trees feigning death, separating onlookers from white, frothing, fatal water. I can watch him here.

I've made the paper, because two children are missing. This makes him more fascinated with the water, so we spend long hours hiking along the river and pausing at various points along it to talk, sitting side by side on the dark craggy boulder faces that line the bank. Right now, we're at the edge of the dark, foaming water, and for the first time, Moor tells me, " I can't swim, you know."

I keep my eyes downcast, thinking about how easy his death would be, the insignificance of the eddies and ripples that would close over his pale head. "Oh, yeah? Does it scare you to be here?"

He shrugs in my peripheral vision, snaps a stick off a decaying tree branch half-buried beneath the mulch in front of us. "Not really. I mean, it's not like I'm afraid of death. I think about it a lot."

I imagine the pistol I've seen on his desk, fingerprints in oil on its barrel. I don't want to tell him he shouldn't, that he has a future, because he might not, regardless of whether or not I kill him. "I do, too," I admit.

"You know the scar?" he asks after a moment. He's referring to the one on his throat, a delicate vein of white across the pink of his neck. I do know this scar, I've touched it with the hands I'm wearing, tentatively when he showed it to me, like it might still hurt him.

"Yes."

"You know how I told you I did it myself? Well, I did. But that's not what I tell everyone. Most everyone else thinks my dad did it...that's my go-to story." He stabs the stick in the soft earth, face obscured by blond hair so that I cannot see what he's thinking, why he chose to confess this to me.

"Why?" I ask.

He shrugs again, bony shoulders in blue cotton. "I don't know. I guess I do it because I feel like there's no, I dunno, *evidence* to prove what an asshole he is. I mean, I have bruises on my chest sometimes. Once I had a bloody nose. But for some reason, it's easier to hide those and make one myself to show people. I don't know." He looks up, squints. "You must think I'm a liar."

I cock my head, listen to the sounds of rushing water and my own nervous, longing breath. "No. I think you're interesting," I say. Then, because it's true, I add, "Anyway, everyone is a liar."

We sit there, live things rustling in gray leaves and the river thrashing in its rut of earth. The quiet din of nature sounds seems to last for a long time, and I try to find a name for the aching I feel in my chest. It's at that moment I feel Moor's cold fingers inch into my palm, rough and dry from working shop and sanding wood.

This is what cold feels like, I think with a sudden jolt of realization. It's not as if I've never felt cold before. Of course, I have. But I've only felt it with borrowed skins, the idea of cold, the endlessness of cold that swallows you when you are immortal. Not this, not the cold of another living thing's hand inside mine. I think of my black, cloven hoof flashing through waves, then look down at skin, joined.

My eyes flicker up to meet his, startled, and I pull away because the reality of sensation hurts. Not because I don't want him to touch me. *I do.* I want his hands, his boy hands, to rove over me unfearful, over my withers and my neck and my haunches. I want him to touch me, in that moment, without getting stuck. Pulled in. Assumed. Consumed. Destroyed.

His cheeks burn as I stare at him, and he jerks his hand away, violent color darkening his grimacing face. He stabs the stick into the wet earth, digging a grave small enough for a pile of picked clean bones. "I'm sorry," he mumbles.

"No," I say stupidly, and reach out. I watch this foreign hand pick out a strand of his white-blond hair, thread through it, and skirt across his brow.

He watches me, tries to figure it out. "It's okay," I tell him, even though it's not true.

Very slowly, he leans across the divide between us and kisses me. His lips are salty, and I touch the heated back of his neck. *This is what kissing feels like,* I think. *This is what warmth is.*

The real me is too black, too green, too wet. I smell of silt and the sweetness of rot and the faint, briny-scaly smell of lake. My eyes are bisected by a reptilian pupil, and I am never warm. I am a horse, by some definition, but not the horse of Chincoteague or the Wild West. Not Bucephalus. Just the horse of forever, of the very bottom of all the bodies of water since the beginning of time.

There is nothing more lonely than being immortal. I've tried to remedy this more times than I can count. The immortality, not the loneliness. The loneliness is not to be remedied.

I have no gills, but I do not drown. I don't know how I live in the water. I've never met another creature like myself, so I'm not sure if it's my skin that breathes, or if I can breathe oxygen out of water, or if I've never actually breathed and I only think I have.

I've become a deer and dashed out onto highways in front of logging trucks. I've become a rabbit and hopped up to a fox, become a fox and thrown myself into a mountain lion's den, attacked a black bear cub and waited for the mother. In the end, it always hurts too much to retain my chosen form, so I change back into myself, yet they end up adhered to the slick black skin of my body, stained in both our blood, and I must drag our combined weight, staggering on splintered legs to the water to drown their dying breath, eat their bitter flesh, lay my head on the shore, and cry until there is no salt left anymore.

I've thrown myself into the rapids of rivers that ended in falls. I've speared myself on the jagged rocks beneath them. I've charged off cliffs, into rock faces. Nightshade turns to dust between my teeth. I've done everything I can think of to penetrate my singular skin, to perforate my insistent heart. Sometimes I bleed, sometimes I sleep, but I always wake up healed. I don't remember how old I am.

It's my skin. How I live, how I hunt. When I'm in another body, I can touch humans, animals, anything, and remain separate. However, the second I return to my original form, my glass-green forever-wet skin becomes impossible to pull away from. Whomever I have touched becomes inextricably connected, glued to me, stuck to an adhesive, and all I have to do is go swimming to drown them. Then they die, and slide off to the black bottom. Their death ends the bond. I wonder if my own death would, too.

My skin keeps me from dying. Nothing breaks it, nothing gets in, and everything inside stays forever protected. I'll bleed from the borrowed skin I wear to try to die in, but every time, I change back just before the heart stops.

———

The next time I see Moor, nothing feels different. We talk, joke, he tells me about the stepping stool he's making in shop, about how his teacher mentioned to him that he has lots of potential. Our elbows brush. I ask him if he's ever ridden a horse, he laughs and says no, thinks I'm weird for asking.

Once we get to his mobile home, we tip-toe past his father, who is sleeping in the recliner in front of a static television. To the front room, down the narrow, claustrophobic, smoke-scented hallway, where I wonder what will happen once we get to Moor's room.

I'm answered as he shuts the door behind us and pushes me down to the mattress, lips all over mine. *This is what kissing feels like. This is what being young feels like.* I push my hands through satin-soft hair damp with the cold outside, hold his head just right so I can lick the outside of his teeth, feel the surfaces slippery and imperfect. "Have you been thinking about this?" he asks, cupping my cheek with a trembling hand.

I turn to kiss the palm, stunned by the humanness of it, and say, "Yes."

"Me, too," he says, and he smiles.

We kiss, and I let myself imagine impossible things. *I could live off of other animals, for a while, until the winter. Pick off drifters and hitchhikers. I could stay here. I could be a boy for a while. I could be young, for a while.*

Moor's hand, warm and unsure, moves to the hot, hard place between my legs to gracelessly rub, and I freeze, grabbing his wrist. "Stop."

He snaps up, eyes wide and terrified, so gray they're almost silver. I see myself in the shined surface of them, nineteen or so, with mussed dark hair and the sharp cut of young cheekbones. Lips swollen, red. "What?" he asks, touching my shoulder now, my ribcage. "Why?"

"There are things you don't know about me," I say, because *I'm worried I'll become my real self beneath you as I come* won't make sense, is too much. I think of his narrow, naked, youthful body adhered to my vast blackness in this bed, and fight hunger, fight sorrow.

"Well, tell me then. I want to know you. You like me, right?" he asks, lips dipping low, close to mine. I catch them in my mouth, kiss him deep and wet.

"Yeah, I like you. I just don't want—to hurt you," I settle on, shoving him onto his back, pushing his shirt up over his pale, gold-dusted stomach. He's hard, pressing against the seam of his jeans, as I reposition myself between his legs to bend my head to kiss the aching line of him. I'm not sure if I've done this before. If I have, it was so long ago that the memory has faded to near nothingness, translucency. It could easily be a dream.

He traces my eyebrow with a finger and says, "I've already resigned myself to the fact you're probably going to hurt me."

He's fire-hot in my mouth, and I think, *this is what sex feels like*.

———

Starving doesn't work, either. I've tried it. I grow too weary to swim, to shift forms. My hide lays stretched out like iridescent black-green wrapping paper over black-green bones. Lakeweed and thrushes grow in my mane. Barnacles form on my fetlocks, destined to remain forever. I hallucinate heaven, but it never comes. I am thin, dying, but I do not die.

I've laid at the bottom of the ocean for years, waiting. It's not worth it. Divers come, eventually, and I lay still as the earth until they tread upon me, then drown.

A young girl gets lost on her way somewhere, I find her picking seeds out of a pinecone, sap on her hands and the pale pink of her shirt. I turn white, my legs lengthen, thicken, and I walk up to her with an elegant neck lowered.

"Unicorn?" she asks when she sees me, breath caught in her throat and the expected glisten of love sliding over brown eyes.

I grow a horn, and she steps closer. *You're very special,* I tell her without speaking, cocking my great white head and snuffling air from my nose. *I wouldn't talk to any little girl. Just you.*

She giggles, trips down the bank, debris sticking in her polka-dot leggings. She has freckles on her nose, and she's missing one of her front teeth. Hand held out, it lays on my nose like a tiny kiss. She doesn't feel warm. Maybe the unicorn can feel the heat of her blood, but I'm cold and hungry inside, thinking of Moor and the salty, half-baked smell of the skin below his navel, the stains he left on his sheets. *I only eat to live,* I think, not to her, but to myself. *Starving won't work,* I think. She doesn't notice, she just stares in wonder.

"You're so pretty," she tells me, stroking the velvety muzzle before her. I lengthen my neck, hook my head over her small back, and bring her toward me, this small dark thing against the snow-promise of so much white.

You're prettier, I respond, nickering. Then I lower my bulk to my knees so that she can knot hands in my thick white mane and toss a leg over my back. I'm bending into mulchy wet earth so bits of organic rot stick to me as I stand. *Close your eyes,* I say, looking over my own shoulder at her shining face. *I'll take you to my forest.*

Without question, she shuts them, grinning because I am exactly what she wanted, I am giving her everything she wished for in her most secret, private wishes. I turn to face the water, its surging sadness bubbling over the banks like tears. Then I change, she sticks, and I dive.

———

I was born a monster. I am immortal, but I bleed. I pick bones clean with pointed teeth, pick teeth clean with pointed bones, and try in vain to reconcile the meaning of these things. In the end, I keep thinking of my heaven, which is no longer the sweet hereafter, but Moor. Just Moor, the *idea* of Moor, the slate gray of his eyes, the scar on his throat, and the malleability of his stolen future. I salivate, and think of salvation.

And then I remember, it is only an idea, too.

———

I tell Moor to meet me by the river, the place where it bends and grows deep and angry. I sit in my boy's body and wait for him.

He touches my shoulder when he arrives, a lingering touch with those cold, rough fingers. I want to turn and catch them in my mouth, I want to think, *this is what love feels like,* but I am too old to know of love, too old to hope for salvation. Instead, I stand, take his hands in my own.

"I have to tell you something," I say quietly after he kisses me, once, on the corner of my mouth.

"You already have," he mumbles. "You think in your sleep. I can hear it. I guess you're telepathic or telekinetic or whatever." There's a lazy smile, a quirk of his brow. "I guess you didn't know, huh?"

I stare at him, things racing inside of me. "No." I didn't. I have never slept around someone before, there is no one but the fish who could have heard me.

"It's okay. I mean, you should still explain. I know you're something else, but I don't know what you are. I know you kill kids, but. I don't care about that, really. I didn't care about anything until I met you, you know."

We sit down next to each other, staring out at the river. His hand stays in mine, cold, rough.

"I don't know what I am, either."

"You look human."

"Sometimes," I say. It's cricket-quiet for a few passing moments, chirping and water gurgling and the peepers hiding in the rocks creating a chorus of small, organic songs. I think Moor must be letting things sink in, imagining inhuman lips on his lips, around his dick, and trying to make sense of it.

"You know, I liked you the second I saw you. You're so handsome. I liked your hair, and your leather jacket. I thought you were from the city or something, that you would be too cool for me. I was so surprised when you started talking to me. Your whole life was like this huge mystery, all the stuff you said about who you were was so vague that it didn't even matter if it was true. The fact I didn't know it all, couldn't know it all, was enough. So whoever or whatever you are, doesn't matter. I still love you."

After a while, I tell him, "I'm a monster. And I'm immortal. Those are the two important parts."

He looks up at the sky, as if there were stars out tonight. "You dream about horses a lot."

"I know," I tell him. Then, because it seems pointless not to also tell him, "I was going to kill you, at first. And eat you. It's what I do."

"I've gathered," he says, shrugging in the way he always does. "I wouldn't have minded. I was going to do it myself, anyway."

We sit there, and suddenly he's leaning into me again, tilting my head back and kissing me, fierce with force and spit and teeth between every swipe of his tongue. He pulls away, breathless, eyes so dark they're very nearly black, and says, "Well, are you going to do it now?"

"Kill you?" I ask, voice a whisper. Of course, I have to. There is no room in the world for a monster and a boy to be each other's salvation.

"Yeah," he says. A kiss. Then, "I think about jumping in this river every day. I'd rather ride something in, instead."

"I could let you live. Move on to another river, another town. If you wanted," I say, because wanting to save him is the human thing to do, and I'm humoring his humanity.

"Neither of us want that," he says quietly. Then he adds, "This, here, is what everyone wants, really. To not die alone. To have some magic thing find them, make them better. To find what it is they love, and let it eat them. "

Of course, he's right. It is what every human wants, it is what *I* want, inhuman, endless, profoundly lonely. Mouth full of pointed, blood-slicked teeth and salivation. I don't want to save him unless he can save me, and he can't. I hold the grief in my gut and wish I had been born something different.

I stand up, haul him to his feet after me. The quiet stretches between us for a long while, and I wonder if he will give me the one thing he can. "Do you want to see me, first?"

He nods, threading hands through my hair. His gray eyes glisten, fill with wet that beads on the bottom lid. An ache spreads in my solar-plexus; something close to love, closer to relief. I have never been seen before.

"Okay. You can't put your hands on me until I'm ready."

There are no stars. I change into myself: mottled sea-color horse with bullrushes for hair and skin that cannot be broken or be touched, ears quivering shells of black, eyes wide, green, reptilian, sorrowful. My hooves cut into the muck of the shore, I drip water onto Moor's tattered shoes, but his eyes do not change.

"You're beautiful," he murmurs, raising his hand like he plans to lay it on the flicker of my throat. I raise my head, dished and delicate and seal-slippery just out of his reach.

Even like this? I ask.

"Yes," he says easily, the stupid, reckless certainty only a young person can have. The certainty that young people get when they think their lives aren't worth living, that magic deaths are better than unmagicked existences. He's wrong, he's wrong, but I am hungry.

Are you ready?

"Will it hurt?" he asks.

Do you want it to?

He shrugs, tongues the corner of his mouth. "I just want it to be real."

I nod, duck down to my knees, and he climbs on. It helps to imagine that I'm bringing him somewhere beautiful.

Jonah's Joyworld

This story was originally meant to be part of a long, ridiculously ambitious novel-length horror project about ghosts and prepositions. It had many characters I imagined converging in a climactic and creative way, but when I revisited it, this particular bit with this particular character was the only part with any guts. I lost the prepositions but it remained a ghost story of sorts, though perhaps not in the way one might expect.

Jonah's Joyworld

Jonah's Joyworld closed at least fifteen years ago. But the big, fiberglass whale at the entrance? The gaping mouth, flaking-off blue paint, the angry eyes that used to open and close, now frozen, forever peeled at a lazy half-mast and stuck under a film of oily grime? He's still around. The rest of the park, too. Just standing there, freaky and rickety. You can see the frame of the old wooden coaster from Marty's roof, if it's a clear night.

I never went when it was open. I mean, it was a theme park with a bible theme. Who goes to theme parks with a bible theme? Not my family. Even though my mom guilt trips us for skipping church, and my brother once went through this weird, moralistic, hunting-is-bad, daddy-killed-Bambi phase, we didn't go. I remember saying, *Jeff, if daddy doesn't kill Bambi, we don't get venison sausages in the morning. Don't you like venison sausages?* Jeff, who was, like, ten and a bitch at the time, whined that hunting was illegal. I probably said, *So is your face*. I said that a lot when Jeff was ten. I might actually still say it.

No one ever took us to Jonah's Joyworld. It was too weird, I mean, what kind of rides do they have at a place like that? Theme parks are supposed to be scary. Getting scared is fun. But the bible is definitely not the fun kind of scary, so we never went. Not even for a birthday party or anything. I don't even think the Christian kids in school went. Isn't gouging people for an overpriced admission to a religious theme park, like, blasphemous? Isn't there some story about Jesus ripping up a marketplace his disciples built in Jerusalem to sell little Jesus trinkets? Isn't money, like, the root of all evil? Whatever, point is, I'd never been. Only seen the ugly sun-faded billboards on the one highway leading in and out of town.

It was Marty's idea to check it out because every fun thing we ever did on the weekends was Marty's idea. On Saturdays, I always sat there staring down the neck of my beer wondering how the fuck Marty thought up this shit, and why the fuck I never did. Sometimes I'd imagine suggesting something anyway, like, let's go shoot bbs at the McLearsons' dog. Or, let's go get really stoned and watch Jeff's snake eat a rat.

But I never actually got around to saying that stuff. And if I did, then everyone was usually, like, no, that doesn't sound fun. Which totally sucked because I was almost sure that if *Marty* said let's go shoot bbs at the McLearsons' dog, or let's go get really stoned and watch Jeff's snake eat a rat, everyone (including Anna Trecall) would be, like, fuck yeah, that is the best idea we've had all night. It was weird how that worked, almost as if people didn't even like Marty's ideas as much as they liked Marty.

Anna Trecall liked Marty. I could tell because she wore this one shirt, the white one with the really low neck, basically every time we went over to his house or someone else's house he might be at. And if he wasn't at that person's house, but she thought he was going to be, she would ask about him and get all disappointed if he wasn't there and put on a sweater.

I liked her in the sweater as much as the white shirt. The thing about Anna Trecall was that she was totally beautiful in whatever she wore. Plus, her boobs weren't even that big, so it seemed really unnecessary that she wore that shirt, but whatever. I wasn't the one she was trying to impress, and I didn't even blame her for it—Marty was everyone's favorite. There was a reason he was my best friend.

Anyway, we were all sitting on Marty's roof, drinking beers. I was staring at mine, trying to come up with a brilliant plan, when Marty beat me to the punch, like always. "Hey," he said, lying on his back with his hunting cap over his face so that his voice came out kind of muffled. "Anyone remember Jonah's Joyworld?"

My brother Jeff, the fucking tagalong, swiped the cap off Marty's face. "The what?"

"Jonah's Joyworld," Marty repeated. "You know, the theme park. Knock-off Disneyland, a few towns over. Cool as hell, I went all the time as a kid before I moved school districts."

I was surprised to hear this—Marty and I became friends the minute we met, but I never heard much about his life before I was in it. He'd been a quiet kid, we played on the swings and dug in the sandbox, and I didn't ask questions because they made him stare at his shoes. His parents were never home, we were allowed to climb on his roof, and that was enough for me. He'd never mentioned god or the bible once. "Dude, you went there!?" I blurted. "I didn't know anyone who went there."

Anna Trecall smacked her lipgloss and tossed her long, red-brown hair over her shoulder. I could smell her shampoo. "I went a few times," she said, raising her hand. "It was weird. Creepy. They had one of those Pirates of the Caribbean rides...with the boats and the water and stuff?"

"A dark ride," Marty offered.

"Yeah, one of those. Anyway, it went through the whale's stomach. Scared me shitless." She leaned her head onto Robin's shoulder, and they swayed a little bit, all shiny and made-up like two dolls. Anna Trecall looked way more like a doll than Robin did, though. She was so pretty, she didn't even seem real. "I remember crying."

"I think all that stuff is still standing," Marty mused, scrambling up to the highest point on the tarry slope of his roof and craning his neck like he was trying to make out something in the distance, even though it was pitch-black out. "The roller coaster is, anyway."

Then he got that look in his eyes. It was annoying because when Marty got an idea, he never delivered it like he *knew* it was going to be awesome. He just was genuinely excited, like a dog, tail lashing. It made it hard to actually be jealous of him because nothing about him was ever hateable. "We should go!" he said, all stoked. "How come we've never done it before?"

"Uh, because it's all boarded up, that's breaking and entering, right? It's probably illegal," Jeff argued.

"So is your face," I said.

Anna Trecall stepped in again, sitting up straight, a glint in her eyes matching the one in Marty's. "Don't the cops have better things to do than drive around the perimeter of an old amusement park looking for kids to bust?"

"And, worst-case scenario, they *do* catch us, they're not gonna *arres*t us or anything. They'll just tell us to go home. And if they give us a hard time, we can make up some bullshit about hearing a crying baby inside. We'll look better that way," Robin offered.

"They're not gonna catch us," I told them. I always go along with Marty's plans, since part of me always thinks I secretly made them up, and he just got to them faster or something, or sucked them out of my brain. "Let's do it."

"Mike!" Marty crowed, then collapsed down to his haunches and hugged me so rough and clumsy that we both fell over, the sandpapery shingles of his roof scraping up my arm. "My man!" Marty did that sometimes, called me *his man*. I never knew what to do with it. Half of my guts twisted in pride, like being second in command to the coolest guy in the friend group was its own sort of honor. But the other half coiled up hot and embarrassed, wriggled away from him like worms under an upturned paver, hiding from the light.

"Who else is coming?" Marty yelled, smelling like beer and wood-smoke and maybe, somewhere way under that, Anna Trecall's lipgloss. I coughed.

Robin and Anna Trecall stood up and brushed their butts off, roof-debris falling into their Ugg boots. "We are," Robin said, though she sounded less than enthused. "Lemme get my jacket."

Jeff grumbled, but he followed us all into Marty's Jeep, anyway.

On the way to Jonah's Joyland, we went to pick up Parker, Jason, Eric S, and Eric L, who were all hanging out together at Parker's house because Parker has ATVs. It was the only reason anyone would hang out with Parker, who had some weird colon disorder that made him perpetually stink like rancid county fair outhouse. We took three cars there and must have looked like a funeral procession or something, these three shitty clown cars stuffed full of teenagers following each other out to the middle of fucking nowhere. I thought we were gonna get lost, but then I saw the whale.

It was the only thing reflecting starlight at the very end of this tar-black parking lot. All the street lamps that might have otherwise illuminated the park had obviously blown out, so the thing was as obsidian as the ocean when you're looking at it from the window of a plane. I've only been in a plane once, when I was four and my grandma died and we flew out to Florida for the service. Still, the black of the ocean at night was so black that I remember it, even now. It was like a solid thing and a vacancy all at once, suffocating and empty, the densest density about to crush you to dust and the widest hole in the entire world, the sort you could fall into forever. Somehow, both of these things, at the same time.

Anyway. The whale. At first it just looked like a boulder, ugly and lumpy and gray. But we got closer, and I could see the texture of its topside, with the fiberglass barnacle lumps. Marty said, "I can see its blowhole," and everyone laughed except me.

I could tell that Marty wasn't trying to be funny because of the way his voice sounded. Like a really young kid, like he was super excited about something. He sounded like Christmas. *Awe,* I thought in my head, trying the word on. *Marty is in awe.* As soon as I thought it, I crushed the thought like a bug. It seemed too intimate, too personal. Like I wasn't supposed to notice my best friend was strung up in sticky wonder, like I was trespassing for noticing it at all.

We parked, and so did the rest of our caravan. Everyone tumbled out of the car, kids in a herd, shrugging on their jackets and whooping at the night. Most of the group started toward the whale, except me. I stood on that ocean-black parking lot cement and let my eyes adjust to the darkness. I wanted to see this place if we were gonna see it. I wanted to be able to take it all in.

Marty clapped me on the back with one of his big hands. "Great idea, dude," he said, even though it had been his idea.

———

We started toward the whale eventually, a little ways behind everyone else. Eric L, who was scrawny, was riding on Parker's big shoulders, and they were screaming about something, their breath leaving plumes of steam in the night. Parker's pants almost fell down, so he dropped Eric to yank them up. Robin and Anna Trecall were standing very close together, hands clasped in each other's jacket pockets, Uggs making their stupid *swishswish* noise as they shuffled along. I noticed that Jeff, the bitch, was still in the car. Everyone else kind of blended together.

The roller coaster's dark silhouette seemed much bigger and more imposing here than it did from Marty's roof, its many-board body curved in places like the ribcage of some huge animal. It made creaking noises that reminded me of the noises corn made when it grew, the eerie crackling sound of lengthening stalks that got even louder in the rain. I shivered. "Hey, Marty," I said.

"Yeah?" he seemed like he was only half-listening.

"You heard this place is haunted, right?" I told him. We were almost close enough to the whale to make out the sign behind it, the blue and yellow box letters spelling out "Jonah's Joyworld" through multiple layers of spraypaint graffiti. The whale's eyes were open mid-blink, like the animatronic mechanism just gave out right in the middle of it moving. It looked tired.

"Yeah," Marty repeated, shrugging. He finally looked at me, hair overgrown and sticking out from under his hunting cap, half a smile twisting up the corner of his mouth. "What, you believe that? You believe in ghosts?"

"Not really," I told him, not sure if I was lying or not. "I just. Don't *not* believe in them, either." We arrived at the old hollowed out box office. There was one of those revolving metal things they have at the entrances to county buildings and public transit, so I pushed on it, but it was too rusted, so we hopped a low iron gate that still had spots of its original mint-green paint stuck on it, flaking like fish skin. "I mean, there's no proof they exist, but there's no proof they don't exist either, right?"

Marty grinned. "I guess so. It would be awesome." He struggled over the wall, landed awkwardly, then looked back to me. "To see a ghost, I mean."

Then his eyes narrowed, the black of them getting shimmery, stars in a rain-wet sky. "Are you *scared*, my man?"

I kicked him in the shin. "Yeah, c'mon, aren't you?"

Snake-fast, his hand struck out and found mine, the fingers twining. He batted his lashes down at me, making a sappy girl face. "Yeah. Protect me, Mike."

I ripped my hand away, wiped it on my jeans, and thought about ghosts. Then we caught up to the others.

———

For a long time, we all stood in a line in front of the whale, too chickenshit to lead the brigade inside. The girls clung to each other. "Ooohh," Anna Trecall said, pointing to the lazy eyelid. "He's giving me bedroom eyes."

Everyone laughed, except me. I didn't like when Anna Trecall said stuff that sounded stupid. The thing about Anna Trecall was that she was actually as smart as she was beautiful. Or maybe not *as* smart, because that would make her basically a genius, but she wasn't as dumb as she pretended to be. I wondered if she thought it would impress Marty, to make sex jokes. I wondered if it did.

The whale gaped at us, his huge mouth open, the inside a burnt red up by the gums and faded everywhere else from sun and weather. Jason shined his huge, bright, wilderness-man flashlight on it, strips of that dusky pink color illuminated in the dancing beam. Otherwise, in the dark, everything just looked black and gray, like an old movie. The teeth were really creepy, they were shaped like *human* teeth. Not sharp at all, just flat and boxy.

Marty read some of the funnier graffiti aloud, and Parker pointed out a doodle of a cock and balls that was poised so that the jizz shooting out of it would land in the whale's eye. Marty climbed gracelessly on top of the whale's head and tried to stick his hand in the blowhole. We all kind of hung outside it, like no one wanted to go in.

Of course, Marty was the first. "Let's go check out this bad boy," was what he said. Everyone, except me, followed.

I ran to the side of the whale, put my hands flat on its cold, smooth, fiberglass side, and used the fin and some fake barnacles as hand-holds to scramble on top. I tried to stick my hand in the blowhole, too. Just because Marty couldn't do it didn't mean it was impossible.

I couldn't do it either (it wasn't an actual hole, just a plastic lip and indentation, like a little donut on top of the whale with the donut hole molded over), but I sat up there for a second before I slid down, looked around. The buildings all seemed low to the ground and oddly shaped. There was the wooden roller coaster, of course, in the distance, and another twisted track of a kiddie ride. Jason's shaft of light rolled over a water ride without the water in it, just an empty flume with a line of sad-looking white boats, then darkness again as the light swung back to illuminate his path. I could hear them all shouting and laughing, Anna Trecall's voice high and tinny and pretty above the rest. My sneakers hit the pavement, and I ran to catch up.

Jonah's Joyworld 71

I almost knocked into Marty because I had too much momentum. My outstretched hands collided with his narrow back in the green army surplus jacket.

"Where were you?" he asked, stumbling but grinning. Everyone looked scared and excited now that they'd crossed the final threshold into Jonah's Joyworld, past the mouth of the whale. Their cheeks were all bright and rosy. Mine probably were, too. Anna Trecall was beaming.

"Climbing the whale," I said breathlessly. "Parkour."

"Yeah," Marty answered, distracted already. "You gotta come check this out. Eric S found the dark ride, with Jonah in it. We found the exit, and we wanna trace it back to the entrance. See if we can get inside, walk the track, check if any of the creepy mechanical bible story dudes Anna and I remember are still down there. It's probably underground, you know?"

The way he said "Anna and I" seemed big, important. It kind of stung. I nodded, agreeing. "Yeah. Underground. Let's go."

We all ran close together in a clump, Jason's big-ass hunting flashlight revealing fleeting, erratic chunks of the park's skeletal remains. It was dark, so we were only getting to see the place in fractions, but from what I could tell, the whole thing was vandalized. Every building was streaked in curse words and gang symbols, all the signs painted over or torn down, every window shattered. We were not the first kids in town to have this idea, after all. I kept tripping on weeds that'd pushed up out of the pavement, and every sound I didn't recognize was spooky, made the hairs on my neck stand up. *Ghosts,* I thought again, feeling like I was in a horror movie.

"Here it is," Marty said, breathless. He stopped, his hands on his knees and waist bent so that he could look inside the tunnel. There was a raggedy-ass, half-falling-down loading dock thing attached to the entrance of the ride, with a faded plastic yellow awning and a sign that read "Jonah's Fantastic Boat Ride!" in an annoying, bubbly script. There was a little picture of a pissed off looking whale, and underneath that, a stick person with a speech bubble saying, "Must be 34 inches to ride." The entrance to the tunnel was, of course, through the mouth of a second whale. This one's eyes were stuck closed, and the pink on the inside of its mouth had faded off completely, making it an even sadder, creepier whale than the first guy.

Marty tentatively climbed the stairs up to the loading dock, his sneakers leaving scuffs in a layer of dirt and leaves and stuff. He stood up, half-shaking, and jumped up and down on the sagging boards. They made noise, and a cloud of dust rose up around his feet, but the whole structure held. "Seems safe," he said, because Marty's definition of safe was kinda dubious. "I think we can all come up. Except Parker. You better stay down there."

"Fuck you," Parker said, and clambered up after Marty.

Anna Trecall was next. Marty held up his hand and pulled her onto the structure. The thing about Anna Trecall was that she was almost as brave as she was beautiful, so she was usually the most willing to follow Marty into things, even before I did. In fact, we probably had the same motives: trying to be close to someone rather than actually caring about the plan or whatever. She probably followed because she liked Marty, I probably followed because I liked her. And when it was just Marty and I, I probably followed because that was the space she'd be occupying, if she were there. I liked to sit, close to Marty, in that Anna Trecall-shaped hole.

Marty hauled me up, too, our hands tangling like they did back at the entrance. The wood was gray and splintered, but it didn't sway or anything. Jason shined his flashlight down the shaft of the tunnel into the whale's mouth, and we all peered down it, but we couldn't see anything. Just the crumbling black rubber conveyor belt thing they used to propel the boats and the plastic siding of the flume. Maybe once it had been a bright, oceany blue, but now it was a really gross turquoise. It reminded me of the color that inflatable floaty things faded to after being left out in the pool too long, sun- and chlorine-bleached. It seemed brittle, weak.

Parker stepped over the little gates where people waited in line to climb into their boats, toward the operation panel that was still standing, all its buttons intact. He stood there, pushing them, even though the circuitry was obviously all broken and the thing hadn't been functional in years. "Cool," he said anyway. "Eric, come check this out." Eric L and Parker were both really into planes and stuff. They wanted to be pilots and were probably going to join the Air Force once they graduated. In elementary school, they played a game called Pearl Harbor where they ran around the playground making engine and explosion noises and knocking down all the younger kids. The buttons on the boat ride probably reminded them of something that reminded them of planes or whatever.

I snuck up on Marty, flicked him on the spot of skin between his collar and his overgrown hair. He spun around. "You want to go in?"

"Duh," I said. "Seen any ghosts yet?"

"Nah. Just you," Marty told me, whatever the hell that was supposed to mean. Then he crouched down, gazing into the tunnel again. "I think I remember there being a couple of little drops...like, it started all dark, then there was a drop. And then you were underground, in the boat. Inside the whale."

I made a face, but Marty couldn't see it because he wasn't looking at me. "Gross."

"Yeah. Bible stories are weird, man." He grabbed a bottle cap off the boards. It was so scratched up that I couldn't make out the beer brand or anything, just the remnants of a red logo. I watched as Marty chucked it down the dark mouth of the tunnel, where it clattered for a long time before it stopped. It was a sad sound, lonely and full of echoes. I decided right then and there that this place was more sad than scary. *Let's go back,* I thought about saying, but before I could share my good idea, Marty made a fist in my flannel. "Let's go," he urged, his hand heavy on my back.

———

Inside, the tunnel smelled like piss. Serious piss. I walked with my arm over my mouth and nose, inhaling shallowly so that I wouldn't have to take any of that gross, toxic air into my lungs. Everyone was coughing and complaining. Eric S and Robin gave up, and shortly after them, Jason. "Peace, dudes, I don't want to die of an asthma attack tonight," he said and handed his flashlight over to Marty, who started walking behind the rest of us to illuminate the dank, smelly passage. Anna Trecall stuck around because she was *that* brave.

"It smells like a cat box in here," Eric L yelled, his voice bouncing off the plastic walls.

"No, dude. It smells like beer when you spill it and don't clean it up for, like, a week," Parker argued.

"Same thing," Anna quipped, holding her delicate nose between two fingers so that her voice came out funny.

"Not the same thing, " Parker told her.

"You're *all* wrong," Eric S said, holding his wadded up jacket up to his nose. "Smells like the shit my mom uses to clean the shower. Some evil chemical that's not bleach."

"Ammonia, dumbass," I yelled, and my voice sounded way too loud in the tiny space. It ricocheted off the walls, making it sound like there were a million mes in there. "Ammonia is what cat piss or *any* piss turns into when you let it sit for a long time."

"Guys," Marty said, suddenly stopping and sweeping the light to the ground beneath our feet to reveal the black, springy mat. Everyone shrieked at the sudden, stinking, oppressive cloak of darkness. I felt someone grip onto my elbow, and it might have been Anna, but it probably wasn't. "Shhh," Marty said, voice very close, breath hot on my cheek. "Look. Look at all the little paw prints."

We scanned the decaying rubber conveyor belt, and sure enough, there were a billion five-toed tracks. Some of them brown and crusty with mud, some of them outlined in dried salt-white, from the stuff people used to melt snow in the winter. We were all quiet, staring at the weird, unexpected sign of life in this sad place.

"See. Told you guys it was cat piss," Eric L said. His voice was uneasy. "You think cats live down here?"

We all shrugged in unison. "I guess so."

A few minutes later, after clambering awkwardly down the slanted ramp of the drop, we saw our first cat. For a while, it was just two hovering green orbs ahead of us, like fireflies in a movie that's supposed to be romantic. "Fuck. Fuck!" Parker and Eric yelled, grabbing onto one another and backing up rapidly enough to knock into the rest of us. "You guys see that?"

The orbs danced away into the darkness, then disappeared, but Marty, who had been checking out the faded and cracked bible paintings on the walls, swung the light ahead of us just in time for everyone to spot the back paws and orange tail skittering down the tunnel. "Kitty!" Anna Trecall said, running after it a few steps but stopping, I assumed because Ugg boots aren't all that comfortable to run in. "Awww. I hope it comes back."

"It stinks," I reminded her.

She rolled her eyes. "I like animals even when they stink."

She didn't have to wait for the cat to come back because pretty soon, there were a bunch more. Our journey from one end of the creepy whale-belly ride to the other got totally crashed by cats. I started to rethink the whole more sad than scary thing because the cats kind of changed the atmosphere. There was this constant pitter-patter of their little paws padding up and down the rubber, the floating pairs of animal eyes in the distance, sometimes in crowds of two or three. "What if they're rabid?" Parker proposed at some point after the second drop. The air was even closer, staler, and smellier down there.

"They're not," Eric L told him. "You're dumb. Cats can't get rabid, only dogs and wild animals like squirrels."

"You guys are both stupid," Anna Trecall said. "Pretty much *anyone* can get rabies."

"Then don't pet any of the cats," I advised. They didn't exactly seem petable anyway, too skittish and suspicious, but still. I didn't want Anna Trecall to get rabies from some stupid feral cat living in the belly of a whale.

"Yeah, I'm fucking out," Eric said then, turning on his heel, fishing a miniature carabiner flashlight hanging from his keys out from his pocket and clicking it on. It wasn't very bright, but it was enough to find his way up by. "You coming?"

"Absolutely," Parker announced, but he was the only one.

Marty was a man possessed, Anna Trecall devoted to him, and me devoted to her. So we trudged on, a party of three. "Come on, guys. I want to see Jonah."

On we went, deeper into the darkness and the air thick with cat piss. I had a headache starting up somewhere in my sinuses, and breathing was starting to become a conscious effort with every stinging noseful. I noticed we had all gotten quiet, no more laughing or shouting or piggy-back rides. It was weird, it really seemed like no one was even having fun anymore. Everyone seemed more freaked out than silly, nervous and silent but determined.

I wasn't excited about trespassing on the grounds of a derelict amusement park like I had originally been when Marty came up with the idea and we all thought it was great. I wasn't excited, but I also wasn't ready to turn back. It seemed completely necessary that we see Jonah or what was left of him. If anyone, even Anna, was like, *let's turn back, guys, it's stinky and cold and I'm hungry and scared and stuff,* I wouldn't have wanted to. Or at least, not all of me. The trip down into the dark ride, us walking along the gloomy flume like we were boats, seemed like it was about more than just exploring the ruins. It felt like a mission. Or at least it felt like that to me. I was going to find a ghost here—I was going to find *something.*

Instead, I found Marty's bottlecap, the red scuffed up one he'd tossed down ahead of us earlier. I leaned down and picked it up. It seemed magical that it had made it down this far into the tunnel, so I privately stuck it in my pocket, next to my wallet and my knife.

———

I'm glad Marty was the first one to see him because Marty was the one who cared the most. Around the next bend in the tunnel, I was too busy watching cats weaving in and out of a pathetic-looking diorama of a desert on the "shore" of the flume to notice, but Marty did. "Fuck, yes!" he crowed triumphantly, running along the conveyor belt, flashlight bouncing.

The rest of us were left in the dark, so we tripped after him, me panicked, Anna shrieking. It felt like I was running through something more spongy and wet than old newspaper and cat piss, so I was glad to meet him in the light, which he was shining on a slumped, mechanical figure in a formerly white robe.

I got that really bad feeling in my stomach, the one when you realize that you have a test in first period biology, but you totally thought it was next week. Or the feeling when you walk into a party and see your ex-girlfriend when you promised your new girlfriend that she wouldn't be there. Or the one when you realize the girl of your dreams is in love with your best friend and not you, and you can't even blame either of them because he's pretty great. If you were a girl and you were given the choice, you'd pick him, too. You know the feeling. That sinking, icy dread.

It wasn't realistic enough to be mistaken for a real man, but still, I half-worried it was one. That shrunken-looking robot, its head lolled onto its chest, wires and rusty metal tubing sticking out of a split in the orangey rubber on its neck. Too small, not at all proportionate, but there he was—the goal of our trek. This was why we walked the track of the dark ride—to see Jonah. We knew this thing would be here. It still made me feel awful to look at, though.

Marty reached out and touched him, pushed his head back so that we could see his face.

"Oh, my god," Anna Trecall said, jumping backward and putting her hand over her heart. "I definitely don't remember it being so *ugly*. Ugh."

The eyes were blank and gritty with age, little glass balls with the surface cracked and unglossy. The lids, the same as the whale's, were stuck at half-mast. "Jonah looks stoned," I observed.

Marty didn't say anything.

I finally choked out my good idea. "I think we should go back."

"Yeah," Anna said, agreeing with me for once. "Are the fumes getting to you guys? They're getting to me."

Marty still didn't answer. He was poking at Jonah's moth-eaten beard, which looked suspiciously and horribly like it was made from real hair. The robe's fabric had really creepy stains all over it, brown and red and yellow like it was a lab coat on a mad scientist. Jonah's curled, inhuman-looking robot hands were holding a scroll. I hated it, hated the robot ruler of this underground biblical cat realm. I wanted to get the hell out of there, I was done trespassing. Anna was starting to back away, and I was desperate to do the same, but something kept me stuck there. Standing in the Anna-shaped hole.

"I'm gonna steal his head," Marty finally declared, and there it was again. *Awe.*

Because Marty said it, it must have been a great idea. Anna Trecall and I looked at each other, we didn't tell him no. Instead, we helped him, as cats watched from the shadows.

It took some serious muscle to twist the thing off. The synthetic skin fell away easily—it was made out of some kind of weird, leathery rubber that reminded me of grade school and punch balls, the eraser-pink kind we used to whack each other with when we played dodgeball in third grade. Those fuckers stung like crazy if they hit you in the gut.

Anyway, the skin wasn't the problem, it was all the hardware inside. None of us knew shit about engineering after Eric and Parker ditched, so there didn't seem like an easy way to untwine the wires or anything. I just got my pocketknife out, and we hacked through it. The whole time, I wished we were laughing, but we weren't. I grit my teeth and breathed sharp and shallow, Jonah's robotic insides cutting into my palms while I beheaded him for Marty, pretending I was beheading him for Anna Trecall, feeling like a knight or something, battling a dragon for a fair maiden. Blood ran down my writs in rivulets, and once I finally pried the thing off and handed it to Marty, his palms got all bloody, too.

He beamed at me, and Anna slow-clapped.

"Thanks, dude," Marty said to me, a gravity to his voice making me feel like this was the last time we were ever gonna see each other, or that he was going to kiss me. One or the other.

I backed away, heart hammering in my chest. "No problem. More awesome than a ghost?"

"Hell, yeah," he said, clapping my shoulder, leaving my blood in his handprint on my jacket.

"Okay, can we go now?" Anna Trecall insisted. And it's the damnedest thing—for the first time in my life, I forgot she was there.

We nearly sprinted out the rest of the tunnel, Anna leading our small pack, Marty bringing up the rear with the flashlight and Jonah's head. No one paid attention to the remains of the ride that much, but I kept on catching glances of it out of the corner of my eyes. Paintings of the ocean. What used to be a heavenly host of angels, I assume, from the wireframes in the shape of wings, the cat turds hardened with white feathers. Bundles of metal and punchball skin flaps and other electronic refuse where other characters had once stood. Green, floating cats' eyes. Graffiti. The ribs of the whale. They all blurred together, and suddenly, there was the hill, and at the top of that, a circle of stars.

We whooped, bursting out of the tunnel after scrambling up the last incline, a whale's fiberglass tail arching up into the sky, marking the exit. The air smelled clean and fresh and almost hurt the inside of my nose, but we sucked it in hard, doubled at the waist. I panted, wiped blood and black smears of oil off my palms. Marty caught my eye, and we both grinned, wild, reckless grins. We hadn't seen a ghost, but I still felt like I had.

It was empty outside. The rest of our friends must have headed to the cars to stay warm while they waited for us, so our party of three made our way to the exit. We got turned around a few times, weaving in between sagging, decrepit, cat-pissy buildings, climbing up onto things so that we could reorient ourselves with the black of the parking lot, the bumpy gray back of the entrance whale. At that point, we passed by the old dead roller coaster, its sign proclaiming "Escape from Nineveh," in red, flaming script. It was less impressive close up, the track apologetic and sullen. I didn't blame it, I thought Escape from Nineveh was a really stupid name for a roller coaster and wanted to ask Anna Trecall if it had anything to do with the actual bible story about Jonah or if it was a totally made up place. She was way ahead of us, though, so instead, I asked Marty.

"Hey, dude. What's Nineveh?"

He seemed distracted, staring down at the disembodied head in his hands. Jonah's mouth had distorted into a mournful, screaming O shape since I cut it off, and Marty stuck his finger inside the hole experimentally. "Umm...it's a place. It was all sinful. God told Jonah to go there and govern the people, but he just wanted to punish them, I think, so instead he fled. Um. On a boat."

"Oh. Is that when he got swallowed by the whale?" I asked.

"I think so."

We walked side by side for a few moments in silence, shoes crunching in gravel and broken glass. I kept feeling like he wanted to say something to me, something important, and whatever it was, I knew I didn't want to hear it. So I scrambled for something to say instead. Always at my futile, repeated game of trying to beat Marty to the punch. I couldn't think of a single word, though, save for *let's go, let's go,* stuck repeating in my brain like an annoying commercial jingle.

"Do you believe in god?" he eventually said.

It made my insides writhe, that same dread feeling from down in the belly of the whale. I swallowed and said, "What the fuck?"

He shrugged, shoulders bunched defensively around his ears. "You believe in ghosts."

"I said I didn't *not* believe in them. There's a difference between that and, like. Believing."

"Okay, well do you *not* believe in god, my man?"

I chewed the inside of my cheek, stomach squirming. I didn't want to talk about god with Marty, not here with Jonah's judgmental cloudy eyes staring at me from under my best friend's arm, not at this theme park, not ever. "I dunno," I said. "Why do you care?"

Another shrug, a frown. "It just seems crazy. Like the universe is too complicated to not have been made by something. But I hate—I hate the idea of some old guy. Sitting up there judging me. You know?" And then Marty looked at me like he looked at me down in the tunnels. Wide eyes, flaying pupils, the blue of them a cutting, blade-sharp thing. My mouth was suddenly dry. *Don't kiss me*, I thought.

It was the scariest thing I could think of. Scarier than the bible, than a roller coaster, than Nineveh, than a severed head, than demon cats, than ghosts. Scarier than god. Marty leaning forward, closing his eyes, and putting his mouth on mine like he put his hand on mine, saying *my man* low and hot and close, where only I could hear it. Kissing me because I was standing in that Anna-shaped hole, ready for it.

Crazily, I thought of kissing *him* instead. That would show him. Like when you so badly don't want a girl to leave you, you leave her first. When you don't want to even look at the fucked up Jonah robot, so you put your hands all over it, stick your knife in its wire guts. But I stopped myself right before I did it, jerking forward, then jerking back, heart pounding, eyes wide. We stared at each other until a horrible creaking sound made us startle apart.

Anna Trecall finally made it to the turnstile by the box office. She put her hands on the rusty bar, pushed it, and it let her through. Then, as soon as she passed its threshold, she disappeared. Wicked out like a flame. I don't mean metaphorically—I mean for real. One second, she was standing up there, Uggs *swishswish*-ing, breath visible on the chilly air, and the next second, she was gone. All that remained was the black of the empty parking lot, stretching out ahead of us like nothing, like everything. Marty's Jeep was gone. The other two cars were gone. My brother, who'd hidden out the whole fucking time, our friends who'd ditched us, gone.

We stood, staring. Then Marty dropped Jonah's head and took off running. It bounced grotesquely, and I skittered away from it, heart in my throat as I chased after my best friend, following him to the whale's fiberglass tail, pale against the horizon. He stopped, tried to wrench the turnstile from its locked, rusty position. Tried to climb up to the blowhole and jump down on the other side like I did on our way in, but he couldn't. There was some invisible fucking forcefield, some barrier, some wall. And with that now-familiar dread feeling mounting in my gut, I knew I couldn't, either, we were stuck. The parking lot black as the ocean, black as tar, black as substance, as absence, had become solid with the night, and it would not let us out of the whale's boxy ugly human teeth.

I felt weirdly calm as I stood there, panting. No escape from Nineveh but no judgmental eyes of god, either. Jonah's head ricocheted off into a dilapidated old food truck, and it was facing away from us now, our friends were gone, *everything* was gone but this, here: Marty's bottle cap in my pocket, a bloody handprint on my clothes. I reached out into the darkness to touch him like Anna wished she could. To take his hand. To say, *yeah I believe in ghosts, I believe in god. Yeah, I'm scared.* To kiss him, maybe, now that no one was fucking looking and the fabric of reality was falling apart.

But when Marty turned around, his head was gone, too. Twisted, oily, crimson-slicked wires jutted out from the collar of his jacket in an aborted stump. Flaps of orange punchball rubber hung in sagging wings from beneath the rim of his hat. He didn't have a mouth, but if he did, it would be open. My fingers would fit inside. My fist could fit inside. My fear would fit inside.

A silent scream lodged itself inside my throat, jaw hanging open but no sound coming out. And you know, it was just like me, to come up with a good idea but say jackshit about it. Keep a kiss hidden and curdled and warped inside the darkest corner of myself, distorting it into something unrecognizable, filtering it through a girl, staring it down the neck of a bottle like the neck of a gun, passing it through a whale's entire piss-encrusted digestive tract so that it could come out the other side, baptized and realized and fully formed at last.

But too late. You can't lick lips that have frozen in time and rotted clean off.

Blackbird

This story was cobbled together from two stories that were about exactly the same thing. I couldn't tell when I wrote them—they felt distinct and unique to me at the time, as things often do when you're obsessed with them. But years later, when I stumbled across each story in the deep bowels of my hard drive, I could see they were identical twins. I strung them together and fattened them up over the course of a bizarre, ill-fated trip to visit my parents. Little of the original versions remain in this, but the overall air of grief and loss lingered like blood on a needle.

Blackbird

Things are different now.

Sheila goes on walks at night and thinks every stick and twig on the sprinkler-glistening sidewalk is a snake. Each time, she flinches. She's never been afraid of snakes before. It must be some sort of primal reaction, a biological corner she's been cajoled into, stripped down to from lack of sleep, the world bleary through her forever tear-clouded eyes.

Her skin is different, too. She's been breaking out like a teenager the last few weeks, sore red spots on her cheeks, dotting her brow beneath the wing of bangs that rest there, shiny with oil. Embarrassed, she buys some face wash, the kind kids with acne use. It makes her skin smell like high school. An acrid chemical burn that brings her back to cheap weed and cheaper beer, guys leering at her from football game bleachers, white dust on a blackboard scrawled in equations. Girls laughing at her when she breaks the chalk. She was never any good at math. Like shadows, the nightmares creep back up on her, and she wakes on the couch sweating, worried that she's missed months of class, that she's seventeen years old again because her face smells like it.

Every day is like this, now. Bad dreams. Holes she picks in her wan cheeks as she stands in front of the toothpaste-globbed mirror, popping whiteheads so big that they splatter against the grimy glass. Snakes, but not actually snakes. Just wet sticks.

And then there's James, who is turning into a blackbird.

James, her husband. The artist. James, with his sold-out gallery shows, James, who gets stopped in the street, always by pretty teen girls in all black and dog collars, mascara tracks down their cheeks, begging for him to sign their tit. Brilliant, beautiful James, rolling his eyes at Sheila over fans' shoulders as he cupped a budding breast and scrawled his name on it in Sharpie. *Can you believe these crazy kids?* his twinkling eyes said, and Sheila never once got jealous. Not until now.

First, there was the selective muteness, followed by the anemia, followed by the weight loss. It was like a domino game, so many falling numbers, bits of James slipping away with each new symptom.

Then the feathers came. Not sweet fluff, like goose down in a pillow, but ugly hairpin sticks. Gray and itchy, poking up from under his skin. At first, Sheila thought James was breaking out, too. Like they both ate something that didn't agree with them or were having an allergic reaction to new laundry detergent. She tried to pop the weird dark lump buried under his flesh, force it out like a sliver of wood, but a feather emerged in a slick of infection instead, wet with pus. Hard hollow core, little black filaments hugging it. Then his mouth lengthened and transformed. He grew a hole in his throat that opened and closed obscenely. *Caw,* he said, mournful, scratchy. The whites of his eyes disappeared, and his pupils narrowed to dark vacant pits mired in gray iris. His toes lengthened, gained a joint, a translucent hooked nail. Ugly, gnarled stubs started poking from his back. *Caw.*

Sheila can't remember a time when there wasn't some sort of darkness inching out from James's cracks like smoke fighting its way through the floorboards of a burning house. It's what made his art special, it's why she loved him. He was bizarre and magic and animal, and always, *always* Sheila felt like it was some grand accident that she ever caught him in the first place. Like you can't really snag smoke in a pool skimmer, can you? But she did. She locked James the Junkie down. Three years and counting, a cheap amusement park moodring on her finger holding the place for the diamond he promised he'd buy later. A document signed and a black mourning veil over her face that he lifted to kiss her.

But now, everything is falling apart in a mess of fluttery damp wings, a smear of egg-white snot in his hair, falling out in clumps like the snags that collect around the drain. He's hatching, he's changing, and she's losing him. Smoke in a pool skimmer. No —a blackbird in a net. Sheila's life unraveling, this secret in their bed.

Sheila lets herself into their house, which is holding its breath. A house like a funeral home, like an aviary. Up the stairs, quiet, her eyes burning as she listens for the crazy in-and-out of James's breath. She hears his bird body shifting on the bed as she pushes through their door, pausing so that she can press her forefinger and thumb into the bridge of her broken-out nose, a pitiful attempt to stop herself from incessantly leaking.

James sits up, rustles. Blinks at her and collapses back into the sheets, his wings crumpled at odd angles behind him, jagged, an inside-out umbrella.

"Sorry," she says, walking clumsy and blind to their bed.

James touches her cheek when she's close enough, clawed fingers on clammy skin. Sheila slides in beside this warm, foreign thing in the vague shape of her husband, and it pushes hollow bird bones against zitty skin, says in a reedy voice, "You're cold."

"It's windy outside," Sheila says, losing her valiant battle against the tears. Sometimes, James can't talk at all, only crow, so those words alone shatter something fragile inside her. "I had a nice walk," Sheila adds, omitting the snakes because she doesn't think James can handle them right now, even though they're bothering her, scaring her as they wind and contract in her chest. Scaring her even though they aren't snakes at all. She reaches, smooths what's left of James's hair away from his brow, trying not to gag at the sensation of pin feather tips under her fingers. They feel like a hundred tiny plastic nipples for a hundred microscopic mouths. *I know I love you,* James said a few days ago in this new, scratchy voice, *but I can't feel it. I don't remember what it feels like.*

Sheila is still recovering from the world-ending blow of that confession, and it makes her move slowly, makes her bones lead-heavy with despair, smoke coughed up from the still-smoldering loss. But she makes herself go through the motions anyway. Of loving, of being loved. She crawls in between sheets and puts her arm around James's weird new ribcage, squeezes the fire-hot skin close to her own chill. His breastbone juts out now, a sharp cleaving line between his collapsed pectorals, sticky with sweat-matted fluff. "How are you?" she asks him, lips against a caved in ear. It's nothing but a black hole in the side of his head now, a round vacancy with interior angles like a bolt.

James shrugs. "*Caw,*" he says indifferently. He's not sad about turning into a bird—or he isn't anymore. He has a bird's feelings more each day now. Sentiment whittling into survival, love into instinct. *Caw.*

Sheila's heart clenches. All the emotion that James is no longer feeling yawns vast and expansive and heavy inside her chest instead, snowballing onto her own human heart and tripling its weight. Emotions grow and mutate, tangling together like tumbleweed, new tails tying into a rat king. She holds James harder, squeezes him. Smoke in a pool skimmer, a blackbird in a net.

Mechanically, James kisses the back of Sheila's hand, because it's what he's supposed to do. It doesn't feel like a kiss, though. It feels like the point of a beak digging between carpal bones, a tongue depressor jammed into the back of her throat.

———

Once James falls asleep, his breathing labored and frantic and wheezing through that new hole, Sheila slips outside into the windy air again, because she can't stay with what's left of him. She steps over a broken twig, imagining it writhing under her, alive and silver in the moonlight. It cracks under her heel as she dials the number, guilt already making her heart drum a beat quicker in her chest.

"Hello?" a voice answers, tinkling and glass-high, even though she's surely just woken up. She's a girl just like any other girl. Her name is May, like spring, like dew. Sheila works with her, and they share their lunches together, joke about the terrible e-coli burgers in the hotel cafeteria, and pick at the wilted romaine. She's fresh out of undergrad, and it shows, something buoyant in her laughter, little squares in the center of her teeth whiter than the rest, because she just got her braces off. She is a girl just like any other girl, except for that she loves Sheila, which makes everything different.

It's not a romantic or sexual love, Sheila is pretty sure. Maybe a big sister love, a mother love. The way an abandoned baby bird imprints on the first thing to show it affection, to vomit ground-up seeds into its mouth.

At work, May got off to a rough start. Sexual harassment, this teenage boy custodian who stole her used tissues and jacked off into them in the bathroom before sneaking them back into her locker, stained and crusty. Really gross shit, reported through tears. Sheila fired him without a second thought, and ever since, May has clung to her. It baffled Sheila at first, since she had never really been clung to. She caught her husband in a net, tricked him to stay until his free-bird's heart made him sprout fucking wings. It feels good to have this shiny girl-burr buried in her hair, snagging. Sheila thought she'd never feel that newness and magic of being loved ever again; she already had her chance, and it's growing feathers, now.

"Sheila? It's four a.m.," May says, dripping with worry. Wet and sticky like a cakepop dipped in soda. It seems miraculous that May's love is so powerful. Sheila can feel it through the phone, feel it by proxy. It's not what she needs right now, but it almost fills the void James's voice left yawning between her ribs. *Caw.*

"I know. I'm sorry," Sheila says. She means to explain, laugh it off, launch into her work-voice. *Girl, you will not believe the night I just had. Did you know birds have these freaky holes in their throat that wink open and closed? If they get food in it, they die. Suffocate. Terrifying.* But instead, she just chokes up, stands there with her hair whipping around her, her zits stinging.

"Are you okay? What's wrong?" May asks as the silence yawns on. Sheila can hear her sitting up in bed, the crinkle of her sheets and the box spring creaking. Then she covers the receiver, says something to her roommate, and whispers conspiratorially to Sheila, "Wait a minute. I'm going into the living room."

Sheila loves that May gets out of bed at four a.m. to listen to her. She loves that she answers, that she's here, that they are friends, girl-friends, that instead of giggling derisively when the chalk snaps and the equation comes out all wrong, May hops out of her girl-bed and pads into her girl-kitchen in her bachelorette pad. Sheila never had a life like that—she slept with a switchblade in a squatter punk house with rapist skins and drug-dealer burnouts until she and James scrapped enough together to move out. She didn't trust other girls; they were prettier than her, which, until she turned thirty, felt like an egregious crime against her existence. But here May is, loving her. Maybe Sheila loves her back, too, loves May for being there while James transforms into a dried-up husk of hollow bone and pinion that she aches to be inside of but can't even look at.

May clears her throat. "What's going on?"

Sheila shakes her head, braced against the wind as she drags her hand through her bangs, digging at the aching bumps of stress and oil on her forehead. She wants to tell her the truth. *James. He's turning into a bird, literally. A fucking bird. I'm losing him. I'm terrified. I don't know how to help him anymore. I'm so pathetic and desperate for love that he can't give me right now that I'm calling you, because you* do *have that love to give. It's fucked up, I know, I know it's fucked up.*

"I've just had a rough night, family stuff. And I guess I started thinking about you," Sheila says. May doesn't know about James and doesn't know about love; she's too young and untarnished. If she did know about love, she wouldn't have answered the phone. She'd be running from Sheila, an unbeautiful woman twice her age, crumpled up like a foil ball, broken out like a teenager, afraid of snakes that are not there. Using her.

"At four in the morning?!" May laughs. Sheila laughs too, a broken laugh over a torn sob. It's all wrong. Everything is different now. Her face is wet and hot, throat tight with how much she wants to hold and kiss and fuck and love James, not the empty, black-eyed bird-boy asleep in their bed. *He's abandoning me,* she thinks of telling May. *He's figured out I'm fucking boring, and he's flying away.*

"Yeah," Sheila says, shaky. Then, after a wind-whistling moment. "I'm kind of a mess here, honestly."

May is quiet for a moment. "A mess? What kind of mess? Did something happen at work?"

"No, nothing like that."

She lets out a sigh; it leaves her lips in a *whoosh* that crackles against the receiver. She works front desk at the hotel Sheila (assistant) manages. And often, when things go wrong, she and the other careless twentysomethings who input reservations into the computer are to blame. Sheila sometimes forgets she's May's boss, sometimes forgets it matters to her —it's been a long time since she was that young, working her first minimum-wage job, feeling like her future hung in the fragile balance. She used to worry May only liked her because she was sucking up for promotion, but she doesn't worry about that anymore. "Thank god," she says. "I thought something crazy happened. Like, you found a body in a room."

"No! No, nothing like that. Oh, god. Can you imagine."

"Inez with her vinegar. She wouldn't even use bleach on the blood."

They laugh again, and a knot loosens inside Sheila. Inez is the head of cleaning staff, and she refuses to use any synthetic cleaner. Lemon juice and vinegar all the way, like she's dyeing Easter eggs. Guests complain all the time.

"So…" May says. "You couldn't sleep? Do you want me to read to you?"

The night stretches on, cold and in front of Sheila like some future she never imagined, icy and unknown. "You don't have to."

"I want to! I'm up! What are friends for?"

Sheila lets out a rattling sigh, watching a family of skunks skitter across the road, liquid in their undulating motion, a mom, dad, and a string of three wobbling babies fighting against the wind. They're cute. Why couldn't James turn into a skunk? She could tolerate that. He could sit on her lap, she could pet his black-and-white wedge-shaped head. "Fine. Whatcha got for me?"

"Umm….a cereal box," May says. "I can give you the nutrition facts."

"No food, I'll feel fat."

"Sheila! You're not fat. But okay, let's see… *Reader's Digest*? My roommate's mom brings us the ones she finishes. They're *so* twee. I never read them, but I bet there's some really dry lifestyle pieces in there for you. "

"No *National Geographic*? *Cosmopolitan*? I love those embarrassing story collections."

"Yeah, here's *Cosmo*, same issue, though, so you already know what happened. Lady's poop clogs the fiancé's toilet. Baby pukes on girl while she's talking to her crush on the bus."

"Ah, baby-puke girl," Sheila mumbles. She's only half-listening to May, staring out at the puzzle of sticks that litter the road, watching the palms sway and and creak and rattle against each other, fronds glittering. Still, it's comforting to talk. To hear a voice.

"Hm, well. There are more articles," she breezes. *"Ten tricks to do with your tongue to drive him wild."*

Sheila says nothing—the silence sticks in her throat, three-sided and sharp like she swallowed a corn chip wrong. It aches. She aches. She thinks of May's pretty pink tongue, the soft slip of it in her little straight-toothed mouth, and then, the horrible air-hole opening and closing down in the dark passage of James's throat. His warbles, his song. *Caw, caw, caw,* like mourners in a line.

"May," she says. "Do you ever feel so lonely you think it might fucking kill you?"

"All the time," she answers, and Sheila can almost imagine her twirling one of those bottle-blonde curls around her finger. Because May doesn't know about James, she's imagining a different kind of loneliness, a nobody-loneliness instead of a somebody-who-can't loneliness. It makes Sheila feel even lonelier. "Too bad I'm so far away," she says then, almost coy. She lives in an expensive crackerbox apartment across the street from the hotel that her parents pay for and has no car. She walks to work. Sheila can stand in the lobby and look into May's window, if she wants to. She doesn't, though, because she doesn't like standing in the lobby. Too many tourists milling around, smelling of sunscreen and airport and rental car air freshener. Too many crows lining up on the railing outside, hunched and laughing, waiting for the night crew to bring out last night's trash to the dumpster.

"Yeah. It really is too bad," she answers after a beat. "I could use a shoulder tonight."

"To cry on?" May asks.

"To cry on. Maybe lean on. I don't know. Maybe even just to look at." Sheila doesn't know what she's saying anymore, men can turn into birds, sticks can turn into snakes. Twenty-two-year-old pretty girls can maybe-flirt over the phone with their zit-encrusted married bosses in their forties. "Am I making sense?" she mumbles.

May shifts, the line crackles. "In a four a.m. sort of way, sure."

The trees rattle their branches, drop more snakes on the ground, and for some reason, the way the air smells makes Sheila think about James. James, a few years ago sitting out on the fire escape of the rundown duplex they rented before they could afford somewhere better, James, smiling and wild and full of life and wonder and brilliance. James, blowing glass, taking photos, tattooing with a needle wrapped in thread and dipped in craft-store India ink. Building designs from pinpricks, hair hanging in his face. Now, his feathers cannot hold a needle, or a camera, or a hand. May reads from *Cosmopolitan,* her voice wind-chime-soothing. *Use the tip of your tongue to write the alphabet. Spelling is fun! You'll have your man's eyes rolling into the back of his head in pleasure.*

Sheila gags a mouthful of spit onto the pavement, and the wind catches it, makes it skid into the gutter in a fat white wad. There is a girl on the phone, she remembers, and she clears her throat politely. *Backdoor bravery: if you're feeling adventurous, try tickling his starfish. Not every man is strong enough to take it, but if you've managed to harness a unicorn, this naughty trick will keep him under your spell forever!*

Sheila closes her eyes, and listens.

Back in bed, James is sleeping. His scarecrow body rattling with uneven breaths, feathers fluttering as he huffs through that almost-beak. He looks smaller, somehow, like he's shrunk since she last saw him. Sheila lies down in their bed facing the window, her spine brushing dead bones and hot skin, her face twisting into a reflexive mask of disgust.

She wishes she could wake James up, uncoil him and pry him apart, dig into him, kiss him until he stops breathing. She wants the real James, the one she loves, the one she remembers. She wants him bleary and confused and beautiful and *human,* burnt red like he's been gone on a long vacation. Sunscreen and airport and rental car air freshener. She wants him to say, *What happened? Where have I been? It feels like forever,* so Sheila can sob and pray and press lips to his paper-thin eyelids. *It doesn't matter. You're back now. You're back. God, I missed you so, so much. You don't know the hell I've been through.*

This is what Sheila wants, so she thinks of anything else. Snakes, high school. Starlight. Kissing young, pink lips, wrist-deep in breeze-tossed blonde curls, even though she's never kissed another woman before. Tourists and their money, visors on their heads and cameras around their necks. The jangle of coins in a register and the smell of PineSol-mopped hallways. An elevator going up, an elevator going down. The way it used to feel to be fucked, hollowed out with hands bruising her ribs and there, that's

James again, so she stops. Blinks tears, opens her mouth, and pretends to scream.

Then her phone buzzes against the bedside table, and she grabs it fast, frantic and clumsy because she doesn't want it to wake James, who will not wake from a long vacation but will wake vacant and unfeeling as he has been waking for weeks now. Bird-brained, blinking. Unable to speak more than a few words. *Caw caw caw.*

Sheila gazes at the picture May texted her, tries to make it out through sticky eyes. Her shoulder, pink and sloped under the strap of a white camisole. She's smiling in the background, so terribly, terribly young. *Anytime you want* is the message underneath.

Sheila grinds her face into her pillow, teeth blood-deep in her own cheek. James's breath rattles in and out. She listens to the sound of a voice lost, of wings rustling beside her, and forces herself to reach out, press her fingers into the dandruffy ruff around James's lengthening neck. A crop is growing there, where Sheila feeds him seed. Funneling it down into that pocket, avoiding the terror of that winking air hole. Going through the motions of loving. Of being loved.

The next morning, Sheila grinds coffee, watching the greased beans like insects whir and decompose under the spinning blade. Then, she shakes the powder into the French press. Pours the scalding water in, steam lifting in ghost-like tendrils. Historically, she was a coffee snob. Liked it with half-and-half, sipped slow while she did a crossword before work. Now, she can't taste anything beyond the bitterness, so she doesn't waste grocery money on creamer. She just fills her thermos, then leaves.

But not before drawing the curtains while James thrashes in the bed, squawking. His body has surely grown observably smaller in the night, his wings grotesquely larger. She remembers learning about the laws of mass conservation in high school physics —that something, even when radically transformed, maintains a consistent mass. She wonders how this pertains to James. If he will split into a hundred blackbirds, a murmuration dancing across the sky. Or maybe the laws of physics don't apply to him at all, anymore. He's transcended his programming, shaken off the laws of the universe as he molts. It would be like him, like his art, to break something so fundamental.

She listens to sports radio on her commute, two teams she's never heard of, static interrupting the host's voice every few seconds so that it sounds like he's coughing. A sick man, reporting trades and scores and plays from his deathbed. The coffee burns the roof of her mouth, and she arrives at the hotel early, sits in her car in the employee lot popping zits in the rearview. Squeeze tight until the skin ruptures, pushing and pushing until all the yellow-green comes out, followed by a pitiful bead of blood. She dabs her face clean with a napkin, combs her bangs back into place to hide it. Her grays are growing in under the black dye, and she thinks of May's shoulder. Unblemished, smooth. Like her own shoulder used to look, back when James fell in love with her, and she drugged him, trapped him, shoved him in a cage.

A seagull suddenly drops onto the windshield, and Sheila jumps. Spills coffee on her slacks, heart pounding so hard that she feels like she's coming apart, like her ribs will fly into bits, like the soup of her insides will spill out onto her lap with the French roast she can't taste. Wet everywhere.

Flapping weakly, the bird throws its head back, blinking in a daze. There's a bright red spot on his otherwise yellow beak, some natural marking a shade lighter than the blood crusted around a wound on his head. That beak reminds her of ketchup on mustard, but still, she cannot breathe, the terror too tight in her chest. Not until the bird goes limp and dies, probably concussed from hitting a window, and she has to wrench herself out of the car and use a stick to push the body off the still-warm hood.

Sheila hasn't admitted this, not even to herself: she is not afraid of snakes, but she *is* afraid of birds.

It began as she was growing up in her dreary New England town. A bizarre fluke, an environmental anomaly one December with birds underfoot. Birds everywhere, crawling and hopping, slick-black and ever-moving so that the ground was alive with them. Think of a sparrow corpse covered in ants, glistening in the sun and shuddering with movement; that's what the world was like, only her suburb was the sparrow corpse, and the ants were sparrows. Not just sparrows—starlings with their dusky spots, pigeons gray and hollow and clumsy, their heads bobbing. But mostly, Brewer's blackbirds. She hated them and their eerie yellow eyes, the almost emerald glint to their feathers that caught in rare moments of sun. Hundreds upon hundreds, all milling about like insects on a dead thing.

Winter was a peculiar season for a bird infestation. Winter was when the birds were supposed to leave the cold, not remain mired in it, fluffing their feathers desperately to maintain heat. They didn't seem like they wanted to be there, agitated and sometimes aggressive. They'd pick at Sheila's mother's heels with needle beaks as she pushed her shopping cart across the parking lot. A seagull took the neighbor's straw hat. A flock of starlings attacked the twins who lived up the block when they were walking to school. People stopped leaving their cats and small dogs outside because the birds would eat their food at best, peck bloody holes in them at worst.

Everyone complained all winter, about slipping in the inch-thick sheen of their shit all the time, the coating of silvery black on the sidewalk pockmarked with flyaway feathers. People got tired of carrying umbrellas to protect their hair from the endless rain of droppings. Everyone complained, but people like to complain. They like to have some phenomenon to talk about, Indian summers and climate change and mysterious flocks of birds that darken the skies.

But Sheila—she did not complain, and she did not like it. She was terrified of the birds. They pulled her hair from its braids and dive-bombed her and stole her doll at the park. They seemed to follow her with their luminescent yellow eyes, mocking her, haunting her. *You can't fly, but we can. We could peck your tongue out and leave you here, no one would ever catch us, or hear you scream. We'd spiral up into the clouds like tornados, like we weren't here at all.*

She thought of them when she left New England for the sun-doused glamor of the West Coast. Thought of leaving them behind, California and all its promise sprawling before her. Art, artists, boys, men. James, with his vampire teeth and tattooed arms, beckoning, allowing her into his world of track marks and collages, gore and gutter dirt. *They can't find me here,* she thought. *I'm safe.*

When she woke up to the commotion, black feathers in the sheets, flapping in chaos against the window, talons flexing like fists—she saw the new yellow of James's eyes like the yellow of her zit-pus. And she hadn't cried then. She'd just ground her coffee beans, made her coffee, drove to work.

But now, with the seagull's white down stuck under her windshield wiper and the wind giving way to rain, she begins to weep.

———

Under the lights in the lobby, May looks tired. "Oh, Sheila," she says, tongue against her straight white teeth with their even pearlier centers. "Did you ever get to sleep last night? Your eyes are pink."

"I killed a seagull," Sheila says, dabbing her eyes with wads of toilet paper she gathered from the bathroom. She wishes she had foundation, powder. But ever since James began slipping away, she's lost sight of things. Her morning rituals, the taste of coffee. She doesn't remember where she keeps her makeup, from back when she wore it. "Can you believe that? I hit it with my car."

"Oh, my god? Well, any bird who gets hit by a car is a dumb bird. They can fly."

Unless they can't, not yet. Unless their flight feathers haven't grown in all the way, pushing out in odd plumes at the tips, like the bristles of a mascara wand. Wide, black, then stuffed back down into narrow tubes. It's only a matter of time before James spirals up, knocks into the ceiling fan. "This one couldn't, I guess."

"Well, you shouldn't feel bad, ok? Also! I brought you this," May says quietly, maybe even shyly, as she hands Sheila a gift bag. There's seafoam green tissue paper exploding out the top, a card reading *for you!* in bubble letters. "It's nothing, really, not a big deal, I'm just worried about you, and well. You've been really amazing to me, here. I don't think I would have lasted at Hyatt without your support, and I'm just so grateful, it's my way of thanking you."

Sheila opens it in the breakroom, breath held in wonder. A box of Zen brand green mint tea. An icy blue bath bomb shaped like the planet Saturn. Lotion in a pink bottle, cherry blossom scent. A bottle of Pinot Grigio with a hummingbird on the label, *Chuparosa*. A nicer, more thoughtful collection of items than James has ever gotten her in the whole of her life. They always scoffed at gift registries and Valentine's Days, *commercial bullshit,* they called it. It all seems so silly now, to have turned her nose up at excuses to celebrate being married. Going to dinner, sharing a box of chocolates, holding hands. The motions of loving. Of being loved.

She smells the bath bomb, puts some lotion on her wrists, saccharine floral and spun sugar. Did May go out and buy this stuff this morning, before work? Or did she already have it all ready, before the four a.m. call, the shot of her shoulder? Even wondering makes Sheila miss James so much that she wants to scream. Like her brain is a betrayal, even though he betrayed her first by turning into a bird. Still, she hurries off to the bathroom to wash the lotion off, shaking. Then she dials home. *Maybe he'll answer*, she tells herself, bile in her throat. *Maybe he'll answer, and all of this will have been a dream. Some fucked up thing I made in my head.*

But of course, it rings and rings, and no one answers. A truth she knows and cannot pull herself out of, thick and clinging like May, the burr in her hair, clinging like the still-there scent of cherry blossom. It lingers even after she desperately scrubs her wrists with handsoap until the skin turns red. A reminder she is loved but not by the person she is losing.

———

All through the day, Sheila checks her phone. Opens it to that photo of May's shoulder, May's smile unfocused behind it. She decides she has to push her away—she's in too deep. The gift is too much, this skin is too much. Just as Blackbird James cannot love Sheila the way she needs to be loved, Sheila cannot love May. She cannot chew birdseed and regurgitate it into her sweet perfect mouth. She cannot accept this *Chuparosa* wine or soak in the stained blue water of her tub. She cannot be that woman, that self-care woman who cares for herself. She can only lock her windows, cage her bird. Pluck his feathers, disinfect his needles.

So, after her shift ends, she finds May outside, standing by the hotel pool. Its aquamarine surface shudders under the still-falling raindrops. "I love watching it," May says, sucking on her vape pen, letting out a cotton candy cloud of vapor from her lipglossed lips. "The storm."

For a moment, that's all they do. Stand side by side in the wet, watching the storm. "Do you want to come over?" Sheila eventually asks, arms around her shoulders, shivering. She forgot a jacket, like she forgot her makeup, like she forgot herself. "To my house, I mean. I can show you what it is—why I can't sleep."

May's eyes brighten, green like traffic lights, *Go.* "Of course. I meant it when I said anytime, girl. I *want* to help." A lifted brow, waggling and plucked. Sheila still can't place if this is flirting or just friendship—she doesn't know, she has no experience, she's never had sleepovers or slumber parties or done another girl's nails. She spent her teen years piercing her own ears with safety pins, chasing men in bands who were older than her dad, spitting at the boots of the girls around her who did the same. Women were competition, not friends. Not lovers. They were her mother, bird-beak scars on her ankles, lying in bed hooked up to a beeping machine saying, *If you leave me now, don't bother coming back, Sheila.* Iridescent black-oil slick and yellow eyes in the rearview.

"So, what is it you're gonna show me?" May asks. Not a wink but long lashes fluttering down to half-mast. Rain clattering off the hood of her clear plastic slicker.

"You'll have to see it for yourself," Sheila explains, breath catching as May links their arms, begins marching purposefully to the car. The seagull body is still there when they arrive, sodden and gray in the rain. "I'd rather show you? I'm not sure I can explain."

"Ooh, mysterious," May says. She looks unreal in the passenger side, mountains of blonde hair frizzed up from moisture in the air, teeth white on white, mouth open and laughing, tracing the alphabet with the tip of her tongue. Sheila cannot look at her, so she doesn't. She stares out the streaked windshield, noticing a crack spidering in from an impact. The seagull, maybe. She hadn't realized it hit so hard.

They drive out of the city and to Sheila and James's suburban house, which is forty minutes down the highway on a good day. But it is not a good day. The rain calls for traffic, and the traffic slows them to a crawl. Sheila white-knuckles the steering wheel, and May doesn't seem to notice, gushing about some couple she checked in at work. "Newlyweds, for sure. So cute. He kept looking at her like she hung the moon, wanted to scoop her up bridal style right there. It's crazy, love is real, you know?"

Love is real. It's feathered and revolting. It hides its syringes, it lies to you about everything, everything. It has a hole in its throat you can suffocate with vomited seed. It's running out of veins. May knows nothing about love, but Sheila forces a smile anyway, thinks of feathers, of slipping in bird shit and bruising her knees. The deposits of soft-serve brown surrounded by milky white and water, caking her bedsheets, her carpeting, the tiles in the bathroom. Blackening her hands. A bullet ringed in electric yellow, and nothing, nothing left to cherish.

When they make it to the house, the rain has stopped, and the sun is out. Too bright, it burns Sheila's salt-scalded eyes as she lets herself out of the car, shaking. The house is a mess. Dirty dishes tower in the sink, the toilets unscrubbed, everything quiet in its layer of dust and neglect and molted down. It hadn't occurred to her when she invited May over that she would *bear witness* to it. All Sheila's shame, all Sheila's secrets. Not just the one big one.

"It's filthy in here, I'm sorry," she explains, setting her keys down in the chipped plaster bowl beside the coat rack. "You'll understand when you see."

"This is *nothing,* you should see my apartment," May says, hanging up her wet slicker outside. The drops chase each other down the folds, hounds after rabbits. Sheila stares, seeing death everywhere. She can hear James flapping around the bedroom, wings hitting walls. Dull thumps, desperate flaps.

She reaches out, fingers fanned. "Hold my hand?" she asks May. It feels like cutting her throat to bleed out onto the carpet, that request, but May does not react. Her hand is soft and pink, like her alphabet-tracing tongue.

They walk down the hall, fingers tangled, Sheila sweating. When she throws open the door, she finds the ritual complete—there is not a half-man, half-bird spasming on the sheets. There's only a dark-feathered shadow fluttering around the ceiling, repeatedly smacking its body against the walls in a jerking, chaotic pattern. It seems terrified. James is nowhere to be seen. No traces of his body, no traces of his mind, just an animal, trapped and panicked.

"Oh, the poor thing," May clucks, squeezing Sheila's hand. "No wonder you can't sleep. How long has it been here?"

The gravity of transmutation has not sunk in yet, but Sheila is crying anyway. Her chest hurts. Her stomach hurts. She does not remember the last time she ate. "Weeks," she chokes out, wiping her eyes on the tail of her untucked uniform shirt. "I've been feeding it, letting it live here, *keeping* it, and I just—I don't know what to do. I'm terrified of birds. I always have been."

May sympathetically squeezes her shoulder. She doesn't know about James, she doesn't know about love. She sees a pathetic fortysomething who lives alone, who can't kill spiders on her own, or unclog the drain. She probably pities Sheila. But because she also loves her, she's eager to step in, to save the day, to kill the spider, to snake the plumbing. "Go in the kitchen, make yourself some tea. Or better yet, open that bottle of wine. I will take care of this little guy."

Sheila imagines May hitting James with the heavy base of the bedside lap. Braining him, crushing him to a mass of blood and feathers and hollow bones. Then she starts crying harder, the sobs turning to hiccups. "No, I want to watch. I don't want it to get *hurt,* I want it to be *safe,* I don't want to *lose it,* but—but."

"Shh," May says, putting her hair up, hitting her vape. "You haven't slept, Sheila, you're not making sense. Trust me, girl. You'll feel better when it's gone."

In the end, it's quite anti-climactic. May opens the bedroom window and gently ushers James out with a broom. He streaks out into the post-storm sunlight, black against white, a comma on a blank page, then erased. He flies like he didn't just learn, there's no lopsided attempts, no drop in altitude, no injured wing. Sheila watches him go, and suddenly, the tears don't come anymore. Like she's a desert, the last drop of rain evaporated up into the atmosphere.

"Do you think he'll survive?" she asks May, wiping her nose on her sleeve.

"Maybe, maybe not," May says. "He wasn't a pet. He made his choice, you know. But he definitely wouldn't have survived here. And sometimes, birds have diseases! You weren't safe in here with it, either. You did the right thing by letting it go before it kills itself or you. Or like, breaks its own neck on the window glass."

Sheila thinks of the seagull. "There are windows out there, too."

"And coyotes and shotguns. But you can't worry about that stuff." Then, again, "You did the right thing."

"Yeah," Sheila says, swallowing. She feels numb, like a bird.

The night doesn't end, her life doesn't end. Things are different now, but in some ways, they're still the same. Sheila has always loved by holding on too tightly to things that didn't want or need her, James always wished to be more (or maybe less) than human. The sky still rains, and sticks are still not snakes. Sheila is still afraid of birds and that hole they breathe through down in the deep pink folds of their throat.

May uses a corkscrew on the bottle. The cork is cheap and disintegrates, so she has to dig it out with a knife and strain bits of it from their glasses using a mesh colander. But the wine tastes good, better the more of it Sheila drinks. They sip and sip, and May turns on music, an old punk record she finds in the bookcase, a band Sheila hasn't heard in years. May twerks from the kitchen to the empty living room where she finds a framed picture on the mantle. It's an old grainy photo of Sheila and James from when they were young and in love, though their love looked different, even back then. Sheila is skinny and sad, her collar bones stand out, her hair is still dyed black. James doesn't have wings yet, but he might as fucking well. "Who's this?" May asks, tossing back the dredges of wine in her glass. "An old boyfriend?"

"No one," Sheila says, shaking her head. "No one at all."

Feeze!

The first version of this I wrote was somehow lacking in irony. It was before I realized all my sanctimonious, insufferable vegan protagonists were not sympathetic in the least. I almost feel bad for what I did to this kid—I hope now, if he were a real person, he'd be capable of telling this story at dinner parties, laughing at himself riotously while eating onion dip with his new boyfriend. It is a gift, to laugh at oneself.

Feeze!

Joey was so pissed off. He was at Chuck-E-Cheese, for one. The place was named after an animal byproduct made by an industry that tortured cows. They might as well call it Chuck-E-Tortured-Cow. Or, Chuck-E-Pus-in-the-Milk. Or Chuck-E-Genetic-Engineering.

Joey jotted these down on a napkin, brainstorming vegan propaganda stickers. His hair, which his mom called the Fuzz Wump because it was styled in a complete lack of style that involved gel, hairspray, and rubbing his head violently into his pillow while he tried to sleep, was in his face. He stared through the tendrils of it at the creepy mouse on his napkin, its ugly face obscured by his fucked up handwriting.

The cheese was just the beginning of the injustice. On top of that, he was at his kid brother's birthday party. Joey wasn't the kind of teenager who hated his kid brother or anything, but that didn't mean he wanted to go to his birthday parties either. He felt awkward. All the moms and nannies kept on staring at him and his Fuzz Wump, at his denim jacket with the Teen Idles patch on the back. The Teen Idles probably sounded like a band of delinquents to them, the moms and the nannies probably missed all the nuance of the pun in the title. They were also probably weak-minded and drank wine coolers at night to wind down. They didn't even know the superiority of the social order he was supporting by wearing a Teen Idles patch.

His brother screamed at one of his friends, the fat one with the robot on his shirt, who screamed back. There were words, probably, but Joey couldn't tell. He couldn't distinguish them over the sound of sad, lonely mooing in his head. He scribbled out Chuck-E-Cheese on the napkin and replaced it with Cruel-tEE-Cheese.

Finally, a frazzled-looking waitress no older than him arrived at the table with the naked pizza crust he ordered. "Um…crust, sauce, no cheese? Is this you?" she asked uncertainly, narrowing her eyes in suspicion.

"Yep, that's me," he said smugly. "It didn't, like, *touch* any cheese, did it?" he asked.

She wrinkled her nose. "Um, no? I don't think so. I didn't cook it, I just wait tables."

"I brought my own *vegan* cheese," Joey told her, unzipping his patch-festooned fannypack to remove the white, uniform block. The label read "Feeze!" in yellow bubble lettering. He loved this stuff, he went through, like, four blocks a week. "Get it? Fake cheese."

The waitress shot him a look, expression exhausted. "Restaurant policy is no outside food," she said, face pinched as she regarded the Feeze!, like she wasn't sure it even really counted as food. "Sorry." Then, after a beat, she added, "And shouldn't you, like…refrigerate that?"

Joey shook his head, pointing to the ingredient label. "Unlike dairy, Feeze! isn't perishable. Nothing nasty in it to go bad. Just fiber and plants."

"Okay," she said, backing away from the table. "Just, like…keep it out of eyeshot of the managers, okay?"

Joey saluted her, wondering if she would look up the product and go vegan tonight after speaking to him. He should really be paid as a brand ambassador, he was probably saving so many cows. "Aye aye," he said. Then, once she was gone, he used his pocketknife to rip open the cling wrap and carefully sliced a bunch of tiny Feeze! squares to put on his pizza crust. It didn't melt, which was to be expected, but it did start to sweat little pinpricks of oil when it came into contact with the warm sauce, so he supposed it was ready to eat.

Three slices into his Feeze! pizza, he heard his mom say, "Scott, you can leave the present on the table."

Joey's head snapped up, and his eyes swept the room. If Scott Graham was here, maybe Clay Graham would also be here. He craned his neck, trying hard to get a good look past the bulk of elementary schoolers milling around the table. *Bingo,* he thought to himself. There, slouching to make himself look shorter, was Clay Graham in the flesh.

Joey didn't really know *why* he had a crippling crush on Clay, but he did. Sure, he was older, and sure, he was one of the four other punks in town who weren't also skinheads, which made him cool. But he wasn't *hot* by any stretch of the imagination. He had terrifically jacked up teeth, legs that were long in a bad, spidery way, and the biggest wrist and knuckle joints Joey had seen in his life. But then there was the fact Joey stared at Clay's hands long enough to make that comparison, so whatever. Joey just liked Clay, so much that it made him nervous.

As a result, they hardly ever talked. The few times they hung out at lunch, Joey spent most of the time spitting on the pavement (even though his mouth was usually dry) and shuffling his feet and smiling dorkily and saying, "Yeah, me too!" a lot.

They made eye contact, and Joey froze as Clay nodded to him, grinning. He grinned back in a hectic, crazy kind of way, his cheeks getting hot. He hated himself for the minute it took Clay to disentangle himself and his freakishly long legs from the kids and parents to walk over to the very lonely end of the table where Joey was sulking with his Feeze!

"Dude. I am so glad to see you here. I was gonna hang out in the parking lot until the cake came, then I was gonna steal some cake and book it out of here with Scott. I'm on babysitting duty," Clay announced, gesticulating. That was another gross thing about Clay that should have turned Joey off but didn't: he gesticulated a lot, but there was very little variation in his gesticulation. It was a repeated motion of him holding his right arm out like there was an imaginary beach ball underneath it and moving it in tiny micro-motions as he talked. Joey could imitate it, and he hated that he could imitate it. Clay had, like, no natural charisma. Or he shouldn't have had natural charisma, but he did.

"Me, too," Joey said dumbly. Then he turned redder, cleared his throat. "I mean, not the booking it with the cake thing. Or the babysitting thing. I'm just stuck here."

"Yeah," Clay said. Awkward, friendly. With that weird hand motion.

"Yeah. Um." Joey dropped his head, hiding behind his hair a little. He wasn't normally a socially inept person, but Clay brought that out in him. "I'm glad you're here, too, though. I've been sitting here choking on how bad the air smells, drawing shit on napkins. It's a sad story."

Clay sat down next to him, cocking his head. He had really huge eyes, and Joey could see himself reflected in their darkness. It was at this moment that Joey noticed around his very dark, very big left eye, Clay had a ring of swollen, red-purple flesh, like someone had tried to punch his lights out. He tried not to stare.

"So, what, you don't like pizza?" Clay asked.

Joey wrinkled his nose. "No. Not *cheese* pizza, anyway, which is basically every pizza."

"You don't like cheese? Who doesn't like cheese?" Clay asked amiably.

"Well," Joey said, hopping atop his metaphorical soapbox of sorts. "I'm a vegan. Which means I don't eat any animal byproducts. Including cheese, or milk, or basically any dairy."

"What's this, then?" Clay asks, pointing to the remaining Feeze! pizza.

"Glad you asked. This is *vegan* cheese," Joey explained with evangelical fervor. "A cruelty-free substitute. It's called Feeze! Get it, like fake cheese?"

Clay looked skeptical. "How does it taste?"

Joey shrugged. "Fine. Wanna try it?"

Clay shook his head. "I'm cool."

Taking a large, dramatic bite, Joey theatrically worked his way through another piece of his pizza, grateful for the way in which the Feeze! was acting as a social lubricant in his moment of need, proud to show how palatable it was. "You should try it," he said through a mouthful. "It's tasty."

Clay raised his eyebrows, then winced because from what Joey could see, it tugged on the tender skin of his black eye. "Okay, I gotta ask…why dairy? I get being a vegetarian, dead animals are sad, but what's wrong with cheese?"

Joey loved this question, so very glad that he and Clay were talking about veganism because Joey was fairly certain that without a topic fueled by rage and superiority, Clay's presence would render him otherwise silent. But there was nothing in the world, not even his weird crush on Clay Graham, that could silence the furious voice of Justice. "Because dairy cows, and chickens on egg farms or whatever they're called, are tortured. They're put in insanely small cages, fed really shitty food, and chickens, they chop their beaks off so they can't peck anything. Dairy cows are given tons of hormones so that they produce tons of milk, and their udders are attached to machinery that makes them all infected and full of pus. So basically, there's pus in cheese pizza." He paused for effect and blinked dramatically, polishing off the rest of his slice. "Gross, huh?"

Clay nodded thoughtfully, playing with a straw on the table with his unearthly fingers. Usually, this was the point in Joey's graphic dairy-tales that people got grossed out. They decided that they were horrible people and made hollow vows to become vegans, or they got all weird and bristly and defensive and talked about how they really need protein because they're anemic or something. Joey waited anxiously to see what Clay's response was going to be.

"Hmm. Well, I guess that's the price I pay for the greatness that is cheese," Clay drawled.

It was not what Joey was expecting. His face fell. "But pus, dude. Pus. In your cheese. Pus in every mouthful."

Clay shrugged. "Pus is no grosser than blood."

"You drink blood?"

"Sometimes," Clay said nonchalantly.

Joey stared. Clay stared back. Then he said, "Here, watch," and pulled his right foot up onto the chair he was sitting on, so that his knee was bent in front of him. Then he proceeded to very carefully roll the baggy black ankle of his pants up to the joint, revealing a very white, very hairy shin and a series of nasty-looking bruises.

"Did you get in a fight or something?" Joey blurted, curious. "I noticed the black eye."

"Kind of," Clay answered, voice distracted. "Went to a punk show. Took some punches."

Joey's stomach crawled, his insides bunching together like they were alive and sentient. Clay Graham and his white, hairy calf should not have been attractive. Clay Graham's bruises, and this punk show where he got punched, should not have made him mysterious and charming. "Oh," Joey said, charmed anyway.

His eyes dropped to the bony jut of Clay's kneecap, where there was a scabbed over thing that looked half-burn, half-scrape. It was red and crusty, thick enough that it pulled the skin around it taut and itchy. "I got this skidding across the cement floor in board shorts," Clay explained, applying pressure with his creepy long fingers to either side of the ugly abrasion. "Let's see if I can get some pus out of it."

Joey's eyebrows tried to fly off his head. "What? No. We're at my brother's birthday party. We're at a table of food," he hissed.

"You care if I profane a table of tortured cowpus pizza?" Clay asked drolly.

Joey had nothing to say to that, so he just got up on his haunches and leaned over Clay's knee, hopefully shielding the grotesque spectacle from his mom's most likely critical gaze. He peered down, heart beating fast at this new revelation of Clay's skin, of his skin in *pain*, his brown-red scab where he had been torn and half-healed over. Clay used a dirty index nail to pry up at the sides of the dried-blood shingle, patient as a surgeon. "Does it hurt?" Joey asked, enraptured.

"Eh," Clay said, peeling a chunk off. A bead of crimson rose to the surface, and he swiped it up with his fingertip before sucking it off, revealing the pink, newly exposed tenderness underneath. With careful pressure on either edge of the new wound, Clay squeezed, and alongside the blood, beads of clear fluid rose to the surface. Joey gasped, bit his lip. His dick twitched in his pants.

"Lymph. Not pus," Clay declared. "Ah, well," he bent his head, then licked the bloody lymph right out of the wound.

Joey decided that this was probably the sexiest thing he had ever witnessed in his fifteen years of life. His stomach twisted, a deep gurgle building in the lowermost cavern of his insides. He was *moved.* He wondered what it said about him that his stomach was dropping and his dick was half-hard against the zipper of his jeans because he had just witnessed Clay Graham licking his own scab at Chuck-E-

Cheese. Probably that something was wrong with him, but he didn't even care.

Clay whipped his head back up, eyes closed, triumphant grin twisting his lips just before he stuck his tongue out. "There you go," he announced. "Do I have permission to eat a slice of pizza now that I've eaten my own pus?"

Joey nodded solemnly. "You have my permission to do whatever the fuck you want," he said.

Then their eyes connected in a very scary way, Clay's flashing, wide and wet like two wounds. Joey felt sick, eyes darting to his lap, stomach churning. Crushes were the *worst*.

"Hey," Clay said. "You want to go to the ballpit?"

Joey looked up again, in spite of his nausea. "Huh? You mean the dirty, germy cesspool of kid puke and hypodermic needles and possibly venomous snakes? I thought you wanted to eat your hard-earned slice of pizza."

Clay stood, shrugging his jacket off onto a chair. He was wearing a white sleeveless shirt underneath it, and Joey could see all the planes of skinniness it clung to. He pinched his own thigh, trying hard to kill his boner, desperate to will away the wobbling sensation deep in his gut. It was a fruitless effort. Maybe a nice, brisk walk to the ballpit might be better for the job.

"Yeah, I'll get to that eventually. But now I wanna play," Clay said. The word *play* made a weird shivery feeling zip down Joey's spine. His stomach flip-flopped again, a sea-sick sort of dizziness crawling over his scalp, making him shudder before he broke out in sudden sweat.

"But there will be kids there. I hate kids," he said.

"Yeah, so do I. But don't worry, I'll scare them away," Clay promised. Then he grabbed Joey's arm, and Joey's gut fell off an internal cliff. Chuck-E-Cheese and its cacophony of colored lights swam around him, carnival-brilliant, and he swayed in place, officially nauseous. "Come on, let's go," Clay urged.

Helpless, Joey followed.

Clay dragged Joey across Chuck-E-Cheese, clamping his wrist in the creepiest, jointiest hand in existence. He wove through the games like an expert, and as they penetrated more deeply into the building, Joey realized that this place was pretty much a casino/hamster cage hybrid for kids. They played games for tickets and exchanged them for cheap-ass toys, or they crawled through multicolored mazes of plastic tubes. He felt like he was in kiddy Vegas. It was overwhelming. It was not helping his stomachache.

"I don't think we're allowed to go in the ballpit. I think we're too old. Or too tall," he complained, not wanting to get kicked out of the place his brother's birthday party was being held at. His mom would probably kill him. He tossed the Fuzz Wump out of his face, tripped between hordes of kids with tickets in their fists, stomach roiling, sweat dripping into his eyes. *God,* he was so sweaty.

Clay shrugged. "It'll be fine. There are three ballpits here. Two are for little kids, and they're not covered so parents can watch. We couldn't get away with messing around in those. But there's one toward the top of that structure over there for older kids that's dark and has, like, an awning. For privacy. I think we have to take that purple tunnel. " He pointed, pale hand swimming against a technicolor, cheese-scented backdrop. "See, twelve and under, we're golden. We can pass as middle-schoolers."

Joey was pretty sure they could not pass as middle-schoolers. He was also pretty sure he wasn't going to fit in the entrance of that purple tunnel. But Clay was already trotting over to it, getting on his hands and knees and sticking his head inside. He looked like a giant, punk hamster. He poked his head out a final time. "Okay. Coast is clear."

Without further ado, Clay disappeared into the chute. Joey made an unintelligible noise of frustration, his guts writhing in protest. He didn't want to be stuck in a tunnel with a child-sized circumference behind Clay, especially while he was nauseated with nerves. But he also didn't want to be alone out here in a room full of mostly eight-year-olds, with half a boner. He would look like a child molester. So, without a better option, in he went.

It smelled overwhelmingly like plastic inside, and he wasn't sure if that was an improvement upon the cheese or not. His mouth watered alarmingly, a burp working its way up his throat. He let it out and felt a little better.

Emboldened, he propelled himself upward, using the joints in the plastic tubing as tiny grip-holds for his tennis shoes. It was kind of claustrophobic, which was not helped by the proximity of Clay's ass mere inches from his face. "Don't fart," he shouted up the tunnel, and Clay cracked up.

Occasionally, a kid would come sliding down next to them, and they'd have to press themselves against the siding of the tube to admit the tiny, germy body. Joey's queasiness spiked every time, a constant ebb and flow, like restless waves battering against an eroded shore. His high-fiber vegan diet made him have to use the bathroom a lot, and he was beginning to regret not taking the precaution before following Clay up into the network of tubes. Now he was thinking too much about tubes and things moving through them—kids like chewed up food in a throat, kids like turds ricocheting out a colon. This was a digestive tract, and he and Clay were stuck in it, lost around hairpin turns and endless switchbacks.

Weirdly, Clay seemed to know where he was going. He kept on taking turns into different colored tunnels and scrambling around corners like he fucking *was* a hamster and lived in a Chuck-E-Cheese. Joey would get lost if he tried to recreate their path on his own, which made him even more nervous. He was at Clay Graham's, a hamster tunnel native's, absolute mercy.

They eventually came to a level plastic platform, and Clay shouted, "Left!" before pointing with his gross, bony finger. Just beyond it, Joey spied a promising rainbow of multicolored plastic balls.

Four kids who looked like they were between nine and eleven crowded the entrance to the pit, sitting there with their chests puffed up like they thought they were tough.

Clay crawled on his hands and knees right up to them, poked one in the ribs. "Hey," he said.

The kid stared at him, eyes wide, until he piped up. "Hey!" he said, but it was not a greeting, it was an affront. He had a *Karate Kid* shirt on that was splattered in pizza sauce, and he had clearly hit puberty early because Joey could smell his pubescent BO. This kid flexed, like he was gonna wax on, wax off Clay in the face.

"How old are you?" Clay asked.

"Twelve," the kid said. "You're too old for the ballpit."

"I'm seventeen," Clay said. "And I have a black eye. So I think you should leave," he told him.

There was a momentary pause, this stinky karate kid facing off with a punk hamster, and Joey was genuinely unsure who would win. But being seventeen paid off because eventually the kid pouted and gestured to his friends. They all nodded frantically and scrammed right down the tunnel, and just like that, Joey and Clay were alone.

Joey could not fucking believe it. Maybe Clay was a wizard or something, had weird supernatural powers that made him seem threatening and/or sexy when he was neither. "That was way too easy! How did you do that?" he asked, staring at the kids' retreating backs.

"Jedi mind trick, young padawan," Clay said, grinning. Then he surveyed the ballpit in all its vacant, expansive, colorful glory. "Empty," he announced, making his stupid awkward beachball hand-gesture before jumping in. "Water's great!"

"Can you feel the germs?" Joey asked, squirming on the edge of the ballpit, feeling like every organ in his body was tied up in furious, gassy knots. He wasn't even *in* there, and he could feel the germs. He could practically see them. He could definitely smell them, the residual rubber-eraser and sweat-

and-sugar smell of children. It was making his salivary glands *pour* like leaky faucets. He had to keep swallowing his own spit, willing himself not to projectile vomit all over the guy he had a crush on. "Personally, *I* can feel the germs," he managed to say.

"Dude, I licked my own knee-pus. You think I have very well-tuned germ sensors?" Clay said, flailing in the rainbow sea of plastic balls. "Pleeeeaassee come in with me. I want to show you something."

That got Joey's interest. What could Clay possibly show him in a ballpit besides kid-puke, hypodermic needles, and possibly venomous snakes? He was curious, so he grimaced, swallowed a thick throatful of saliva, and jumped in, too.

Immediately, he regretted it. The second the balls touched his arms, his stomach tried to turn itself inside out. He puked in his mouth a little, swallowing down the sour tomato chunks before he surfaced, kicking and screaming.

"Fuck!" he bellowed, clawing through the nasty plastic toward Clay, scrambling up his long-ass body and clinging to him like a koala. It was so not his plan to hang onto Clay like that, he just wanted as few balls as possible to touch him, and the best way to achieve this was to put the majority of his body on something that wasn't balls, so the only option was Clay. After a few seconds of panic, he realized what he was doing and flung himself off, backward into infected plastic. "Whoa, sorry, dude," he coughed, tongue tasting horrible and acrid. The shock of the balls at least seemed to kick his digestive system out of its funk. He didn't feel like puking anymore—the urge passed with the hacking, swallowed mouthful of it. Crisis averted.

Clay laughed. "I don't care, you can use me as a jungle gym all you want, " he said. " Joey believed him—Clay's arm had actually been supporting his weight when he was on him. The ghost of it still burnt on Joey's lower back, warm and solid. Interesting. Promising.

He struggled against the horrible suck of plastic balls, treading rainbow plastic, trying to decide if revealing his embarrassing feelings was a worse fate than contamination. He chose contamination in the end, resigning himself to catching a hundred diseases so he could keep sort-of flirting.

"So, what were you going to show me?" he asked, voice echoing in the cavern. "Because you better show me quick. This is so disgusting, I can feel myself getting scummier by the minute."

"Nothing," Clay responded, grinning with his awful teeth. "Just wanted to get you in here with me."

Joey's mind flatlined into wordless, outraged static as he reached out and smacked Clay, hard, on the arm. Just flat-out walloped him. Clay looked genuinely shocked and caught Joey's wrist when he went for a second hit. "Dude, I'm covered in bruises. Watch where you punch me," he said, but his voice was wheezy and weak with laughter as he wrestled Joey away, kicking blindly under the sea of balls.

"You are such an asshole. Is this what you do to people, make them swim in dirty balls?" Joey yelped, arms pinwheeling in the cesspool of kid-nastiness. He wasn't actually mad, though—his crush on Clay was winning out against everything else, and he was totally getting off on messing with him now. The cessation of his nausea left him feeling invincible, powerful. He'd gone through the terror tubes and survived without puking. He could do anything now. Even reach into the balls to pinch Clay Graham beneath the clicking ocean of multicolored plastic.

Clay snorted, then smacked at him. In a moment of perfect entropy, their hands locked, holding one another at arm's length as they play-fought. The tension between their locked elbows kept their bodies apart until Clay suddenly bent his, sending Joey crumpling into his chest. "Gotcha," he teased, wrapping his freakishly long, freckled arms around Joey's shoulders, clasping them, and dunking Joey into the balls face first.

Joey would have screamed, but then his mouth would have been open in the ball-sea and he would have gotten ball-germs in his mouth. So instead, he just kicked wildly in panic, trying to free himself from Clay's inexplicably strong grip, nails scrabbling against any flesh he could reach.

Clay yanked him out, then dropped him back into the pit of plastic with a rattling click. "You're such a little germaphobe. No pus in your pizza, no ball-germs in your mouth."

"Blech," Joey panted, running his tongue fervently against the roof of his mouth. "Not *those* kind of ball-germs," he said before he realized what a not-cool thing that was to say.

Clay should have paused. He should have made a weird face, he should have given Joey time to fumble over his thoughts for a minute to come up with a witty retort to make his Freudian slip look like an intentional joke, instead of the mortifying exposure it was. Instead, Clay didn't miss a fucking beat. He narrowed his eyes and said, "Oh, yeah? The other kind is fine, though?" One of his eyebrows was raised, and he was smiling. Joey was almost sure he was flirting back.

"Uh," Joey said, trying to keep his head above balls and not drown, astounded by the revelation that he *might* get lucky. "Yeah. The, uh, other kind? The not-seven-year-old-snot kind. Is preferred."

Clay nodded sagely, brow still cocked up into a delicate V over his eye. "I see." Then he swam away from Joey, doing an inelegant back-stroke through the multicolored plastic. "We're in the wrong kind of ballpit for you then," he called over the distant din of screaming children.

Eager to see if he could push this, Joey awkwardly doggy-paddled over. And once he was close enough, Clay reached across the divide and fisted his hand in the front of his shirt, hauling him close. *Bingo*.

"Can I tell you something?" Clay asked, voice low.

Joey treaded balls. "Um. Do I have a choice?" His cheeks burned, and he audibly gulped. "You're holding me in place."

Clay loosened his grip but only minimally. "I didn't eat a slice of pizza because I hoped I'd be kissing you later. I didn't want to subject you to the pus of tortured cows."

Maybe there was a parallel universe where Joey was actually a suave, clever fifteen-year-old. However, if there was, he was currently not occupying it because his response to that incredibly hot come-on was, "Just your own pus and blood."

Clay cocked his head. "Hm. Good point." It was comforting because it wasn't suave, either. Though Joey supposed he shouldn't expect anything different from someone who thought it was a good idea to try and seduce a guy in a ballpit at a Chuck-E-Cheese's during his kid brother's birthday party.

Joey recovered quickly. "No. I mean, I don't care. About your pus. Or your blood." His voice dropped to a whisper, and he stopped resisting Clay's tugging arm, letting himself go slack and pliable. "I actually thought it was really fucking sexy. When you licked your knee. I know that's weird, but I did. Whatever. Guess I'm weird."

Clay's gaze dropped, and he laughed nervously. Then he flattened his palm across Joey's chest before sliding it up his shoulder and around the nape of his neck, where it rested with tentative weight. "Sooo…," he asked, drawing the word out. Their legs knocked together, Clay's thigh sliding between Joey's, inevitably brushing against his chubbed-up dick. "Can I? Kiss you with my pus and blood mouth, I mean?"

"Fuck, yeah." Joey was *so* proud of himself for fighting his nausea down long enough to do *this*. Totally worth it. He nodded emphatically and closed his eyes, smelling Clay all around him. Clay's deodorant, Clay's hair gel, and then, just before their lips collided, the sweet, Pepsi smell of his breath. *Bingo.*

Clay didn't waste any time shoving his tongue past Joey's lips and flicking it against his teeth. Joey got the distinct impression that Clay hadn't kissed a lot of girls because there was basically no preface of romance or tenderness or any of the stuff you had to bullshit your way through when you were kissing girls just so you could get your hand up under their bra. Clay was all tongue and teeth and palms scraped over Joey's back, his thigh working between his legs fervently like one of those dime-fed horsey rides outside liquor stores. It was fucking great.

Their bodies slid together to a chorus of wet sucking noises and the muted click of plastic balls shifting together to accommodate their motion. Clay's hands tried to curl through Joey's Fuzz Wump but met too many snags and knots and tangles, so instead they slid down Joey's sides, one digging into his lower back and sneaking fingers past the waistband of his jeans so that could grip his ass through his boxers. "Oh," Joey groaned, arching his back and pushing his ass into Clay's palm in encouragement. Those spidery fingers found their way *into* his underwear then, parting the sweaty crack, petting the tight furl of his hole with needy strokes.

Jesus Christ. Joey was about to get fingered in a ballpit. He could not believe his luck. "Damn," he mumbles. "Forward."

"Yeah," Clay said breathlessly, catching Joey's mouth and kissing him again, sucking on his lower lip before tilting his head back for air. "I think you're so cute. Always check you out at lunch. Your little ass in those skinny jeans with all your patches. Drives me crazy."

Joey's stomach twisted, then lurched. He thought it was arousal, at first, so he shimmied closer, squeezing all the plastic balls out from between their grinding bodies so that he was flush against Clay, riding his thigh, rocking back toward the finger at his hole.

But then the sensation happened again, and this time he noted with a spike of horror that it was *not* a good lurch. It clenched lower than his stomach, deeper. A pain ricocheted through his abdomen, sharp and septic. His eyes flew open, and he thought back, inevitably, to the unrefrigerated Feeze! and his high-fiber vegan diet. "Fuck," he said.

Clay thought it was a sex-fuck. "Mmhm," he mumbled, chewing on Joey's shoulder, grabbing his ass, roughly groping him up against the canvas side of the ballpit. "What do you want me to do to you?"

Goddamnit. Joey wanted Clay to let him *go*, was the thing. He needed to get to a bathroom, pronto. The entire Feeze! pizza he'd wolfed down had rapidly made its way through him in record time, tumultuous through his stomach, liquid fire through his guts. He hadn't avoided imminent disaster by not puking—he'd worked his body into a *worse* frenzy, pushing the sickness from one end to the other. His body needed to get the Feeze! out, and if it couldn't come up, there was one remaining option. He wasn't gonna puke all over the guy he had a crush on. He was going to *explosively shit himself into his hand.*

"Sorry—*fuck,* sorry, I really want to make out with you, but I gotta—" His own stomach cut him off, a guttural sound like approaching thunder rumbling out of him. The burp smelled like Feeze!, a horrible harbinger of what was to come. Panicked, Joey tried to clamber off of Clay's thigh, but the balls made it impossible. His colon shuddered, his intestines heaved, sweat sprung to his temples, and his vision careened like a washer's spin cycle. All the while, poor Clay's finger stayed nudged up against Joey's hole, hand trapped in his tight jeans, totally clueless.

It was coming, and there was nothing, *nothing* Joey could do about it. His life flashed before his eyes. Then, he let loose.

Torrential was the only appropriate adjective. The way weather guys call rain *torrential* during monsoon season, they would have used the same ugly word to describe the shit-storm that broke loose in Joey's boxers. It was a monsoon of shit. Coffee-thin and very chunky, little undigested bits of his quinoa and spinach and tofu breakfast in a watery brown sea of pizza and liquified Feeze!

"Fuck," he wailed. It felt *good* was the worst part. Like, yeah, it was the most horrible thing that had ever happened to Joey in his entire life, but the relief in his stomach as the horrible pressure was finally being released felt almost orgasmic. Burning hot lava filled his jeans, shooting down his legs forcefully, getting in his sneakers as he scrambled helplessly through the balls.

Clay just stared at him, mouth open, hand open, full of it. He looked like one of those blow-up sex dolls, mouth hanging in a little O of shock. He remained frozen for a few seconds before he started flailing, kicking Joey off and backing away, shitty hand still stuck in his waistband. When he finally wrenched it out, he gawped in horror at the mess in his palm before he started to gag. The wet, horking sound of it accompanied Joey's frothy, chunky farts, and together, the sounds mixed, bouncing off all the plastic in a terrible cacophony of corporeal reflexes.

Joey had one goal: get out of the ballpit as fast as fucking possible, sprint in his shitty shoes to the parking lot, and run the fuck *home* so that he could kill himself or fake his own death or something. He didn't even want to get to the Chuck-E-Cheese bathroom, he needed a *shower;* it was down his legs, in his socks, squishing up from the pressure of his pants and slithering in wet rivers up his back.

But the balls were frankly a *lot* easier to jump in than climb out of. All he could do was tread uselessly, locked in place, swimming in his own filth. Balls churned around him, rainbow streaked in miserable brown and then, spectacularly, *pink* as Clay retched beside him. The thick, sloppy puke that shot out in a geyser was the color of the Barbie aisle at Target. Like he ate nothing but cherry slushy and strawberry Starburst before he came to this party. Cotton-candy streaked in bubblegum. Joey shrieked and tried to escape the line of fire, but all the motion did was make him rip another shit, more liquid gushing out of his blubbering hole and into his clothes.

He swam and swam, desperate to get away. From Clay, from Clay's puke, from his own ocean of shit and the foul latrine and sewer stench of it. After what felt like an eternity of helpless wallowing, he *finally managed* to make it to the tunnel entrance and haul himself up into it from sheer force of will, leaving brown handprints on the edge as he scrambled, brown shoe prints as he climbed.

"Wait!" Clay shouted. Joey looked over his shoulder—there was a string of snot hanging from Clay's nose, his eyes were wide and watering and bloodshot like he was crying through the vomit. Joey was somehow still attracted to him, to his long, creepy-weird, shit-stained fingers he was holding up, starfished out as far away from his body as he could possibly manage. Too bad Joey fucked *that* up forever. "Don't *leave* me in here," Clay begged, but Joey couldn't stand to remain, inhaling the sinus-burning stink of his own hubris. He looked away, then slid down the tunnel without another word.

The whole long plastic thing, from mouth to anus, was streaked in shit when he emerged on the other side. The kids he sped past were screaming, gagging, crying. He heard the distinct splatter of throwup against plastic and launched out the other side of the tunnel, hitting the ground running. That whole freaking play structure was about to become a hazmat zone, and he didn't want to be there when it happened. He kept his eye on the prize—the sliding double doors leading out of this cheese palace hellhole.

His shoes squelched wetly with each step, shit bubbled out from the legs of his jeans, leaving a trail that he was desperate to outrun. Chuck-E-Cheese security had already spotted him, too dumbfounded to close in yet, so he had to get out of there before they tackled him and made him pay for his crimes. Outside food. Almost-sex in a ballpit. Getting shit all over the ballpit and a ton of the tunnels. Starting a chain reaction of puke in the hamster cage.

He decided in a fit of madness that his pants were too heavy, so he stripped down—unbuckled his belt and let the soaked, shit-heavy denim hit the floor with a slap. Then he kicked out of his shoes, feeling lighter and freer now in nothing but his loaded boxers. Chunks fell down his legs in messy rivulets as he sprinted, reduced to a near-animal state of pure survival, pure adrenaline. He leapt clear over a pizza party like a gorilla escaped from the zoo, then he burst out into the parking lot, escaping in a gust of outhouse-laced air-conditioning, his mom and his brother and all his brother's little friends staring at him in slack-jawed horror. *Bye forever,* he thought.

Joey tore off into the night smelling like a slaughterhouse, choking up a sob from somewhere so deep that it might as well have been his asshole. As it hit the air, it sounded suspiciously like a tortured moo.

The Place

For most of high school I was obsessed with the Gerard Manley Hopkins poem "Spring and Fall." I wrote four separate pieces that were inspired by it, but because I was still a child myself, I couldn't really capture the feeling of the poem at all. It means something different to be a child obsessed with grieving the looming curse of growing up than it does to be an adult observing the same tragedy with retrospective hindsight. So, these pieces were left to collect dust, as they were not very good.

Many years later, I plotted a long, horrific fairytale featuring two sisters who could access a parallel universe where they played a bloody game called Thrall. However, before they were sisters they were cousins, and one was named Margaret after "Spring and Fall," which I was clearly still haunted by. This piece deviated, but those two cousins needed a home.

This one grew from a combination of these seeds: my teenage musings on a beloved poem, the early, discarded scaffolding of what would later grow to become a much darker work. This story isn't dark, it's only bittersweet.

The Place

Spring and Fall
To a young child

> Márgarét, áre you gríeving
> Over Goldengrove unleaving?
> Leáves like the things of man, you
> With your fresh thoughts care for, can you?
> Ah! ás the heart grows older
> It will come to such sights colder
> By and by, nor spare a sigh
> Though worlds of wanwood leafmeal lie;
> And yet you wíll weep and know why.
> Now no matter, child, the name:
> Sórrow's spríngs áre the same.
> Nor mouth had, no nor mind, expressed
> What heart heard of, ghost guessed:
> It ís the blight man was born for,
> It is Margaret you mourn for.

Gerard Manley Hopkins

"It's easy to go to," Margaret promised. The garden sprawled around her, glittering green dotted in flowers, fat bumblebees swarming the lavender, and hummingbird moths zipping in haphazard paths from yarrow to yarrow. Summer and all her promise teemed like a pond, the good kind you could swim in. Clear water and tickling fish and violent chartreuse scum but only around the far edge, making it safe to wade in by the rope swing without having to touch it. I loved June more than anything in the world. A school year could be dreary, boring, skull-crushing. But then June would come along, and with a wave of her magic wand, she'd make it all right again.

"So let's go," I told Margaret. Brave, endless Margaret. Popsicles and sunscreen and sprinklers on the mind, chlorine-bleary around the periphery of her vision. "Show me how to get there."

"Alright but—you can't tell your brother," she whispered conspiratorially. Leaning in, sweet hot breath on the shell of my ear. "Or any boy. It's just for us."

This only delighted me further. Margaret was a year older and therefore infinitely cooler than I could ever fathom or aspire to be. Copper corkscrew curls that glinted like pennies at high noon, freckles on her nose and eyes like green apple candy. She did ballet after school while I was forced to attend boring old Bible study. There was nothing that could have made me love her more, could have wheedled further loyalty from my heart. "I won't tell anyone," I promised, crossing myself with chubby fingers, meaning it. "Girl cousins only."

We grinned at this—we were the only girl cousins in the family, and something about that felt sacred. She stood, solemnly brushing her hands down the grass-stained front of her pinafore. "Alright, you start like this. Put your hands up."

Four palms, ten fingers, lifted skyward. I copied her, stumbling when that cloud-stricken blue swelled over me. "Now, close one eye. The left one. Put your right foot up, stand on the other like a flamingo."

A ritual. Complex skips and jumps while rotating in a circle. A chant with magic words. I wish, I swear the ghosts wouldn't dare. Creep down the hall like a kitty kitty paw. Leap to the left! Leap to the right! Spin in a circle and turn off the lights!

Breathless, I gasped. The sky darkened. Sudden blackness eclipsed that vivid blue, the river—where had a river come from—suddenly rushed backward, white foam cascading over slippery rocks, leaves tumbling to the grass with a strange gust of sugared wind. Margaret's otherworldly red hair coming undone from its ribbon, chills erupting on my skin and my teeth chattering in my skull. But somehow, I wasn't afraid. This was just the game. And the game was how you got to The Place, and The Place—it was beautiful. Nothing bad could happen there. Junes upon Junes upon Junes, summer forever, girl cousins only.

———

She was right, it was easy to get to. Once you got the hang of the ritual, the steps and the words and the order of everything, it only took a minute or two to arrive. And you could stay there for hours without any time passing at all in the real world. The dreary, boring, skull-crushing world. We'd caper with fierce glossy unicorns and stay up all night drinking potions and saving princesses and climbing to the tall tippy tops of trees to look down upon the glorious kingdom. We could fight battles and slay monsters and send armies to die in our names while we feasted in the banquet hall. The Place, Our Place, with its enchanted forests and snow-dusted mountains and perilous oceans and bustling, magical cities. Serpentine beasts that roiled in great swamps, fluttery soft moths the size of polar bears, twisting cobblestone pathways between miniature castles. It was a brilliant secret, and we kept it dear. Lifetimes passing there while that summer ticked on, day after day. My brother played slip and slide and tee ball with the neighborhood kids in the meantime, and sometimes asked me and Margaret where we got off to. We'd just giggle, fingers tangled and sticky, my tongue pressed into the gap where my two front teeth had fallen out last month, knocked out by a sharp iron bayonet used to keep the fae from invading. "Nowhere," we'd sing-song.

A few years later, it became harder to find. We remembered all the steps in the ritual and did the dance dutifully. Legs crossed, hop hop hop, fall on your bum and pop back up.

"What's not working?" I asked on our third try, frustrated. Margaret's hair had bits of dead grass in it from tumbling to the ground so many times. She frowned, picking some out.

"I don't know." Then, a terrible pause, Margaret's eyes cast to the left and her cherry lip chewed between rows of white teeth. "Do you still believe in it? The Place, I mean?"

I stared at her. It was July, a burning hot one so fierce my clothes stuck to me with a layer of sweat, rivers snaking down the backs of my knees. "Of course I do! Don't you?"

She shrugged. A pinched expression, something uncertain glinting in her green eyes. They seemed less green this summer, the vibrancy dulled to a sage-brush softness, like in getting older, she sacrificed some of her brilliance. "I mean, yeah. But like. Do you ever wonder, if we just made it up?"

I thought back to all that transpired in The Place: the hot, copper slick of dragon's blood slippery on our fingers, dripping from cursed blades. Glorious gifts presented by fairy queens, exotic fruits that gave me stomach aches lasting well into the school year. Scars I still bore, trophies collected from the things we had slain, hanging above the stained glass windows in the palace gameroom. Bones, and battering rams, and those bayonets. "We couldn't have," I said firmly. "It was real."

"I know it was real," Margaret agreed, kicking at the grass. "It's just. We can't tell anyone else about it, and sometimes I wonder if it was all in our heads."

We looked at each other, something unspoken stretched taut in the stagnant, sweltering air between us. "One more time," I begged. "Let's try one more time, okay? I'll show you. It was real."

She nodded, then took my hand as we went through the motions. And almost like the magic itself took pity on us, the sky cracked and blackened. Margaret shrieked, I cheered. We danced in a frantic circle beneath a downpour of blood-crimson rain, fat droplets that fell heavy like acorns from oaks, stinging the skin of my arms. The Place unrolled before us, like a tiger's tongue from a fanged mouth. Cruel white-trunked trees, the whisper of glorious danger calling us back to our kingdom. *The princesses have returned. They are here to vanquish our enemies. Prepare for battle, don your armor, lay roses at their slippered feet.* We raced up the tongue, shoes sliding on the spongy red, and then we disappeared down its throat, cackling.

Margaret and I lay on the trampoline in my backyard come August, passing a tightly rolled joint back and forth. Her hair spread out around her like a copper halo, our ankles close without crossing. The night was a chorus of crickets and traffic, cars slamming by on the sun-warmed road, sending buffets of hot air toward us as they passed. The smoke was green and numbing in my throat, I coughed and rolled over. Margaret patted my chest. "Don't hurt yourself, kiddo."

I grimaced at her—I was turning seventeen in a month, and I did not feel like a kiddo. I felt old, exhausted, ancient. An uncertain future stretching ahead of me, knowledge that my upcoming school year would be spent slaving away on college applications meant to seal my fate. Margaret had already been through that gauntlet and was leaving in the fall for a prestigious art school back east. It choked me to think about her departure, so I didn't. I told myself she'd be here like she always was, that nothing was changing, that we'd spend our summers together like always. To cope, I dulled my anxiety with weed and stolen beers. I was always better at believing the pretend stuff, anyway.

"It's pretty," she mumbled, glancing up at the hazy sky. There were no stars, just the usual gray-black faded to an indigo tonight, a strip of periwinkle hugging the mountains. "The color of….hm. Violet icing. On a fancy cake."

I blinked, mind fuzzy, tears not yet prickling. When I swallowed, my throat burned. "Remember… those games we'd play? All the crazy foods? High-ceilinged halls full of pastries?" I ventured. Saying it loud felt like telling a secret.

She laughed, a tinkling sound like shattering glass. "Oh my god, sort of. You always made up the most insane stuff. What did you call it, our summer thing?"

"The Place," I murmured.

"So fun," she said, closing her eyes. "I should make art of it, in school. Paint those wild skies you would describe, and the, um, lizard things? We would pretend to ride on?" Pretend. A bitten, two-beat lie, or maybe not. Maybe I didn't remember anymore, maybe it had been so long the past was obscured like the stars, indistinct like a dream. "Our noble steeds. They were sort of like dragons."

"Right, or iguanas…giant iguanas. With wings. Talons. God. And we rode them into battle, to kill evil fairy armies, or something. There was so much *murder,* and blood! Aren't little girls supposed to play with Barbies? We were weird."

I, personally, did not think we were that weird. It was essential that we fought those battles. Essential that we protected our kingdoms, our people. But I said nothing, throat too thick, Margaret still prattling on. "We'd just sit around for hours, while you talked and talked. It was so vivid. Like being there." She reached out across the trampoline and held my hand. "I wish, I swear the ghosts wouldn't dare."

I swallowed a sob, tried to keep it silent in my chest, each breath aching. "Creep down the hall like a kitty kitty paw."

"Leap to the left!" she giggled, kicking up one foot, then the other. "Leap to the right!"

And then, like the *amen* bookending an incantation, like the period on a page, like the termination of childhood: "Spin in a circle and turn off the lights!"

I shut my eyes and prayed for the sky to go black, but nothing changed.

Prodigal Son

This story is one of two in this collection that was originally fanfiction (Feeze! is the other, believe it or not). I very rarely adapt my fanfiction, as I tend to write things deeply mired in canon. However, in this case the story is so wildly and unrecognizably derivative from the source material I'm almost positive no one will guess what it began as (unless they already read it in its original form). This story is only a few years old. I wrote it in an empty house with a woodstove that I couldn't keep a fire going in, so it will forever remind me of the smell of lighter fluid and burning newspaper, smoke pouring into an icy living room, so thick my eyes watered.

Prodigal Son

The bar is smoky, so your eyes sting when you see him for the first time.

Young, but not too young. You watch him fumble with his wallet to show his ID to the bartender, who barely offers it a second glance before sliding him a PBR across the counter. The boy's blond hair is the same gold of beer pouring into a glass, a straw-shade tinted red under the neon Budweiser sign he's sitting beside, topped off with pale foam like Sun-In highlights.

You think you'll only look at him. His pretty pouting mouth and barely-there freckles and the column of his neck disappearing down into a well-worn flannel. He's the sort of boy you like best—bravado slapped over shy bones like caulk into fist-holes punched through old walls.

But after a few furtive looks around the bar, his eyes fall on you. And like something from a porno, he gets up, one hand shoved into the pocket of his Levi's and the other tight-knuckled around his glass.

"Hi," he says, sitting down at your little table in the back. He looks even younger up close, and you wonder if that ID was a fake. There's a nervous cloud around him, and he rakes a hand through his hair, cheeks pink as he says, "I don't normally do stuff like this, but, um. Are you, like. Cruising?"

It's very charming how clumsily that word fits in his mouth. Your endearment to it soothes the sucker-punch of what he's throwing out there, naked and dangerous. "If I wasn't, asking like that could have gotten you into a world of trouble, kid," you say.

Relief slackens his shoulders. "But you are, aren't you?"

You take a measured sip of your sidecar, pretend your heart isn't speeding. Pretend it doesn't still scare you to be clocked by a stranger. "I wasn't planning on it tonight. But I could be convinced to make an exception," you decide.

He swings his legs, and you notice he's too short for the barstool. You think of Little League and stolen bubblegum, things from your childhood you never got to pass on from one generation to the next, forcing you to hunt ghosts in the boys you find, the boys you fuck. "I heard this bar was *that* sort of bar. Not, like, a *gay bar* gay bar, but the sort of bar you could…well," he shrugs. "I don't really know how to do it right, sorry if I sound like an ass."

He doesn't sound like an ass, that's for sure. Only stupid, naive. The sort of fool who'll end up curbstomped or dragged behind a bumper, a rookie queer who waltzes right up to strange men and asks if they're looking for sex with other men, like he doesn't know any better. It's laid so bare that part of you *wants* to entertain it. *Wants* to believe this is the way the world works, instead of in code and in bathroom stalls, between bruised knuckles, on drugs. "Listen," you say. "Maybe you should try one of those gay bars. More your speed."

He shakes his head. "Oh, I've been. Not what I'm looking for."

You cock a brow. "And what is that?"

The look he gives you turns your stomach, transforms you into a dumb, sizzling thing. Big cow's eyes up through pale lashes, some dizzy shade of blue you've only dreamed about. "Real shit," he says after a beat. "Just. Something real. All those guys at those clubs—they're shiny and shaved and high as hell. Air-brushed, sort of, like pinups in a magazine. Plus, they all *know* each other already. Feels like high school again. Being on the outs with the cool kids, I dunno. Reminds me of giving handys to the football players who wouldn't look at me in the halls."

You're surprised. You thought this was his first time ever, that he'd spent years jacking it alone in his room and only now just plucked up the courage to come try it out for real. But maybe not. Maybe you and this kid have more in common than you realized, a whole life of shadows and secrets and dirty knees on back alley concrete.

"I'm old enough to be your father," you say, because it's the last thorn sticking in you. You *are* a father, even if you've never met or seen your son. He was the outcome of your very last, pathetic attempt at denying who and what you were. You thought skipping the condom would make you a man. It didn't. She left town still pregnant nineteen years ago, and you stayed behind, drinking in bars, in code and in bathroom stalls, between bruised knuckles, on drugs.

"I think that's hot," the boy says, like it's a simple thing.

Maybe it is simple. Or maybe those blue begging eyes have your dick half-hard already, and it's been a while, you can't see clearly enough to find your self-preservation in the rubble left from the imploded life you could have had, if you'd been born different, without sin. "Alright, then," you say, polishing off your drink in a determined gulp. "In that case."

He lights up like Christmas, leaves the rest of his beer to grow warm in his glass, and follows you home. Like it's simple. Like this is the way the world works.

———

It's only there in your room, flat on your back with him perched on your hips in nothing but his tented briefs, that you get a name. "I don't like my real name, it's a geezer name," he says breathlessly, grinding against you in desperate bucks. You're not even fucking yet, but this boy moves like he's hungry, like he's *starving*. Like he's waited his whole goddamned life to sit on an old man and rub his hands through the salt-and-pepper thatch of chest hair, an acolyte at the feet of a saint carved from marble.

"Thought you liked geezers," you say, squeezing his thighs. You're in heaven; he's so golden and sweat-dewy, his hair unwashed and his ass plump and perfect as he rubs it into you.

"I do," he says. His smile is sly and crooked, not unlike your own. "Don't wanna be named after one, though. So I changed it."

"What to?" you ask, getting your hands in his underwear, sneaking curious fingers into the sticky heat of his crack. *Damn.* His hole clenches tight under your finger, so you rub it, and he keens, arching his back, deep and slutty.

"Uh, Flash," he bites out, rocking back into your touch. "*Fuck.*"

You scoff. "From geezer name to what…race horse? What sort of name is *Flash*?" you ask in a low voice, teasing him as you dig insistently into that perfect, twitching furl.

"Flash like, um, Flash Gordon? Loved him as a kid. Plus, Always wanted to fuck a quarterback. Never happened, though, so I decided maybe I could just, like, become the one of my dreams instead."

You peer up at him and sort of see the resemblance. Shock of blond hair, toned shoulders, a good throwing arm. "That reference seems too old for you. And didn't Flash play polo?"

He shakes his head, teeth milk-white and brilliant in the dark, the sweat-damp sweep of his hair sticking to his brow. "Nah, you're thinking of the comics, old man. I mean the movie. From the '80s. It's great, you should see it sometime." Then, after a beat, he throws his head back to show off the flicker of his throat, bobbing around another bitten-off, *"Fuck."*

You watch him transform into something crumpled and whining at the tips of your fingers, his cock leaking so the dark patch in the threadbare fabric clinging to the crown widens. "God. Tight little hole, isn't it? You like that?"

"No one's ever touched me there," he admits in a small, almost apologetic voice. He collapses onto your chest, licks over the hair, matting it down before sucking a nipple in his sharp mouth. He doesn't ever stay in one place very long because he's too curious, so eager to get every inch of you under his tongue, a magpie hunting for coins and jewelry and other shiny stuff to hoard. "Can I sniff your pits?" he eventually asks, shy, like he thinks you'll deny him. "I can smell you. Smell so good."

You raise an arm over your head easily, cock throbbing beneath his weight. "Have at it."

He dives in, presses his burning face into the ditch of your pit to inhale, and like something holy is transpiring, time slows. Your long lonely life is whittled down and reduced to this solitary moment, this young boy's nose buried in you, the rhythmic tide of his breath sucking in and out as he fills his lungs. Your hand finds its way from his briefs to the long planes of muscle framing his spine, up to his skull where you tenderly cradle him, and it reminds you of something, though you cannot think of what. You only lie there, distantly moved, staring up at the ceiling of your bedroom.

Eventually, an image comes to you—the cup of your hand against his head reminds you of paintings you've seen of the Virgin Mary, the way she holds the infant Jesus to her breast. Maybe this realization should disgust you, but it doesn't. You pet his hair, murmur *that's it, good boy, take your fill,* like a mother might speak to her nursing son. Like you might speak to your *own* son, if you knew him.

"Can I lick it?" he asks, pulling back with his eyes wet in the dark, the shimmer of your sweat shining on the tip of his upturned nose.

"Yeah, baby. You can lick it. Go ahead, make out with it."

He does, groaning as he sucks, rutting against your lap in shuddering, indulgent thrusts. His tongue is so wet, his body glistening silver in the moonlight, and *fuck.* You could die right here. Live eternally in this moment where a boy locks up on you and comes, just from the taste of your sweat.

He doesn't say anything, only pants, shivering as he kisses down your body, a pathway like a navigator plotting his way home in stars. When he makes it to your cock, he just kneels there for a few moments, inhaling, drooling, sucking you in. "You like the way that cock smells?" you ask him, stroking his hair again, the halo of blond between your spread thighs. You look enormous next to him, thick and hairy, a black twilight shadow contrasting to his brilliant sun-spilt afternoon.

"Love it," he murmurs. "Smells just like mine. You know, I used to sneak off to the bathroom in middle school and jack off, then sniff my hand all day, during class. To tide me over for when I could get home and do it again. Even then, I loved the smell of cock."

"What a dirty boy," you chide. "What did you think about, when you touched yourself?"

"Old men," he confesses, cheek pressed to your cock, red against red. There's a twist of a smirk, on his mouth, licorice sweet. "Daddy issues, I guess."

"That's okay, baby. I'll be your old man."

You groan as he starts to lick you, a handful of careful swipes before opening wide and swallowing you down. He doesn't know what he's doing—gags a few times, eyes streaming, and you feel his teeth more than once, but *goddammit,* it's the enthusiasm that counts. He's crying on your cock, worshiping it, making it shine with his spit until you can't take the aimless roving anymore. You hold him down, fuck his throat, overflow like a bay after a storm. And as you feed him your come right from the source, he nurses all over again. You think about Mary. You think about Jesus.

Once you've finished, sleep comes fast, sideswipes you shortly after he passes out at your hip without showering, the stink of sex cloying in the air. And you've picked up younger men before, you've had plenty of one-night stands. You're not sure why this one feels different, but it does. Like you know him already, like you remember his bones against yours, his mouth on your skin, his dirty hair fanning out on your chest in gold thread.

———

When you twitch to life, he's kneeling on the foot of your bed in the dawn light, eyes wide and pleading, a framed photo from your mantle pressed into his chest. You can't see what it is, but the knowledge he took it ices your blood over all the same. "Don't be mad," he says. "Please don't be mad."

You sit up, very suddenly awake. "What did you do?" you ask him.

"I got up early, went to take a piss, and got tempted to snoop around because—I dunno, because I like you and I wanted to know stuff about you and —I saw, I couldn't *help* but see that— that you have this picture, um, of my mom?" he says, which doesn't make any sense. You blink at him, baffled. Why in the hell would you have a picture of some strange boy's mom? Some strange boy whose real name you don't even know? "It's one from when she was young. I have the same picture. I knew she grew up here. It's why I came back, actually, because I was looking for—because I was trying to find—"

My father sits unsaid and horrifying between your bodies, flashing in neon like the Budweiser sign at the bar. *No,* you think, even though you've already figured it out, already done the math, already placed the blond of his hair and the twist of his mouth and the shape of his nose in the last three seconds of silence. You sit there, staring at him. *No. That can't be how I know you. That can't be why you feel like home. Should have known love doesn't happen like that—only blood, only DNA, only regret.*

You get up and begin to pace, stomach churning, but not as much as it should be.

"Don't be mad," he says again.

"Did you know?" you bark out, because *god,* if he suspected it—if he knew your name, had seen a picture of his father when he was younger, and *still* followed you home—a wave of dizziness crashes over you, and you brace your hands on your dresser, listening to the creak of your bed as he stands.

"Not—not really," he says weakly. "I wondered. When I came up to you at the bar, I was between those two questions—did you have a son nineteen years ago, and do you wanna fuck. I don't know why I settled on the second one, it was—stupid. I guess. I shouldn't have—I *should–*"

"Kid," you say. It's a reflex, it's what you call every boy under thirty you take home and take apart, but this time the full implication hits you. *Kid. Son. Kid. Son.* Why is it that only *now* you're asking yourself why you use those words in bed? Why you have a soft dirty spot for boys around nineteen? Why you're just shy of your fiftieth birthday and have never had a real, honest-to-god relationship with a man your age? You sit down, sink to the floor without looking up at him. "You need to leave. Get the fuck out of here."

"But. Please. If you really are my dad, you can't just—" he starts, like it's fucking okay to call you that after he's sucked the cock he came from. You gag, then retch unproductively before wiping your spit-wet mouth on the back of your hand, mind spinning, foam on the hardwood. You can still feel him in your lap, you can still hear that steady murmuring breath as he huffed your pits like he wanted to crawl inside you. You wait for disgust to hit your body, for your gut to turn itself inside out. But maybe you're broken, because nothing ever comes.

"*Leave*," you say one last time, standing and pointing to your door.

He listens and skitters out like a kicked dog, like a kid who just got caught stealing bubblegum from the convenience store after a Little League game. You remember the scorch of summer, the smell of your own dirty hair in your own dirty cap, what it was like to watch the older boys pitch around the dugout, sweat marks in the underarms of their uniforms and your throat thick with some nameless want. How you'd pretend your dad would come to your games, even though you never knew your dad. Just like your son never knew his.

Once he's gone, you smell your hand and find the faint whiff of his ass still lingering under the rest of him, beneath your chewed nails. His sweat, his skin, his cheap cologne. Like your son in middle school, you inhale, hoping it will tide you over, even though you're sure there can be no next time.

A day later, you get a text from an unknown number.

Hey, it's Flash, from the bar. Can we please talk?

You stare at it, insides coiling up, hot and sickening. You're still waiting for the full horror of what happened to hit you, and still, you feel nothing but numb. You shut your phone off and toss it into your dirty sheets, then go online and type in *dad x stepson raw fuck* to see if you can get off to it. Maybe this is some kink thing that can be nullified with porn, maybe the reality can be cured by the artifice. But instead, the dialog is so fucking cheesy you can't even get hard, so you shut your laptop before any dicks even come out. You keep thinking about the cornsilk softness of your kid's hair, wishing you had been there for him in some *other* way, before *this* happened. Wishing you could dig up the past, like a dog in someone's garden.

Before you know it, you're a little drunk and that phone is in your hand again.

did you ever play little league? you type before deleting it letter by letter.

how did you get this number?? you send instead.

It takes him seconds to reply, like he's fucking waiting.

Told you, I'm a snoop. I sent myself a text from your phone while you were sleeping. you don't even have a lock code. you should get one of those, old man, otherwise you'll get hacked.

Old man. You scrub a hand over your twenty-four-hour beard, horrified by how casual this interaction is, how wide open and bleeding he's stayed. And as hard as you've tried to bleach it out, you remember what it felt like to fuck into his wet, eager, sloppy mouth, the way he whined around his dad's cock like he couldn't get it down his throat fast enough. How you told him *I can be your old man* like you *knew.* Maybe you did know. It seems unfair to tell him he can't call you that *now,* after you gave permission, but it still sets your teeth on edge to read those words.

I don't think we should be talking. I think we fucked up the only chance we had at a normal father&son relationship.

why does it have to be normal? I'm not normal. are u?

You stare long and hard at that. Of course you're not normal, but there are plenty of not-normals out there who draw the line at fucking their sons. Or playing ball with their sons they're pretending they didn't fuck. Or having catch-up dinners with sons who don't want them to forget the fucking part—sons who flirt over text message. Or maybe that's not even what he's doing, hell if you know. You didn't raise a boy, you don't know how they text their fathers, you can only speak for the way a Grindr chat goes when you're over forty meeting up with a kid under twenty. All you know is code, bathroom stalls, bruised knuckles, drugs.

You don't text back. You lie there in your bed, sniff him from the sheets, and make yourself come thinking about *dad x son raw fuck,* the real deal.

You hate yourself after. Ignore two days' worth of increasingly desperate texts from him, all begging, pleading, pitiful, sweet. Like his tongue in your pit. His hole like a ring on your finger. You think of the freaky perfect way his skull fit into your cupped palm, then pray to Mary for the first time in your whole life. A father to a mother, like she might have some sage advice for you, parent to parent.

But the line remains silent, nothing but a dead-ass dial tone.

You could block his number, but you don't.

You could train your brain to give him up and spit him out, but you don't.

Instead, you run away from it, tunnel out from under it, pave over it. You're *pissed,* you think there should've been a failsafe, some warning siren in your DNA that gets unlocked if you're about to fuck your blood relative's mouth without knowing it. You feel like god has failed you. That he should have stopped you, smited you, *told* you. That you shouldn't have wanted Flash so bad in the first place, Like there should have been something that felt wrong, or off, or *obvious* about it the second you let him kiss you.

God shouldn't have made his hole feel so fucking good against your finger. God shouldn't have let you think his beer-spit tasted so sweet. It shouldn't have felt like heaven, so maybe there is no god, maybe there is no heaven. You've never believed in that stuff anyway, really, unless you were desperate.

You got in a car wreck a few years ago. Your fault, you'd had a few at the bar and drove home anyway, swerved and hit the guard rail when a deer dashed out in front of you. No seatbelt, so your body was thrown from the shattered windshield upon impact, and as you bled out on the pavement, you prayed for god to let you live, even though you knew you didn't deserve it one bit.

But you did live. You didn't even come out that worse for wear, just a few broken ribs, a concussion, some abrasions that bled and scarred. A goddamned miracle, like some guy upstairs was listening. In the ambulance on the way to the ER, you remember thinking, *I'm a believer, now, I'll pray every day, not just when I need something, not just when I'm gonna die.*

You forgot all about that moment until now, of course. Even when you cough and those old broken ribs ache, you don't think much about god, but it's funny how things turn out. Because *now* you're praying every day. *Now* you are devout. *Deliver me from evil,* you say over and over again, because it's the only part of the Lord's prayer you know by heart.

Instead of being delivered, you dream about your son coming in your lap, the sound he made like he was dying. You dream about his golden hair, same color yours was before it went gray and receded early, in your thirties. Like a blanket of ash settling over a golden field during wildfire season. Like snow putting out a fire.

———

The sweetness leaves his texts, like he's figured out that won't work.

look. the least you can do is meet up for coffee ONCE to talk to me. gimme some answers. seems like the decent thing to do after abandoning my mom for nineteen years because you're a faggot.

You feel guilty enough that you can't let that one slide, so in spite of yourself, you answer.

She left, ignored all my calls. I figured she didn't want me in your life, which, given how fucked up this is and i am, was probably for the better.

It takes him a while to respond, and in the meantime, you pray. You touch yourself, and you pray. You think of him between your thighs, about his mother's maybe-premonition, and you pray. No one answers, but you do it anyway, sending signals out into the ether, shooting blanks.

Im sorry i called you a faggot. Obviously i am 2. is the first text you get back, followed shortly by *please just meet up with me again? Wherever you want. I'll do whatever. I won't be crazy, I promise.*

And there have got to be a million better ways to deal with this, but you're tired, and you're lonely, and even after opening your windows and washing your sheets, weeks later, you still catch notes of his sweat in your bedroom. Maybe it's your own sweat, though. Maybe you smell the same, like father like son, and the thought makes you at least twice as hard as it makes you sick, and there's nothing you can do about any of it, so.

you got my address, kid. I'll be home all night.

Omw he sends back, and you wait, god's name on your tongue like a tab of acid.

———

You think that maybe when you see him, the want will dry up like a seasonal spring in the dead of August. That *knowing* he's your son and mulling that over for the last few weeks will have cured you, and the final step to unlocking peace will be standing in a room with him again. Feeling strictly and distinctly paternal. Apologizing, and Flash accepting that apology. Maybe it will be something you both laugh about, even. A terrible mistake, a shocking coincidence, but an honest, innocent thing. Maybe you'll move on from it. You'll play ball in the park, go to dinner, show him old photographs, send each other Christmas cards. You'll find out if he ever played Little League, you'll hold him close and feel nothing wrong or dirty when you say, *I'm so sorry I was never there, son.* That void in your heart, the one that gets bigger every year, will finally have something inside, stretching to fill it.

But that's not what happens. You open the door, and Flash stands there on your cement landing in tight black jeans and a white V-neck, his blond hair combed back neatly away from those sin-blue eyes. There is no failsafe. There is no warning siren. There is no god. Swift as a reflex, you want him bad as ever, your eyes flicking immediately to his mouth like tuning forks over water.

"Hey," he says, awkwardly shifting his weight. The air crackles between your bodies, and you wonder if he can feel it, too, or if that's all you. If you're that fucked up you're generating a whole goddamned electric storm for your nineteen-year-old son. "Um, thanks for seeing me. Like, thank you so much, really. Can I come in?"

You gesture into your living room. "Sure," you say.

But he doesn't walk past you to the couch, like you have imagined him doing every time you thought up all your speeches and apologies. It's not just you, it *must* not be, because his gaze flicks up and down your body before he's stepping past the threshold of your home, then kissing you. This boy who named himself after a fictional quarterback space hero from a comic book. This boy who is running from himself. This boy who went to his mom's hometown and fucked the first old man he met in the local dive bar. Messy and reckless, like father like son.

It's not the way a son kisses his father. He slides his tongue right in just like he did that first night, a home run. So eager and impatient that your teeth click together. You don't even *think* to shove him off —instead, you push your hands through his hair, mess it up, cradle his skull like he is your *boy*. He *is* your boy, you think. The claim rockets through you, hot and terrible as he presses flush against your body in one long, yearning line. "Fuck, I just—I couldn't stop, I don't even *care—*"

You realize you don't care either. You kiss him hard to shut him up, steer him to your couch, put him there and lay him out and suck a mark onto his neck so there's proof you were here for your son. You loved him, you loved him right out in the open. One sudden dirty rush to make up for nineteen years of silence.

Kneeling over his body, you tongue-fuck his sweet plush mouth until he's moaning, grinding against you, making fists in your clothes murmuring "*dad, dad, daddy, please,*" in a little boy's voice. He feels smaller than you remember, soft and breakable under you, clinging to your big shoulders, like you are not just some man he's picking up in a bar, not just a father, but a fucked up, kaleidoscope melted crayon mess of both. *Real shit*, he had said when you asked him what he wanted. *Something real.*

"I'm here, baby. I'm sorry about before," you whisper into his hair, meaning *the past few weeks* but also *the last nineteen years.* He feels like a kid who threw up, who had a nightmare, who crawled into your bed in his footie PJs smelling like fever sweat. Your responsibility, for better or for worse, the past catching up and sinking its teeth into your flesh with one final, fatal, snake bite.

He rubs his face into your shirt, mouths over your Adam's apple. Tongue wet with spit, face wet with tears. "I lied, when you asked me what I thought about when I touched myself, back in middle school. I said older men, but what I *really* meant was my dad. I thought about my dad, like, specifically. I didn't know him—you—but I imagined it anyway, him loving me, *you* loving me, I guess. I thought he might look like Flash Gordon, for some reason. My mom said you played football. That's all she really knew about you."

You shake your head. "Baseball," you tell him. "It was baseball."

Then you unbutton his jeans, get your hand around his cock, stroke him gently, and tease him until he stops trying to chase his orgasm and just softens into your sweaty palm like a melting Hot Tamale candy and its red dye 40 smear. It's a beautiful thing, the way he lets himself feel the pleasure, sinks beneath the aimless rhythm of being touched. A hand on his cock, back and forth like playing catch, like chewing bubblegum. *That's it, that's it,* you think, loving how sticky he gets, how much pre-cum leaks out of him for you to lick up. He closes his eyes, sucks the inside of his cheek, your good boy.

When he comes, he whimpers, and you kiss him through it. Play with him until he goes soft, tuck him into his briefs like you're tucking him in for bed. Then you cover his mouth and nose with the palm of your hand, let him sniff.

It feels profoundly natural, like being a father, caring for your son, letting him smell his own cock on his daddy's hand. You wonder if you've been recreating the dream of this specific intimacy with every younger man you've ever fucked, and he feels like the pinnacle because he *is*. You wonder if he's done the same damn thing in reverse. Maybe none of this sits wrong in your gut anymore because it's *not* wrong. Maybe god loved his son so much, too, and this is what it is, to pray. To be answered.

The King of Hearts

This story is both the oldest, and the least edited story in this entire collection. I wrote it when I was seventeen, and what came out of me then has changed very little from what you will read here, today. I resisted the urge to heavily revise it, as I wanted evidence that when operating at my best, I have always been a compelling writer interested in depicting real and complex human themes. I think over-editing this piece would suck the magic out of it, that weird, raw embarrassing high school magic.

The King of Hearts

Did you know that the King of Hearts is the only card king without a mustache? I always noticed it when I was a kid, that he was the nicest looking king. A cad, a charming cad, but a cad nonetheless. Back then, I thought mustaches made men look predatory, or irreparably sad. Cowboys out on the open range, lonely outlaws with their hidden upper lips. The King of Hearts should have been my first indication that I was not cut out to endure the sadness of sad men. When you and I first met, we were kids. You were smooth-faced until you weren't, then you used to shave every morning with a straight razor. That was before you grew scruffy and thin, like someone pressed their lips to yours and sucked out the will, deflated you like a popped balloon.

I've always liked useless facts. People who don't know me very well buy me books with useless facts in them for Christmas, the kind of books people keep on toilet tanks to read in between the tired, warped magazines when they forget to take their fiber. I have a shelf full of those books, and most of the facts repeat 100 times, recycled from edition to edition. The useless fact that people remember about me is that I like useless facts, which is why there is so much repetition on my toilet tank.

People buy me those books the way they used to buy you 80s arena rock merchandise. Somewhere down the line they must have heard you liked Metallica, so you ended up swimming in shirts. They made up half your wardrobe, so it only reinforced our friends' assumptions that this was your entire personality. The truth was that you liked lots of other music, too, you were just too polite to ever say anything.

Most of those shirts probably ended up in the local Goodwill. When I forced you to move out, you had a sack of stuff to donate, and I seem to remember a lot of it being white elephant gifts that built up over the years. KISS action figures, AC/DC vintage lunch pails. An Aerosmith guitar strap, even though you didn't play guitar. I remember because I could only look at the piles, never at you.

Did you know that the word "lethologica" means not being able to remember the word you want to use? We played too many games of Scrabble when we lived together, so many that I got sick of losing to your quick mind and huge vocabulary and cut-throat use of all the triple word score spaces. I remember you saying, *even the worst words are winners when you have the triple word score.* When I refused to play Scrabble with you, you'd play with yourself, dumping all the little wooden tiles all over the coffee table and trying to use every single one, inventing words when necessary, a Webster's Dictionary open on your lap.

My name, Rette, means "rescue" in German. My dad was a policeman who worked in the K-9 unit, and he told me they used commands in foreign languages to control the dogs, usually Hungarian and German, *Schutzhund* training, it was called. He died when I was young, so I forgot about that word until I found the fact in one of my books. Then I wondered if I was named after a police dog command. In German, Rette sounds soft and exotic, but when my friends say it in their harsh American accents, it sounds like a curse. Rette, like wreck like red like reposition like pay your rent, Rette. I miss the way you said it soft, Rette, like wraith like ray like rain. You were an unrealized singer, you'd trip through the bedroom hallway and hum mindlessly but never onstage. Still, your voice gave me chills. Made me sit down on the piano bench, bowled over, moved by the high sweet clarity. Did you know that karaoke means "empty orchestra" in Japanese?

I fell in love with you when I was twenty-two and you were only twenty. At the time, it didn't feel like a new thing, it felt like a thing that was inside me always, something laid in my mother's womb for me to collect and keep dormant until I turned twenty-two and you turned twenty and we shared a house in the city with two other guys from school who came and went like everyone else does.

Did you know that every human spends a half-hour of their life as a single cell? I'd just graduated and didn't know what I wanted to do yet, and you were contemplating dropping out. College was expensive, and we were so young, so aimless, floating to and fro with no real direction. It made sense that we'd eventually crash together. It was like I woke up one morning and couldn't live without you, I was a one-celled scrap of meat pulsing in a mess of endometrium. Then, just like that, my whole past made sense. My whole future. You weren't my childhood best friend anymore, you were the answer to my idle wandering. Maybe I put too much pressure on you to save me from ennui.

Back in those days, you didn't sleep. You called it insomnia, but I think you *tried* to stay awake, downing mug after mug of coffee and cola until your eyes got crazy and bright, and you'd say every single thing you thought, regardless of whether it made sense or not. I think you did it because it made you feel drunk, which was exciting for a square kid like you who didn't even have champagne at Christmas.

We'd stay up all night talking about everything, art and music and philosophy and religion and people we knew from our hometown. I remember cookie dough in someone's kitchenette once, and you with no sleep stumbling toward me, a dangerous dollop of it on your finger, smearing it down my forehead and licking it off. No one knew why I didn't get angry. That was then, some New Years that's not new anymore, that thing between us that's not new anymore.

You were a quiet kid, a sweet teenager. And later, a gentle lover. I thought being with another man would hurt—blood on knuckles, some battering ram stretching my body in a place too tight to be stretched. Cops in alley ways, poisoned blood and white powder. It was 1991, and everyone was afraid. I ran from it the same as you, but we circled back together to face it, eventually, and it was soft. Soft like your shaven upper lip. I remember you placing your hands on my shoulders and rubbing our cheeks together like cats, yours smooth and fragrant like baby powder, mine slightly stubbly in a way that made me feel embarrassingly unclean next to you because I still saw you as a cad, a charming cad, but a cad nonetheless.

In those days, I thought you were the King of Hearts. When you breathed, I pretended it was the sound of every speck of blood rushing inside of you, the sound of your secrets coming in and out between your teeth, the sound of every fish swaying back and forth in the ocean. The thought you could make all those sounds amazed me. They drowned out the cops, the poison, the sniffing. It was like magic.

Did you know that cats sleep sixteen to eighteen hours a day? I noticed when it started. We'd finally bought our own place a few years ago, and over the course of those years, you went from being an angry, brilliant, beautiful, young twenty-year-old college kid to a sad, rent-paying adult. I guess I did, too. That's what happens when you get older, it's the same old story, nothing new, nothing revolutionary. But maybe because I loved you so much, it felt different. Peter Pan meant to stay the smooth-cheeked King of Hearts forever, up all night talking, scheming, singing in that clean alto.

But it wasn't like something outside was making you sad, it wasn't like something I could change or fix. *You* got sad. Inside sad, fundamentally sad. Something you were made of died. I didn't know why. You didn't know why. It was like a switch in your chest, flicked by god's thumb.

You started sleeping, and you hardly stopped. You'd fall asleep on the couch, or in the double bed with the slate-gray sheets, or on the bathroom floor wrapped in a terry cloth robe with a two-day beard, or on the Scrabble board with your hair all fanned out around you and the tiles scattered like forgotten prayers to cure lethologica, five-letter words that even I knew the meaning of, all the triple word scores empty.

We tried a lot of things to get you back, things like sitting on a gingham couch talking to a woman named Carol about our slate-gray sheets every Monday. We tried orange prescription bottles that clogged up the medicine cabinet like too much hair in a drain. We tried "checking in," me asking you things every morning over breakfast that you only picked at like, *How are you feeling? Why are you feeling that way? What can I do to help?*

Did you know that forty percent of party guests will snoop in medicine cabinets? Did you know that if you keep a goldfish in a dark room, it will turn white?

Now every time I see a Motorhead shirt at Goodwill, I smell it to see if it used to be yours. I can never tell. You hardly wore the ones you got rid of, and all those places smell alike, the combined scents of a million people, the combined breath of a million fish all swaying in the sea. I wonder where you are, how many of my useless facts you remember. Did you know that "fear" in German is "*angst*"? Perhaps my father should have named me that. I was too scared to take care of you anymore, too tired. I was afraid of every Monday, the way my younger self was afraid of cops and blood and my dead father.

I missed you. I missed your soft cheeks. I missed you singing "Rette" like I was a police dog and you were my handler. Making this rough, calloused thing impossibly gentle.

When it finally occurred to me that we had already died, I was reading on the right side of the bed, and you were sleeping beside me on the left, starting your tenth hour. Earlier, you had woken up, rolled over bleary-eyed and five o' clock-shadowed and told me, *Did you know that most people choose Monday to kill themselves?* I stared at you for a moment, not recognizing you, seeing only a white goldfish. I answered that I didn't know, but that was a lie. I'd read that before, in one or several of the 100 fact books stacked on the tank of our toilet, gathering dust.

You went back to sleep, and I watched you for a long time, realizing then that with your newly mustached lip and newly scruffy cheeks, newly muted voice and forever empty orchestra, you'd lost all your magic. You were unreachable and unrescuable, despite my name. I had to leave.

I still hear your voice singing in the kitchen when I forget you're gone. *Rette* like ray like wraith like rain. I missed you then. I still miss you today. I wonder where you are, these days. If you're in some hospital, miserable but safe, or with some new man, happy but in danger. I don't know why I see other men as dangerous, but I do. Loving someone doesn't seem worth it, when anything you love can die. Can die while it's still living, light snuffed out, every fish inside the whole sea pausing on a held breath. You were my one shot, my last shot. Now I thumb through old books, and remember. Venus is the only planet in the solar system to spin clockwise. The Japanese have a word for when we eat even if we're not hungry, *kuchisabishii*, which literally translates to "lonely mouth." Pigeons can differentiate between a Picasso and a Monet. Snakes can predict earthquakes. Birds could not live in space because they need gravity to swallow. Thanatophobia is the fear of death. Cherophobia is the fear of happiness.

Absolute Zero

Absolute Zero *is not a short story as much as it is a novella. I wrote the vast bulk of it my final semester of college, but as I began nearing the story's inevitable climax, I shied away from finishing. Only several scenes away from my intended and outlined end, I ground to a screeching halt, and for years, it sat like this. Nearly completed, untouched. Every few years, I would drag it out and read it, marvel at how funny and painful it was, then kick myself for refusing to finish. Why had I abandoned a perfectly good story on the final stretch? Why was it so hard to write those last few scenes when I knew exactly what was meant to happen? What about this particular piece had me so paralyzed?*

When I began the process of selecting stories for Salivation, *I didn't initially include this one as a possibility even though it is very explicitly about hunger and loneliness, so it thematically seemed like an obvious fit. I told myself it was too long, but I knew deep down the real reason was that although I was successfully finishing plenty of older works, something about this one felt impossible to surmount. Still, for the sake of being thorough, I pulled it from the shelf and dusted it off and read through it. When I arrived at the end, it became achingly clear why I couldn't finish this piece: I loved Jake, the main character, so much that I did not want to let him go. Ending his story meant ending his suffering, but also, ending his hope, and I didn't want to do that to him. I wanted to keep him in his self-made purgatory of hunger and loneliness forever, hopeful and blind and young. I knew how this story was supposed to end, but I'd grown too close to this character to follow through on my plans for him. I wanted to spare him and myself.*

Luckily, I've grown older. I can see Jake's future with utter clarity, and know now what I could not know then, which is that he would be fine. So finally, ten years later, I cut him loose and finished this story in time to include it in Salivation. *I hope some of you love him as much as I do.*

Absolute Zero

I have this nightmare sometimes that aliens are making humans think the world is beautiful. It's wake-up-in-a-cold-sweat kind of terrifying.

In the nightmare, no one knows it's aliens at first. Everyone thinks they're finding the world beautiful of their own free will. Like, Mark and I, for instance. Mark and I are staying at my dead Granny's house in the mountains, and we're supposed to be sleeping, but instead, we wake up together and go outside because we're both totally compelled by the beauty of the world to wake up and go outside. We want to go dance in the moonlight and worship the trees and stuff.

And even though it is completely out of character for both of us (we went hiking this one time and nearly died of heatstroke, and there ends all stories about our transcendental interactions with the outdoors), we both think it's because we want to, not because aliens are beaming mind-melting rays down on humanity from their spaceships.

So at my dead Granny's cabin in the mountains, Mark and I dance in the moonlight like when we were kids, playing naked in the sprinkler before we knew what naked meant. Then we get on our hands and knees and dig holes, because this is another thing the aliens are making humans do: dig holes to find them something important, some chemical or mineral to mend their spaceship, I don't know. It's a dream, so that detail isn't important.

We dig in the wet black earth, and Mark says something like, "This is so amazing, how we both want to do this. How we both think the world is so beautiful, and we've thought so this whole time and never told one another, and now we both just really want to dig these holes."

And I feel predictably warm and fuzzy because my feelings for Mark are all fucked up (even in this dream), so I say something mushy like, "I know, so amazing, dude. We're, like, the same person. We're meant to be."

And all around the world, this is happening. People are dancing in the moonlight and digging holes to find metal alloys or ore or worms or whatever for the aliens, and realizing the world is beautiful, and claiming these are totally original impulses. That they *want* to. That their connection over this shared act is authentic, like one individual connecting to another individual over their individual desire to dig holes in the mud, because humanity is way too terrified of not being individuals that they can't admit that maybe some external force is making them do something.

This is probably why the aliens in my dream chose humans to do their hole-digging, because they know other species would be suspicious of their sudden joint mentality. But humans have a joint mentality already and don't realize it, or at least they deny it, so the aliens decide they're a good mark, a good species to do their dirty work, they know humans will write some fiction about connection rather than admit they're being controlled. Humans are manipulable.

In my dream, I'm just like the rest of them. I'm just so thrilled there's something that Mark and I are authentically connecting over. I have dirt under my nails, and I don't care. Everyone is walking around with mud on their hands, and instead of being, like, "Hey, isn't it weird that we're all digging holes and turning into hippies, maybe there's something bigger going on here?" they're just, like, "Oh my god, you like to have dirty hands, too? What a coincidence! We should be friends!"

Humans are so lonely and desperate for connection, but they're so unwilling to admit they all share the same pain that comes from not being individual. There's a word for this. I think it might be paradox.

I only recognize that I'm being controlled by aliens when my parents and my little sister run outside, too, and start dancing in the moonlight and talking about how beautiful the world is and getting down on their hands and knees and digging until my mom's nightgown is black and translucent with filth and my dad's work slacks have grass stains on them and tears in the knee and my little sister's pink nail polish is coming off in chips. Nothing in the world could ever make me believe that I share hopes and wishes and desires and dreams with my family, nothing in the world could ever make me share *anything* with them, because I'm an individual, and they're not, so I know at that moment that something else is making me do this.

I back away, dirty and cold, and watch my family and Mark dig and dig and dig. And I look up into the night sky and see a fleet of UFO shadows on the moon, the shimmery silver beams of beauty-drug raining down on humanity like the northern lights from hundreds of shining saucers. And then I wake up.

———

My alarm goes off, and I feel the same sickness and anxiety that floods through my solar plexus every time my alarm goes off. I roll over. I stare at my gray ceiling, gray naked skin tangled in my gray sheets, and think, *I can't go to school today. Today is the day I really can't go. I just can't do it. I'll die,* just like I think every morning.

Then I get up, slide gray-naked from gray sheets. Feet hit the cold floor, toes curl, eyelids stick together with mucus. I blunder around clumsily until I find last night's boxers and sweatshirt piled like gray snow on the floor and put them on quick as I can because I fucking hate being naked, hate forcing the air to see my naked body, hate forcing my body to touch naked air, hate feeling bad for both of them having to witness the other because neither of them would care if it wasn't for my brain. I hate the whole thing. I'd rather forget I have flesh than never go to school again, which is saying a lot because I really, really hate school.

My dad is making toaster waffles. I can smell their distinctively fake, freezer-y smell from my room. My sister is screaming, probably because someone is trying to get her shoes on, and she throws a fit every morning because she's one of those shoe-hating five-year-olds. I used to think it was because she's a girly-girl type and only likes those cheap plastic dress-up heels and jelly sandals, practical shoes just aren't girly-girl enough for her, but then one time she said it was because shoes "choked her feet," and when she wore shoes, she "didn't know where her feet were going." She's incredibly babyish and stupid for her age, so I doubt she meant anything by it, but I thought it was kind of profound. I still don't want to hear her scream in the mornings, though.

My ears ring. I brush the sour taste out of my mouth, chest still aching around that sick-donwanna-go-to-school feeling. I used to skip school a lot more, but because Mark is on behavioral probation now and actually has to pay attention to his attendance, I don't have the same motivation. I'd rather do not-fun things at school with Mark than fun things not at school with myself. Fun things quit being fun without Mark. So, I stopped skipping. It's hard to have fun alone. It's hard to have fun, period. Or be alone, period, for that matter.

Brush. Foam. Spit foam. Brush. Spit foam. Rinse foam down the sink. Rinse face. Hate the uneven topography of it under my hands. Spit. Rinse. Repeat.

I put on clothes without thinking. It's easier for me to do things with my body if I don't think about it, if I move on autopilot. Buttoning my pants, for example. I can't loathe how much I have to strain the waist of my jeans across my middle if I'm thinking actively about something else, or in this case, actively about nothing.

I tie my shoes and walk to the kitchen, trying hard to be invisible. There is breakfast, if I want it. Toaster waffles and a pale, out-of-season cantaloupe, cut into wedges with salt on it. I know there's cereal, shredded wheat for my sister because she only eats three foods, and shredded wheat is one of them, but I don't want any of it. I take my jacket off the hook by the door and shrug it on. My sister watches me and doesn't say anything, her face too screwed-up and pink with having just bawled over the shoes on her feet that she's not ready to talk. Any word could crumble her veneer of composure. Her lower lip sticks out.

My dad is bustling around, making coffee and taking up half the kitchen because it's a small house, and he's a big guy. He has his cellphone in one hand, the paper in the other, even though he reads the paper on his cellphone these days and only keeps the actual paper version of it around for the sudoku puzzles he does on the train. He makes a noise that could be a greeting, I don't know because he has unbuttered toast between his teeth, and it's making all his words fuzzy.

I nod to him. That's enough for my dad and I. We have both accepted that we live on totally different planes of existence and have nothing in common, so we don't bother trying to pretend that we love each other or even like each other. I'm not the son he expected, and he's not the dad I would ideally have, so we're just people who live together and stay out of one another's way. It's not a bad set up. I know kids who have it much worse.

My sister starts to scream again, her legs held out like toothpicks, stiff and awkward and heavy with their white sneakers. My dad drops his toast, curses. "Sarah, we've talked about this. Shoes are a non-negotiable," he tells her, like five-year-olds understand what non-negotiable means. My mom is yelling from the bedroom, where she is sleeping off her Wednesday night hangover; tomorrow, she'll be sleeping off her Thursday night hangover. She's very consistent, except on Saturday, when she starts drinking at eight instead of five, which leaves only two hours of prime time before she passes out. This leaves her functional enough to go to church with our inauthentically cheerful neighbor, Delia, and judge the rest of the family for not caring about God.

I don't say, "Bye, dad, bye, Sarah," then shout, "Bye, mom!" There are probably kids who do this, but I'm not one of them. I don't want to eat their instant food, wipe their automatic kisses off my cheek. I don't want to be seen, or heard, or loved. Not by them. They're not the worst, but it doesn't mean I have to like them. Leaving my house means going to school, which is also not the worst, but I don't like it, either. Mark is the in-between. He's not a savior, he's not perfect. He's just less not-perfect than either home or school. It's why I choose him from this buffet of less-than-perfect things every morning.

It's early, and he's probably still in bed. Still, I make my choice. Jacket on, backpack on, Adderall in my pocket and not in my gut because I don't take my medication anymore. I slide out the door, and no one says goodbye to me, either.

One time, we went on a vacation to Hawaii. The big island, everyone calls it, even though it's not a very big island at all, compared to Australia. I don't remember the vacation very well. I know I got sunburned, that we ate shave-ice a lot, not those bullshit sno-cones they sell at fairs and ballgames but the authentic kind with the really fine ice and the scoop of vanilla underneath. I also know that this trip was the first time I sucked dick and the last time I swam in front of anyone.

I was around eight, so Sarah hadn't been born yet. I was still the kind of kid who talked, who played Little League and had friends and ran around in the backyard playing pretend games. Mark and I had so many pretend games that I look back on now and realize were really weird. There were ones where one of us was the kid and the other one was the kidnapper, and we would take turns tying each other to Mark's fence with the torn tennis net and pretending to smoke in each other's faces. I definitely remember getting little-kid boners when we played these games, so it wasn't like the dick-sucking incident made me gay. I don't think it made me anything. I know I stopped swimming in front of people, but it's very possible these two things weren't even related.

Anyway. One day, I was just running around like a crazy thing on the beach, pretty much unaware of my body except for that it felt good when it was tied to Mark's fence. Then the next day, I realized there was a difference between being naked and being not naked, and swimming required a kind of half-nakedness that felt weird in public, so I didn't want to do it. My parents thought it was because I had a sunburn on my shoulders and was being cautious, so my mom kept offering to get me a higher SPF, slurring her words and holding the Banana Boat in one hand, a Mai Tai in the other, golden and glistening with a spear of pineapple swirling in the glass.

I did have blisters on my back, but that wasn't why I didn't want to take my shirt off. I just didn't want to be half-naked. Nakedness was a thing on my mind, because the day before, I had seen a man naked for the first time.

It went something like this: every day of this Hawaiian vacation, my parents would get tired by 5:30 and just sit around the pool with Mai Tais talking with other grown-ups. There were a few other families at our hotel with kids, so my mom and these other moms would paddle around the shallow end of the pool with their babies screaming in floaties, or sit around the edge of the jacuzzi complaining about how hard it was to lose the baby weight, especially when it was your second or third. Which was funny because my mom had me eight years ago, and I was not a baby, and I was her first, but. That was just how my mom talked. She made everyone else's experiences about her.

I befriended the older kids of these families, and we would all start going insane and stir-crazy right about the time our parents started turning into half-drunk corpses. We wanted to go to the beach and snorkel and eat shave-ice and explore. We didn't want to be in a *pool,* we had pools at home, we were in freaking Hawaii, we wanted to swim in the *ocean.* Luckily, a few of these kids were sixteen or seventeen, and our idiot parents trusted them to take the rest of us down to the beach and watch us while we "waded around" or "looked for shells." What this actually looked like was the teenagers staying with us for two seconds before booking it along the beach to toss frisbees and throw themselves into the sand in spectacular formations to impress girls in bikinis, who they would then disappear with until dark, when they'd eventually collect us again, smelling boozy and salty and intoxicating in their mystery.

The rest of us, who ranged from seven to twelve, would wage war, attempting to splash and drown and bury each other and anyone else we could get to play with us in the sand. There were bloody noses and lots of cursing and biting and ritualistic sand-crab sacrifice. It's actually incredible no one but those sand crabs died.

What did happen instead of death is that one evening, when everyone was running around screaming and raising hell along the beach, me and this girl wandered off to see if we could scrounge our change together for otter-pops. There was this guy. We called him otter-pop man, and I had a miraculous crush on him before I even really knew what a crush was. He was in his late twenties or early thirties, with a broad, toned chest dusted with golden hair and reflective aviator sunglasses. I thought he looked like Indiana Jones and simultaneously wanted to be near him and talk to him but also got weak and fizzy-feeling when I thought about actually doing it. He had a yellow cooler he filled with otter-pops that he sold to kids for outrageously low prices. I now recognize that he was not in this business for the loose change but for stupid pretty-boys with negligent parents.

The girl I was with, whose name I can't remember, gave otter-pop man a dime. He gave her a grape-flavored otter-pop, then she scampered off, feet flying and sending up rooster-tails of fine white sand into the air. I remember being worried he wasn't going to give me one because I only had a nickel. I handed it to him with a shaking palm, suddenly shy and hot-faced now that I was alone and close to him, close enough to smell his sunscreen and fascinating man-smell. The sun was setting, but he still had his aviators on. He smiled a white, even smile, and told me that he would give me a free otter-pop if I came with him a few minutes so he could show me something.

In retrospect, my eight-year-old self was an incredible idiot. It all seems so obvious, now, like a fucking after-school special about taking candy from strangers. But at the time, the only fear I felt was the excited kind, a thrilled, Halloween-night fear where there's something dark and scary and adult going on, and you desperately want to be a part of it, you feel so special to be near it, but you don't think it can actually hurt you.

That's how I felt. Special, to have my small smooth hand in his big rough one as he led me to the bathrooms on the boardwalk and asked my name, asked me about where I was from, what I did at recess, who my best friend was, my favorite subject. He was so nice, so friendly and normal-seeming, like Mr. O, my music teacher at home whom I also had a powerful, unrealized crush on. Eventually, otter-pop man stopped at the latching handicap stall next to the row of ankle-height showers you use to rinse sand from your feet. We went inside.

It must have smelled terrible in there, but I romanticized this memory for so many years that I forgot that part, the nostril-burning sewage and ammonia stench of a boardwalk bathroom. In my memories, I only smell salt and sand and surf and sunscreen. He latched the door and took his aviators off. He had ice-blue eyes.

"Have you ever seen a man naked before, Jake?"

This question was surprising, but I knew it must be some special and private and adult secret I was being let in on, that it would make me seem less interesting and mature if I didn't know, if I seemed innocent. So I said, "Yeah."

He smiled with teeth, eyes light and flashing under the fluorescence. "Oh, really? Who?"

"My dad," I half-lied. I *had* seen my dad naked, kind of. In a towel, on his way from the shower to his bedroom. Or in his own bed when he kicked the sheets off in the middle of the night, and I snuck in to sleep on the floor because I was scared by some nightmare. In a hazy, half-remembered way, I had seen my dad naked. I think. It didn't seem like nakedness, because it was my dad.

"Did he show you? Or did you see him by accident?" otter-pop man asked. His hand was rubbing over the front of his tented swim trunks. I stared, fascinated. Wanted to step closer, wanted to feel his big rough palm rubbing over *my* swim trunks. His cheeks were flushed, and he kept on licking his lips.

"I don't remember," I said. Then, "By accident, I think."

"Would you like to see a man naked? Are you curious?"

It was like he *knew* me, like he *knew* the thing I quietly, secretly obsessed over. The thing that kept me up at night, wondering, the tingling in my skin when I struggled against the tennis-net knots, Mark's fake-smoking breath warm and sweet on my face, the slats of his fence biting into my tender back.

"*Yes,*" I breathed emphatically.

Otter-pop man laughed. "That's perfectly normal, you know. But some people don't think so. They think it's bad and wrong, because grown-ups...grown-ups are afraid. They're afraid of things that are different. So, you can tell *me* about this, but you shouldn't tell anyone else. They wouldn't understand."

I nodded, because I think my mouth was too dry to talk. I felt safe, concealed in here, like my own private only partially acknowledged fantasies had come to life and swallowed me.

I watched as otter-pop man slid his black swim trunks down his thighs, over his hard dick, fascinated. I remember everything about it in perfect clarity. The thick, heavy redness, the way his eyes were half-lidded, the glint of blue like sea-glass. I remember him telling me it was okay to touch as my hand moved beyond my control. I remember him gasping, I remember his huge hand stroking my cheek, smelling sugar-sweet, like popsicle, I remember the palm cradling the back of my head and holding my skull still as I sank instinctively to my knees. I remember him petting me, patient as I figured out how to have his dick in my mouth without letting my teeth scrape, how to bob my head and use my tongue. I remember being dizzy-sick with my own erection, my own hand hot and sandy sliding under the elastic of my shorts to jack myself off.

I remember about half-way through, after I'd had a couple dry shaking orgasms and was still nursing at the head of his cock while he called me pretty, that I suddenly realized what the fuck I was doing and how mad my parents would be if they knew about it. I started getting antsy, and nervous, and wanting to stop. I tried to pull away, but he told me he was almost done, and if I could just keep sucking a little longer, he'd give me an otter-pop, and I could go home. That I was such a good boy, I was doing such a good job. He held my head down, nails biting behind my ear. He looked sad and desperate and suddenly everything hurt. My eyes streamed, I gagged. Coughed and gagged, almost threw up, right there on his man-dick.

Then the whole ocean was exploding in my mouth, hot geysers of sour stickiness, and my throat spasming and hurting like I swallowed water down the wrong pipe. Toilet paper stuck to my knee, salt in my eyes, me coughing over and over again. Being so freaked out that the teenagers had already come to collect us, and I wasn't there, and my parents were going to kill me because I had just put this man's penis in my mouth and really liked it until it was scary and I hated it. I remember being so worried about getting in trouble.

I don't remember where he went after he came, though. I remember standing up, shaking all over, and eating my lime otter-pop even though I was nauseous, my throat so sore and stinging. I remember looking in the dirty, graffitied mirror to make sure I didn't look different, because I was so sure I had to look different after doing this thing that everyone was going to look at me and know what I did and get me in trouble.

I found the rest of the kids, relieved that they didn't even realize I was gone. Eventually, the sun set, we all went back to the hotel, and my mom reprimanded me for getting my knees so dirty and smelling like shit. "That ocean," she said, pinching her nose, "isn't as clean as they say it is in those books the travel agent gave us."

That night, I was so afraid to jack off, but I wanted to so badly. All I could think about was what a naked man looked like, how I wasn't supposed to tell anyone about it because some people didn't think it was normal. I kept thinking about how different *my* naked body looked, how it must look different now, how I had to keep my shirt on in case someone saw where he touched me, where he'd stroked my shoulder blades as I sucked. In retrospect, I was an incredibly naive and stupid eight-year-old.

The next day, I didn't want to go swimming.

"Porn," is what Mark said when I ask him what he was doing last night.

"You didn't answer my texts because you were watching porn?" I say. We're in the cafeteria, which smells like sweaty kids, things frying in grease, salt, and ketchup. Mark has a chocolate milk and a sad, bleeding sloppy joe on his tray. I have an empty cup. I'm hungry and nauseous at the same time, which is how I often feel, in the cafeteria, and around Mark. And just always, I guess.

Mark is chewing. He shrugs. "No, they were unrelated. I was watching porn, but I also left my phone somewhere. I just didn't see your texts. I fell asleep and then found my phone in the morning, all blown up with stuff from you."

"I was really bored."

"I was, too. If I had seen them, we could have gone to the park." Going to the park is Mark and my primary pastime on weekdays when we're actively avoiding homework. I'm never sure what we do there. I guess it's usually some combination of walking around, pretending to pretend to play (but actually playing) on the jungle gym, throwing rocks at tree trunks from varying distances, jimmying the soda machine to try forever in vain to steal change and sodas, talking about people from school we hate but have never actually met. It doesn't matter what we do there, the fact we have a destination is enough to make it feel like a thing.

"Oh," I said, stomach aching and roiling over its emptiness "Next time, check your phone." Then, "What kind of porn?"

"Dunno. Lesbian porn."

"Ah," I say. Lesbian porn is the most discouraging kind because there are no penises anywhere. I, unfortunately, am bestowed with a penis, so I can't really make Mark's lesbian porn about me.

The cafeteria echoes with screaming kids. There are football bellows and excited girl-shrieks, sometimes in unison, or back and forth like a demented call and response. Mark and I are sitting at the edge of the table closest to the soda machine, where our other kind-of friends sit. I call them kind-of friends because I don't really know who they are now, I only know them from grade school. They were the kids Mark and I hung out with then...baseball practice kids, chess club kids. There's Evan, who used to be really gross and throw spitballs at the ceiling. Like, the ceiling above his desk in fifth grade was a total decoupage of spitballs and eraser dust and little bits of pencil lead. He was the fucking spit *artist* of our fifth grade class. Now he likes computers or something, I don't think he spits anymore.

Then there's Milo, whose real name is Rourk, but no one calls him that because what the fuck kind of name is Rourk? He used to be really popular and cute and everyone, including me, had a crush on him in the second grade, when he was this fearless dodgeball champion. But puberty made him pimply and awkward, so then he started hanging around with us. His hair is marmalade orange, so at some point he got the nickname Milo from that weird Japanese movie with the marmalade orange kitten and the pug puppy. Now he *also* likes computers or something. He's since dyed his hair brown, but the name stuck.

And yeah, that's the extent to which I still know these guys, spitball memories and ghosts of their current interests and hair colors all decoupaged on the ceiling like fifth grade art. Mark is the only one I actually know, and even that is debatable. Sometimes it's hard to tell if the web I have connected in me that makes me like Mark is made up of strands I created because I've grown up with him, or if they're things his real-life-now self has spun. Like, if I met Mark today, I probably wouldn't like him. I'm not even sure I'd notice him. He's just the one who I've told myself I know, the one I told myself I liked. He's been around the longest, so he stuck. Like a spitball.

"Dude, are you gonna eat?" he asks, digging his elbow into my side. I like that he touches me, it reminds me that it doesn't matter who or what spun the web. It's a real thing. I glare at him.

"Obviously. Just not the shit they serve here," I tell him.

He raises one of his eyebrows, then lets the whole thing go. I'm half-relieved, half-hurt. The thing is, Mark would respond to my eating habits differently if I wasn't a) fat, b) bestowed with a penis. That's just the way the world works. Starving is by no means a universal symbol for anything. It depends on what country you're in, what color you are, what's between your legs. If I was skinny and wasn't eating, Mark would make a joke about me being anorexic without actually thinking I *could* be anorexic because anorexia is something only skinny white girls get, and I'm a guy.

If I was a fat girl, Mark wouldn't say shit about my eating habits. He would be secretly pleased. He would be thinking, *It's probably a good thing she's not eating. She could afford to lose a few pounds*, because of course, fat girls can't be anorexic, either.

But since I'm a fat *guy*, all I get from Mark is a raised eyebrow. Fat guys not eating means absolutely nothing. I am null. Void. Absolute zero. By being excess, I become nothing. The excess weight and skin and fat and inches between my legs make me invisible, free to starve in silence. It's not a bad set up. There are probably people who have it much worse. This is male privilege, probably.

There was this girl I remember a few years ahead of us in middle school who had to go to a hospital and get force fed through a tube in her stomach because she was basically dying of starvation. Everyone noticed that she kept getting skinnier and skinnier, but because she was black, nobody thought she was anorexic until it was too late. If she had been a white girl, she would have been thrown into therapy the second her hair started thinning and falling out onto her sweater. But people are stupid. They have these images of starving children in Africa, they don't think black people can starve in any other way. People have very clear ideas in their head about who can starve and who can't, what it looks like, and it's really fucked up. But the nice thing is that I fly under the radar. No one's gonna force feed *me* through a tube.

Not to say I'm starving. Or that I'm in danger of dying. Being fat-white-guy-invisible is entirely different.

"Jake. You're not fat. You know that, right?" Mark says through another full mouthful, like he's reading my mind. My eyes snap toward him, fixed on his familiar face with its sad, scruffy, teenage attempt at a beard, his ice-blue husky-dog eyes. He has a huge zit on the right side of his nose, white and glaring and begging for my nails to close in on it, apply pressure until blood follows pus, and I feel cleaner by proxy.

"I never said I was."

"He's just big boned," Evan chimes in. Evan's mom is morbidly obese and rides around on a motorized scooter. I wonder if that's what fat means to him, if anything less pales in comparison. But what they're both saying is half-true. Like starving, fat is just a word, it doesn't mean anything real, anything universal. I don't tip any scales into unhealthyland, I don't break a sweat on stairs or take up two seats on the bus or anything. I'm not skinny, but I'm not Evan's mom. Still, all of that is relative. My body looks disgusting, feels disgusting.

"Shut up, Evan," I snap.

"But, like, Jake. You don't have to lose weight," Mark says, gesturing toward the cafeteria and its yawning maw of boiling oil and high-fructose corn syrup and aimless wandering kids. "I can hear your stomach growling, dude."

"I'm not trying to lose weight, Mark. Fuck off," I say, like I'm exasperated, like I can't believe he's talking about something so stupid, something belonging to another species, the skinny white girl disease. On the inside, the web is collecting in on itself, folding and rolling into a sticky ball of yarn, a fist of why-I-like-Mark. I'm null and void and invisible, and he's still sticking his greasy fingers in and digging, like he cares. But he doesn't care. He's acting out of habit, he's doing this just so he has something to talk about, because in all likelihood, Mark isn't a real person: he's an automated answering machine. He's no less of a robot than anyone else.

"Yeah, but if you were, you shouldn't. That shit's dumb, dad bods are in."

There are lines above his dark, bushy brows at the tails of his husky-dog eyes, the blue chased to thin ring around his huge pupil, dilated from my Adderall. One of his hands, big and loose-skinned with its purple tracery of veins under the surface, squeezes the empty chocolate milk carton until it's a shade of its former shape. I stare at him, bewildered, and think that if he's a robot, he's a lovely one. A lovely illusion. "Okay. Fuck. I'll go get some fries. Just to make you happy."

Mark grins. There's food in his teeth. "That's better."

Nobody knows. But if they did, they would probably think the puke followed the boners, rather than the boners following the puke, which is how it actually happened. I was just as surprised as any of the people I've never told.

It wasn't like I got turned on and then accidentally threw up, forever solidifying the memory of arousal with the sound of my own gagging. I've read that's how some paraphilias start, a kid accidentally exposes himself to a girl on the playground, she's shocked and horrified and runs away. Everything attached to that memory—the humiliation, the rush, the widening of her eyes, the blush on her cheeks—solidifies and becomes connected to orgasm, then this kid grows up into a teenager who whips his dick out at cheerleaders, then into a trenchcoat-wearing creep in a dark alleyway, forever longing for a replication of that first time, the playground and the mary janes running away, the giggling and the shame.

It wasn't like I was jacking off as a kid, then someone punched me in the stomach, and after that, everything about nausea became boner-inducing. The vomiting came first. The boner was a surprise. Maybe this makes me a True Freak, as opposed to a Freak on Accident.

The first time was in the fourth grade. It was a Saturday, and I was at the mall for a birthday party for this kid I sometimes hung out with before he moved to Arizona. I think his name was Kyle? I don't remember. What I do remember is that his older brother Brandon, who was probably thirteen at the time, was insanely hot. He was there, probably dragged along by their mom to his kid brother's birthday, which was a pizza and laser tag party. The incident occurred post-pizza, pre-laser tag, everyone waiting for their tokens to go into the laser tag part, me too busy staring at Brandon, fantasizing about sucking his cock. He was one of those effortlessly fit thirteen-year-olds, the naturally tan, naturally windswept, blond-haired angel children parents love and other kids hate but also secretly want to be. Or suck on, in my case.

Brandon was wearing a Superman shirt and totally aware of the fact I thought he was the coolest thing ever, trying to act funnier than he was to impress me because he wasn't old enough to know it was a gay thing and not some pure admiration thing. He had this soda, a Sprite, and he was putting his finger on top of the straw to hold the Sprite inside the tube. Then he was dangling the straw over his mouth, releasing the pressure, letting the soda drip onto his tongue. He probably didn't know how weird it was making me feel to watch that straw hovering over his pink cupid's bow lips, he just knew it had me captivated for some reason, and he was clearly into the attention.

Fixated, I watched him do it over and over again. Sprite, straw, mouth. Sprite, straw, mouth. Sometimes he would miss, and the clear, fizzy soda would drip over his golden chin, or the corner of his jaw. I wanted to lick it off. He would laugh, the flash of his tongue swiping it away before my fingers could do stupid things without my consent. Sprite, straw, mouth. Sprite, straw, mouth. Widening dark spots on Superman blue. Sprite, straw, mouth. Then, cough. Choke. Wrong pipe, or something.

Brandon dropped the straw and doubled at the waist, hacking desperately. He had obviously inhaled the soda, but I was too locked in on his cheeks and their increasingly dark flush to really identify what was happening. His eyes watered, getting pink and wet and drippy. He looked like he was going to cry, and my dick was stirring in my cargo pants.

There was sweat in his blond hair, and then. The first wet, frothy mouthfuls of stomach-slime, streaks of pizza sauce making it pink, coming up in fat loogies.

After that, he was just full-on puking all over the shiny marble floor of the food court. Noisy gagging sounds, chunky, tomato red splattering, spreading fast like spilled milk. Little flecks of it on my once-white Skechers. My hand was in my lap, squeezing unconsciously, lips worried between my teeth as Brandon held his stomach in both hands and just emptied himself out, acid and pizza and Sprite and garlic bread and little floating green specs from the few bites of forced-salad. The whole place smelled like puke. People were looking at us. It just made me harder.

I was five seconds away from coming in my pants, right there in the mall, but Brandon and Kyle's mom knocked into me from behind, rushing toward him with napkins, face screwed up and brows knit in rage. Brandon was just spitting now. I caught one last glance of his pitiful red face as she shielded him from my sight, and he was crying, ashamed, embarrassed. I let out a hissing sound and shook as I came, dry. No one noticed, they probably thought I was just grossed out.

And I was, obviously. Puke is disgusting. I've never been under any illusions that it's *not.* I wouldn't be turned on by it if it was airbrushed and scentless and clean. The nastiness of it...the bacteria and the half-chewed, half-digested horror of something that's supposed to be *inside* coming *out* is part of *why* it's so hot. I wasn't supposed to see that part of Brandon. He didn't want me to. But I *did.* He couldn't control himself, he couldn't *stop* himself from being disgusting. He had to let himself go, vulnerable and shuddering and wilted and shamed.

And that was the first time I remember getting really turned on by someone puking. There were times before that, times I was fascinated or intrigued. Craning my head and neck around in the classroom to stare at the kid who'd just upchucked on their desk or on the tire swing, or whatever. I wanted to know if it hurt them, what color it was, what they'd eaten, how long it had been down. But I never got hard from it, just interested, morbidly curious. But with Brandon, I came in a food court, so clearly it isn't just cute boys or puke on its own. It's cute boys puking. It's the intersection.

I didn't make this obvious connection until later. There were other times, times I couldn't sleep and got out of bed in the middle of the night to tiptoe into the kitchen and eat everything in the fridge out of boredom and self-loathing. Usually, on those nights, I'd stick the handle of my toothbrush down my throat and puke it all up. And inevitably, I'd end up getting hard. I'd have to sit there, mouth sour and bitter and slimy, hand hot and shaking on my dick, jacking off until I jizzed on the toilet porcelain, shaking and exhausted, back sore with retches and snaps of my hips, thinking of whoever my latest obsession was puking their guts out in the middle of the food court. Often, it was Mark.

Lately, it's always Mark.

I'm more weirded out and ashamed by that than I am by the whole vomit thing.

———

Instead of going home, Mark and I walk to the park after school. It's called Hiddleson Park, because it's on Hiddleson street, but we call it Peacock Park because there's a fountain by the soccer fields with a statue of a peacock in the middle of it. The fountain never runs in the winter, but there's always a few murky, mosquito-breeding inches of water in there from the rain. The peacock looks like he's mired in tar, but this is our favorite place to sit, on the edge of the peacock fountain, where we get eaten alive by mosquitos.

It's raining big, fat, warm drops of rain this afternoon. They hit my arms and almost hurt, even though they're slow moving. Mark tilts his head back and tries to catch them in his mouth. "Ahhhh, tastes like acid," he says, which is what he always says when he tastes the rain. We thunk our backpacks down in the dugout of the baseball diamond. We can stay dry there.

I prop my feet up against the adjacent chain-link fence and watch the dusty red baseball dirt turn muddy and blood-colored under the rain.

"Hey, Jake. Do you think a girl with really big tits, like double Ds, could smack herself in the face with her tits if she did a slam dunk without a bra on?" Mark asks me.

"A slam dunk, like in basketball?" I humor him because there's nothing else to do.

"Yeah. But without a bra."

"Why do you think I understand the physics of boobs better than you do? I've only touched them that one time. At the party with Melissa, when she gave me the rest of her strawberry daiquiri."

"You felt Melissa's tits for a strawberry daiquiri?! You are so gay. Those aren't even good drinks."

"I like them. I mean, I don't prefer them. But it was a shitty night, I was gonna take what I could get."

We're quiet for a moment, the sound of the rain and some guys shouting while they play frisbee in the distance filling what would be silence. Mark's eyes are closed, and he looks really thoughtful. I'm staring at him, trying to figure out why I find him attractive. I do this a lot, since it's the greatest unsolved mystery in my life. I have a mortifying weak spot for Abercrombie model types, '90s kid movie love interest types, the Jonathan Taylor Thomases of the world. And while Mark's cute by most people's standards, he couldn't model for Abecrombie in any universe. Not blond, tan, taut, or tall enough. He's pale, dark-haired, light-eyed. Those light eyes flicker under the lids. "Yeah, but the boob question. Do you think that happens? Just, like, if you had to make an informed guess."

I shrug, rolling my eyes because I cannot for the life of me wonder how this information is going to benefit Mark's life. "I don't know. Probably. If they're big enough."

"Yeah. What about, like, Isabella Duncan's tits?"

"I've never seen them, dunno how big they are."

"Oh. Yeah." Mark stretches like a clumsy, ugly cat. His pale and hair-dusted stomach shows in a fluorescent strip above this black jeans as his Gorgoroth t-shirt rides up, and I think about how badly I want to open my palm and slap him there, leave a stinging red mark. Or make a fist and punch him. One Halloween in middle school, I punched Mark so hard in the gut that he threw up all the candy he'd just eaten. It was mostly chocolate brown, with spots of Twizzler red and Lemon Head yellow, Sweetart blue, and two green, half-dissolved apple Jolly Ranchers in it. I remember it in technicolor detail, I can't tell you how many times I've come to the image.

"I think I fucked Isabella Duncan last weekend. I'm trying to figure out if it was a dream or not."

I feel a little empty, a little nauseous. All I've had to eat today besides those few fries is water, which isn't food. My face stays blank, because I've been keeping myself null and zero for so long it's easy. "How can you think you fucked someone?"

"I was really, really stoned."

"Isabella's gross. There had to be someone better there."

"Yeah, but I was really, really stoned."

"Gross." I try to picture it, an idle attempt at pushing my nausea to the limit. There's no point in actually throwing up if I'm only full of water, but sometimes it's fun to hold back puke, to deny myself the relief. It's a habit, and I've done it so much that I don't really get turned on by it anymore unless I'm extremely full of food and extremely nauseous, but lesser versions are still fun, even if I don't get hard. "But you don't remember?"

"Not really. Like, all I remember is telling her that she should get on top to make it easier for me because I was really tired and lazy. And she said she couldn't because if she bounced on my dick, her boobs would hit her in the face. Which doesn't seem real. It just seems like an excuse."

"She said that?"

"Yeah. I mean, I think. Unless I was dreaming."

"She said that, and you still fucked her? Dude. That's disgusting. I don't know how you stayed hard."

Mark shrugs again, slouching against the cold metal bench in the dugout, Converse sliding in the gritty muck with a crunch. "Yeah, I dunno. It wasn't that bad. If it actually happened, I mean."

The rain comes down harder, hammering noisily on the wooden roof. I shudder, cold and queasy, headachy and weak with long-burning hunger, face tingly and numb. I rub my cheeks with my palms, clench my teeth against how awful it feels to touch my own skin. "Why don't you just ask her about it?"

"What if it didn't happen? I don't want to put the idea in her head, you know?" He laughs a little. Just a low, stupid snicker. I start laughing, too, because besides being gross, the image of Isabella's huge, bouncing tits hitting her in the overly made-up face with the trashy drawn-on eyebrows is also kind of funny. We crack up, wheezing, and I feel sicker and sicker.

"Seriously, dude, is fucking Isabella better than not getting laid at all? Because that's kind of pathetic." I tell him once we've stopped laughing. My mouth waters. I swallow the spit.

"I guess it doesn't matter if I can't remember it," he says, which is pretty logical. "Though you were right. I probably had better options."

Mark is what I like to call an opportunist. It defines him better than any words that would otherwise suggest sexual preference. If an opportunity arises to have sex, and the person is not ugly or Mark is under the influence of some natural or chemical substance that impairs his judgment, he will take advantage of the opportunity. It's possible that Mark has fucked around with more guys than I have. Not because he prefers them, but because of opportunity.

Here is where everyone wonders why Mark and I have never fucked around. Here is where they think that the opportunity has never arisen. Here is where I explain that it has. That it does, frequently. When there are no better options, and Mark's shitfaced, clumsy, beer-breathed, bloodshot.

Here is where I explain that I'm the opposite of an opportunist. I watch trains approach fast and rush past, the buffet of air hitting me, knocking me over, ticket crumpled sweaty in my fist. Here is where I explain that I don't take advantage of opportunity, because I'm fear-paralyzed and need someone else to tell me what to do, how to do it. Mark's gone for the mouth so many times that I usually block him with a palm, shove him to the bed, take his belt off so it doesn't cut his drunk stomach while he rolls around on the mattress whining, then I leave. Lock myself in the bathroom. Jack off onto the floor while I puke into the toilet.

I'm a missed-opportunist, because Mark is an opportunist. I want him to try shit with me not because it comes up, but because he wants to. But that doesn't happen, that's not the way he thinks about sex. And it's definitely not the way he thinks about me. I dig my elbow into the bare part of his stomach. He doubles around it, squirming away. "At least I used a condom. In my dream, or in real life. Both are kind of impressive," he muses.

"At least," I agree. My stomach growls, the sky rains.

———

Mark and I became friends in preschool, coincidentally, because of puke. When I'm having a good day, I think of it as a sign. When I'm having a bad day, I think about how pathetic it is that I need signs to think something is meaningful.

I used to hang out with this other guy in preschool, before I met Mark. His name was Aaron Horning, and he wore a bandage over his left eye, but no one teased him about being a pirate or anything, because he was huge for a preschooler and bullied everyone into being mostly terrified of him. He was a "smear fingerpaint in your hair" kind of asshole. The other kids stayed away from him, but I didn't, apparently I was a fucked up masochist even at the age of five.

He never beat me up or anything, just bossed me around and called me a baby because I spent a lot of time crying. I was really sensitive. I cried about pretty much everything. I cried in *Pocahontas* when she jumped off the rock and Meeko the Raccoon followed her because I experienced sympathetic bellyflop pain when he hit the water. Maybe I was hyperempathetic and therefore evolved. Maybe I've just been a sissy my entire life. I don't know.

Anyway, I probably hung around Aaron because he called me a baby and paid more attention to me than anyone else did. He was always finding things for me to do for him. Dig holes in the sandbox so he could bury the classroom toy dinosaurs. Hold my hands out for his dirty tennis shoe so he could climb on top of the big-kid jungle gym we weren't allowed to climb on top of. Hold his jacket like a fucking coat rack while he stole a tricycle from some smaller, weaker kid.

See, I was a smaller, weaker kid. I knew that. But unlike all the other smaller, weaker kids, I knew there was no use trying to fight the already existing institution of playground power dynamics. I knew it was easier to be Aaron Horning's bitch than it was to be one of the nameless schmucks he stole tricycles from. Anyway, I kind of liked being a coat rack. And I definitely liked being called a baby. It made me feel like life was simple. It meant I knew my place and didn't have to experience the terror of trying to prove I was different or better than the kid crying in sympathy pain for a cartoon raccoon. I was just a baby. That was okay, I knew how to be a baby.

Anyway, one time Aaron Horning got the stomach flu and puked all over some girl's hopscotch game. I remember his puke. It was pinkish and liquidy with Hawaiian Punch and dissolved the sidewalk chalk lines of the hopscotch boxes. The girls screamed, ran away. Aaron got sent home, and I was suddenly worthless, devoid of tasks. There were no coats to hold, no games being played where I had to be the baby and pretend to sleep while Aaron tried to kiss whatever girl was being the mom. I was totally lost. I wandered around crying, because crying was my solution to everything.

Then this stupid kid came up to me. Curly brown hair, blue eyes, scabby elbows. This really obnoxious, hyper little boy everyone knew about because he was obnoxious and hyper and was always breaking things and fidgeting during rest-time and flapping his arms around making explosion sounds and interrupting the teacher when she told us about space because his mom worked at NASA and he was space-obsessed and knew fucking everything about the solar system. He ran up to me like a fucking rocket, jumping up and down. "Want to play wormhole?!" Mark asked, bouncing. He didn't seem to notice I was crying. I wiped my nose, bobbing my head to keep up with the way he was popcorning around like a yappy little dog.

"How do you play that?" I asked cautiously. If Aaron was here, he wouldn't permit me talking to other boys. But he wasn't here. He was throwing up somewhere.

"You, you, um, you get on the swings and swing as high as you can swing, like *really high*, then you jump off and pretend you're propelled by jet expulsion and getting, s...sucked, sucked into a *wormhole!*" he explained with a series of complex hand gestures, bouncing all the while. I eyed him suspiciously, because he was using words like "propelled" and "expulsion," and I didn't know these words. He sounded smart.

"Come on," he said, grabbing my arm and dragging me into a standing position. "I always see you playing with Aaron. He's mean. You're nice. You should play with other nice people."

It felt good to hear someone call me nice. I wanted to correct him, tell him that Aaron wasn't mean, he was just insecure about his eyepatch. (Which was a story I made up to explain Aaron's meanness; he never indicated to me on any occasion that he was insecure about his eyepatch. In fact, the only thing he ever said about it was that it kept sand out of his eye when he kicked sand into other kid's faces, for which he seemed thankful.)

"I'm Mark. I like space and lizards," Mark told me, breaking out into a jerky, erratic run to the swings. I struggled to keep up. "You should play with me, instead."

And since it was easier to be told to do something rather than to decide for myself and suffer the consequences of possibly failing, I said, "Okay," and blew my nose into my shirt. Fate sealed, up into the wormhole.

―――

I get home just as dusk fades to darkness. Let myself in quietly, sneak past the living room where both of my parents are watching TV. The kitchen smells oily and fishy because tuna casserole is baking in the oven. My shoes make wet squelching noises on the linoleum, but no one notices.

Walk down the hallway, stop at the bathroom. Toilet seat up, knees on the ground. The TV is loud, so I don't worry about turning the faucet on. I push my sandy hair out of my face, stick the handle of my toothbrush down my throat. My hungry, aching stomach spasms, and the first few familiar mouthfuls of stomach sludge up into my mouth, faintly yellow. I spit. Gag. Spit a few more times. My gut is trying hard, but there's nothing in there. Something about this is hot, too, my body working so desperately to bring something up but finding only emptiness. It's not come-in-my-pants hot, though. Just dick-twitch hot, get-a-chubby-that-goes-nowhere hot. Mostly I do it from force of habit, just to make sure I'm still empty.

Then I really gag, and a ton of water comes up, all the water I've had all day. I cough and hack, my eyes watering. It's not the same release as food, it doesn't feel as satisfying or consummate or complete, but it's something. The lingering grossness of the park and school feel gone, swimming and foaming in the toilet. I don't bother flushing.

Toilet seat down. Rinse my mouth out with tap water. Wipe my face on the hand towel. Let myself out.

I find Sarah in my room. "What are you doing in here?" I ask her, my voice so loud and unreasonably angry that she jumps, eyes wide and glassy. They have something around them, something dark and glittery. Makeup, maybe. I can't tell, it's too dark. I flip on the overhead light.

"My mirror is too small," she whines. Then I notice she's in front of my full size mirror, the one I spend time trying to forget about. She's wearing one of her bathing suits that's too small for her now, a pink two-piece because my parents are fucked up and think it's okay for toddlers to wear two-piece bathing suits even though beaches are full of men with otter-pops. And she *is* wearing makeup, grotesque purple smudges of it above her eyes and blush from the cheap compact she got as a party favor somewhere. Her sandy blonde hair, same color as mine, is pulled back from her face in a glittery clip.

"What do you need the mirror for? And give me that," I scold, noticing she's perched on my desk chair with the puke and jizz stains. I roll it out from under her, and she tumbles but doesn't fall, pursing her lips into a fake-cry pout.

"I dressed up."

"Yeah, I noticed. You look like a clown. Now get out."

Then, my five-year-old sister cocks one hip, makes a face, and pokes her little kid belly-pudge with her index finger. "I'm sooo fat," she says, her voice an exact imitation of our mom. I freeze.

"Sarah. Don't say that," I tell her. I try to say it gently, in a big brother way, but I've never felt anything but mild annoyance or mild amusement toward Sarah, so it doesn't come out right. I'm not one of those brothers who is protective of their younger siblings, the kind of brother who gives a shit. But still. I don't want her standing in front of a mirror prodding at her baby fat. I don't even want her to know what the word "fat" means. She's just a kid. She'll have plenty of time to learn about that stuff later.

"I'm fat! Fat fat fat," she says gleefully, just to piss me off, hopping up and down. Both her nipples are showing because her bathing suit triangles are way too small. I want to cover her up, but I don't want to touch her.

"Stop. You're a brat."

"Fat brat," she chimes, pleased with herself.

"Do you even know what fat *is?*" I ask her. She stares back defiantly, the look of a kid who's just been challenged by someone older and wiser than her, but she knows the answer is gonna be *right* and will show them all.

"Yes. What mommy is. And you." She's outrageously smug. I roll my eyes at her. My mom is not fat. She's a middle-aged, self-hating alcoholic, but she's not fat. Not compared to the statistical American average or anything. And my fatness, though completely valid in my brain, is a debatable reality. I'm not skinny, and I'm not muscular. Which doesn't necessarily mean fat.

"No. Fat is Evan's mom."

"Oh," Sarah says, sticking her finger in her mouth. I watch her contemplate the image of Evan's mom's mass of rolls undulating atop her motorized scooter. The air hangs between us, smelling too sweet, like cheap, fruity, little-kid perfume. Time to go.

"Now get out." I stick my hands under her armpits and drag her screaming from my room.

Mark and I were having a sleepover in the fifth grade when I told him I was gay and specifically gay for him. We were both on this sleeping bag I had unzipped on the floor, one of those nice, flannel-lined ones for camping. It was late, easily past midnight. I had a stomach ache from too much popcorn and sour straws. Mark was still going strong with the junk food. The conversation inevitably turned toward girls.

"Man. Wanda is so hot," Mark said, spraying popcorn crumbs all over the sleeping bag.

I wrinkled my nose. "Yeah. But her name is Wanda." Popcorn hit my face, courtesy of Mark's hand.

"Who cares? She actually has tits. Also, she's the only girl in the whole class who wears those shorts with the rips in them."

"Those shorts are stupid. Why would someone wear something they bought with rips in it?" I argued. Wanda wasn't supposed to wear those shorts. There was a rule that you couldn't wear clothing that was torn, she was breaking dress code.

"Duh, Jake. So boys can look through the holes at her thighs."

"Gross," I decided. I didn't want to look at Wanda's thighs.

"Yeah, well who do you think is hot? Every time I say a girl's hot, you have some stupid reason why she's not."

"That's because I don't think girls are hot," I told him. I remember thinking that I should be freaked out about this conversation, that I should panic because what if he found out I liked boys and I liked him and we suddenly stopped being friends because he didn't want me to like him? But I couldn't even make myself care. My stomach ache was more important.

Plus, it seemed like a really weird thing to stop being friends over, and Mark was nothing if not dog-loyal. I imagined telling Mark that I thought about him when I rubbed my stiffies at night sometimes, and I just couldn't see him being pissed off or grossed out. I could see him laughing and making fun of me, for sure. I could see him taking his pants off and waving his dick at me just as a torture method. I could see his ego swelling to dangerous proportions. But I couldn't really see him getting *mad*.

"What do you mean? Everyone thinks girls are hot."

"Um, no. I think Zack is the hottest person in our grade," I told him. This was true. Zack Anderson had white-blond hair and a mole on his cheek and could make the net swish from the free throw line every time. He was really nice and finished his math quizzes early, which meant he was smart. Or at least good at math quizzes.

Mark was silent. Even his popcorn chewing stopped.

"Zack *Anderson?*" he said, sounding horrified.

"Yeah." I said, swallowing the saliva in my mouth. My stomach was so pissed off at all the sugar and butter and salt. This stomach ache was awful, which meant it was great.

"But." There was a pause. Then, more popcorn hitting my face.

"Would you stop that? I'm, like, five seconds away from puking, dude."

"But I'm *way cooler* than Zack! Like, if you're going to like guys, why aren't you into me? I'm your best friend," Mark complained, getting up on his elbows to glare at me. I wanted to puke in his face, but instead, I just laid there, next to him, staring up into his narrowed blue eyes.

"Shut up. I do like you," I told him, shoving him away by his shoulder.

"Oh. Okay, Good," Mark said, sighing and collapsing next to me. Then, "Do you think your mom will notice if we steal shit from her liquor cabinet?"

I don't remember if we stole booze from my mom that night. I know we did later. I know we still do. I know we've both drunk so much stuff from there that my mom finds the empty bottles in the morning and cries because she feels bad for drinking so much and forgetting about it, which is what she thinks happens. Then she hides the bottles from my dad, so he won't think she drank them. I've come into the kitchen and seen her crying at the table in her robe, her hair up in curlers, so many times. Once I asked her what was wrong, and she said, "Nothing, sweetie. Thanks for asking," and wiped her eyes. She hadn't called me sweetie in years. It was weird. I remember being relieved she didn't know Mark and I had drunk her shit.

It was good to know I was getting away with *something*.

On Friday, Mark and I go to a party at Bret Jarvis's house. Bret is a football player with a girlfriend. Everyone knows the type. Thick-necked, stupid, friendly. Danielle is skinny and tan and brunette, with clotty mascara and lipgloss. She plays volleyball. Neither of them are exceptionally attractive, or exceptionally nice, or actually interesting in any way besides the fact they have money and big houses where they can throw parties when their parents are away on business trips. They are entirely average high schoolers.

You hear about the football-cheerleader royalty stereotypes. These cruel, beautiful kids with their drugs and their cars and their sex and their madness, but see, I've never met anyone like that. My experience is that everyone in high school is exactly the same. Everyone is lonely. Everyone has a shitty family. Everyone wants to get laid. Everyone is prescribed something chemical and ineffectual for their personal brand of apathy. Everyone believes they are special.

The differences between the people I know are pretty superficial. For example, I like dick and puke and French decadent poetry. Mark likes tits and cheap beer and Swedish metal. Bret Jarvis likes football, *Call of Duty*, and Danielle. Danielle likes mascara, lipgloss, and Bret. My mom likes church and the Food Channel and vodka. My dad likes sudoku and the Orioles and kobe beefsteak. Sarah likes Hannah Montana and neon colors and swimming pools. But interests don't define people. People wish they defined us, but they don't. They're just coats to put on over our naked selves so that we forget we're all the same half-frozen temperature.

I'm not really friends with Bret or Danielle, I don't really know if this is a birthday party or a celebrating football victory party or just a get drunk to forget the world sucks party. It doesn't matter. Parties, like people, are all the same. Mark and I go to them because they each have things we like.

"I hope they have a keg," Mark tells me. We're walking from our suburb to the ritzier, neighboring suburb where Bret's house is by cutting through a park that isn't Peacock Park. It feels weird to be in a different park, different grass with different playgrounds and different haunting orange lamps and different moms with reflective trackpants and terriers on retractable leashes. My arm bumps against Mark's, but we don't feel each other's skin because we're wearing jackets. It's dark, and leaves crunch under our tennis shoes.

"They will. Do they ever not have kegs?"

"I dunno. I've shown up after all the drinks were gone."

"You'll find something," I tell him. "I probably won't."

Mark goes to parties for the cheap beer. I go for the puke and the dick. Mark thinks I go just for the dick. I've never actually made out with a guy at a party or anything, but I love watching athletic-looking guys take their shirts off and drink until they're sick. I wish I wasn't so influenced by popular culture that I ended up irreparably attracted to surfer-blond hair and polo shirts and calf muscles, but unfortunately I, too, am like everyone else.

Sometimes I tell myself that I like going to these parties, not because I'm attracted to guys like that as they are, but because I'm turned on by watching them undone, dirtied, humiliated. That it's not *them,* it's their dethroning. But of course, if a guy like Bret Jarvis came up to me totally sober in the locker room or something and started making out with me, it's not like I wouldn't be into it. It's not like I'd need to push him off and choke him with my dick until he puked to turn me on. My balls are not as noble and subversive as I wish they were.

"Dude, even if there was some guy who was wearing a shirt that said 'I want to lick Jake's ass,' you wouldn't get your ass licked," Mark tells me.

Mark is under the impression I could get laid if I tried harder. He might be right, but opportunists don't understand missed-opportunists. He doesn't get it.

"Hey, Mark. Fuck you."

"Just sayin'..." He trails off. We find the sidewalk on the other side of the park and turn onto it. There are houses, identical and in a row, two stories with lawns and garages. Sometimes the lights are on, the window shades open, and we can look in and see what TV programs people are watching, what they're eating for dinner. And that's all anyone is doing in any of the houses, watching TV and eating.

I try and imagine what it would be like to actually hit on guys, flirt, whatever it is that people do with other people to let them know they want to fuck. It all seems so foreign and artificial, this dance people do because someone told them it was how to communicate. It feels like a cakewalk. You walk in a circle of numbers until the music stops, and sometimes, you get a cake. It doesn't make logical sense, but lots of people are eating. Others are starving. Others are puking it back up.

I'd be the one standing on the sidelines, watching them puke. Whatever. Let them eat cake.

"We're getting close," I tell Mark eventually. I can feel a bassline resounding in my shoes, hear the distant clatter of laughter, shouting, and bad electronic music. Then, we spot a group of girls in torn shorts and college sweatshirts, their hair up in messy ponytails standing on a lawn in front of a driveway with a bunch of parked cars.

"Is there beer inside?" Mark shouts to them.

They all turn around and look at us warily, grouped together like meerkats with their necks craned, goosebumps on their bare legs. If it's cold enough for sweatshirts, then it's too cold for shorts. Some girls like Mark because he's cute, even if he's rude and awkward and sleazy. I think girls would like me better if they knew I was gay. They'd want me to give them fashion advice and go shopping with them. I could revolutionize the world of fashion by telling every girl that I think donut bikinis are the next big thing in swimwear. Every girl would go to the beach in fried dough. I'm so serious. The cultural capital imposed onto you if you're gay by stupid girls is incredible. It's why I don't tell anyone unless it comes up. I have no desire to revolutionize the world of fashion.

Finally, one of them says, "Yeah. In the kitchen there's punch."

"Sweet," Mark says. "Thanks."

"See, wish granted," I mumble. I can smell cologne already, hear the bellows of guys like Bret doing weird alpha male things in the house. I wonder if any of them are drunk enough to stumble yet.

"You have any wishes?" Mark asks.

"Ummm..." I think, dragging my hand through my hair and cutting across the lawn instead of taking the paved walkway to the door. The planters smell like manure. I scan the bushes for barf splatters, but it's still pretty early in the night. "Dunno. World peace."

Mark cracks up. We go inside.

The summer I was ten was the last summer I was skinny. It was also when I sucked dick for the second time.

There was a Little League tournament at Healy Field Park two suburbs over, and it was probably the hottest day of the summer. I was miserable at Little League and spent a lot of time warming benches or playing as far in the outfield as the coach could put me without getting charged for child negligence.

It was late in the afternoon, and I hated baseball. Sweat was running down the backs of my knees in rivulets, the red dust of the diamond would stick to me there. Between games, Mark and I ate ice to cool down. We didn't even have the energy to stick it down each other's shirts, it was so hot. Girls in short-shorts and white see-through tanktops would walk by, older sisters and stuff. Mark would follow them with his eyes but was too busy complaining about the heat to say anything about them. David Henry asked us if we were gay. Mark said, "He is," pointing to me with his thumb while he sucked Capri-Sun out of a pouch with the straw jammed in the bottom.

I don't remember why I was alone. Maybe I was walking to the bathroom or something. I just remember this kid in a baseball cap yelling, "Hey, you!" behind me. I didn't think he was talking to me until I felt his sweaty hand on my elbow. "Hey, you," he said again.

I turned around. He was around my age, some other Little League kid on some other team. He had a gap between his front teeth, brown freckles on his nose, and a Cubs baseball cap. I don't remember if I thought he was cute or not, it was too hot to think about cute guys. "What?" I asked him. There was sweat on his forehead.

"I heard you're gay," he said, like this was supposed to clear up why he was talking to me. I narrowed my eyes at him, figuring he probably overheard Mark in the dugout. I rolled my eyes. I was bad at baseball, and I wasn't athletic, but that didn't mean I couldn't fight. Mark and I wrestled on a fairly regular basis, and I came up victorious around fifty percent of the time, which isn't bad considering he was bigger than me. If this kid wanted a fight, I could fight. I preferred the Aaron Horning type of bully to the beat-up-gay-kids-at-Little-League-tournaments kind, but you didn't choose the type of bullies who found you and gave you a hard time.

"Yeah, so?" I asked him.

He grinned hugely. I stared at the gap. Then he leaned in and lowered his voice. "Have you ever sucked cock before?"

My eyebrows arched up. Not what I was expecting, here, in public, with little kids running around and whole families with baby strollers and coolers full of snacks. "Once," I told him.

"Did you like it?" he asked. He started walking with me. I didn't know where I was walking at that point, wherever I had been planning to go was forgotten, and now I was just walking to get my legs moving, to get away from the teeming bleachers where people could hear us. I was excited. My heart was in my throat. We walked to a clump of trees hidden from the field.

"Yeah," I said. "It was weird, sort of scary. But I liked it."

"I sucked dick once, too. My babysitter's boyfriend slept over, when I was a kid. He sucked mine, and I sucked his," the kid whispered, even though we were out of earshot, his Coke-sweet breath on my face. I swallowed, a sick kind of desire coiling up in my belly. My face was suddenly hotter than the rest of me, which was remarkable, because I was pretty much melting.

"Did you like it?" I asked, dry-mouthed.

"I liked getting my dick sucked. I didn't like doing it to him, though. It tasted weird, and when he jizzed, it choked me. I kind of threw up. It was gross."

I shivered. I didn't think that was gross. "Do you want me to suck yours?" I asked quietly, my hands shaking, preteen dick hard in my baseball pants. I had totally forgotten about my Little League game. My coach had probably forgotten about me, too, so it didn't matter too much. "You don't have to do it to me."

"That's what I was gonna ask you." He grinned.

"Let's go to the playground," I said, swallowing. "I can do it in the tunnel. No one would see."

He shrugged, gesturing to the grass under our cleats. "I don't think anyone can see us here, either. There were trees. No one would notice, especially if I lie down."

I nodded. "Yeah. Okay. Lie down."

The kid, whose name I never got or don't remember, clambered awkwardly down onto the grass and unbuttoned his white pants with the red dirt smudges on the knees, then pulled his dick out. It was small and brown and hairless, sticking to the skin of his thigh sweatily. I peeled it off, feeling its dark, hot weight in my palm. It twitched, got a little harder. I leaned down over his lap and made my tongue soft and flat to lick over the tip. He tasted like salt.

His head fell back, and he said, "Feels good. Sick."

I didn't say anything, just opened my mouth wide and slid down as far as I could. His whole dick and balls fit into my mouth. He smelled strong and sweaty and musky, the way my underwear smelled after PE. I liked it, even though it was gross. He thrust into my mouth a little bit, making these high-pitched whining noises while I lapped at him. "Move your tongue more," he told me.

I felt like a cat drinking milk out of a saucer or something, my tongue curled and my hair in my face while I licked him, sweat dripping down from my scalp. My own dick was achingly hard in my pants, so I ground my hips into the dirt to relieve the pain of it a little.

"Now!" the kid yelled, and suddenly we weren't alone anymore. A bunch of boys shot out of the trees to our left, cackling and pointing and screaming, "Faggot!" The kid I was sucking off shoved out from underneath me, pants around his knees while he rolled around in the grass laughing hysterically. I was dazed and turned on and confused as to why everyone was laughing at me and not him. I mean, I had his dick in my mouth, but he had my mouth on his dick. That was at least as faggoty as what I was doing. I probably was supposed to be embarrassed. Instead, I was just mad that I had to stop sucking cock. I stood up, knees shaking. I glared at him, because he had most definitely been enjoying it, and here he was, betraying me. I could see a little glint of shame in his eyes, but I might have only seen it because I wanted to.

"Look at his boner!" one of the kids screamed, pointing to my tented pants. I looked down, too. Dry grass clung to my shins and cleats. It was oppressively hot.

"He loved it! It was giving him a boner!"

"What a faggot!"

They all laughed. I stared at them. I knew this whole thing was supposed to be funny, I knew I was supposed to be humiliated, but all I could feel was the frustration of my dick wilting. I thought about how violently Mark would tear through this crowd of idiots if he were here. Then, I realized I was crying. Big surprise. Crying was never something I had a lot of control over.

I ran away, because that's the only thing to do when you're crying in front of a group of kids who are laughing at you and you don't know how to fight.

That was the last summer I was skinny. I became known the following school year as "that skinny fag" by the other kids and "the child sexual predator" by their parents. There were so many stories circulating about how I would make boys take their pants off and trick them into letting me molest them that parents didn't want their kids to be in the same class as me. There were three boys removed from my class and put into other schools that year and five girls (which is completely fucking absurd). My parents cried a lot.

Everyone knew about that Little League tournament and what happened there, or at least some stupid fucked up version of it, but there was no formal evidence that it was me because the other boys wouldn't come forward. It became rumor, legend. People whispered about me, and I never got invited to birthday parties anymore. People said things like, "I always knew that Jake boy was...off." Mark was the only one who stuck with me, because he loved the drama of having a controversial best friend.

In short, sixth grade was miserable. I couldn't change that I sucked that kid's dick. It happened, and it wasn't proven, but people knew what I looked like. They knew I played Little League that summer, they knew I was skinny, that I never talked about girls. I couldn't change most of that.

But I *could* gain a ton of weight. That's when I started binge-eating. Then, if people were like, "Have you heard about that gay kid in the sixth grade? If you fall asleep, you'll wake up with his face between your legs. No joke. I heard his name was Jake. And that he's skinny," then whoever they were talking to would say, "Jake? I know Jake. He's kind of faggy, but he's not skinny."

It was easy because I was kicked out of Little League and had nothing else to do but sit around my house, stuffing my face. Funyuns, Fritos, Nilla Wafers, Wheat Thins. Nabisco rivaled Mark as my best friend. All that shit about being sad and eating your feelings by downing a pint of Dryers? It's true. Can't complain. The pantry and everything in it was always there for me. I widened, softened.

Getting chubby kind of helped but not as much as I wanted it to. Plus, being fat made people hate me for other reasons, which made me hate myself. I figured that things would change once I was out of elementary school. Middle school seemed bigger, more promising. Like it wouldn't be such a big deal to suck dick. Like there would be lots of guys who wanted to have their dicks sucked. I hadn't figured out yet that everything in the universe was made up of the same shit with different names.

I'm standing against the wall in Bret's ritzy living room just kind of watching everyone be stupid. There are the junior varsity girls in sweatpants with spray tans and messy blonde ponytails, laughing hyena-loud with their red cups in hand. Then there are the neon girls, with their reflective American Apparel type bralets under the blacklight glow of white wife-beaters, glowsticks around their necks, booty shorts riding up between their ass cheeks, shutter shades pushed into their hair. I'm watching all the different breeds of girls flit around, acting stupid and making the guys act stupider, when this kid passes in front of me. He has freckles on his nose and a gap between his two front teeth. Most kids I know have parents who care a lot about tooth-gaps and pay to get that shit fixed with braces but not him. If he had been like most kids I know, I might not have recognized him.

But he isn't, so I do.

I imagine him five years younger, freckles on his nose, smelling like Big League Chew and puberty sweat. My hand, without the rest of me consenting to it, shoots out and lands on his built shoulder. "Dude," I say.

He stares at me blankly, eyes bloodshot and hazy with whatever he's smoked. He stumbles. "Uh, hey?"

I let him go, shaking my head. The inside of my mouth tastes salty with memories, and I smell the sun baking the grass golden, even though there is no sun and no grass anywhere. "Sorry," I tell him as he leaves, a line through his forehead. "Just thought I knew you."

One of the neon girls strips down to her orange safety-cone-colored bra and teal underwear and is dancing on the bar. And by dancing, I mean undulating her hips in the general direction of some guy's face. Everyone is clapping and cheering, and her cheeks are flushed visibly, even in the dark. I watch her ass swing back and forth like a pendulum. I try to get hypnotized by it. Instead, I get a little motion sick.

When people live their lives, they don't stop much to analyze what they're doing and why they're doing it. The world moves too fast, and people are too busy hanging on by their final strand of sanity to take a break and wonder what the fuck is going on. At least, I don't. I just plug on through, so bored that I feel barely alive. It's crazy how everything can hurtle on so fast that stopping seems impossible, but at the same time, all I feel is empty.

Occasionally, I have these moments where I move in slow motion. Where the train stops at a station and the conductor tells the passengers they have time to go outside for a smoke. To reflect on what's happening. To ask why they're bored while they watch all the trains full of other bored people slam by in blurs.

As I watch the neon girl's boyshorts ride up inside the crack of her smooth, tan ass, thinking about Heasley Field grass sticking to my kneepads and stubby preteen dick in my mouth, everything stops. The laughter and cat-calls sound underwater. The bass in the music slows down to a heartbeat. I feel like I'm in a womb in Bret's kitchen, a womb full of whales all making whale noises at their dancing whale goddess. She kicks down a red cup full of something brown and fizzy, and it falls like a slo-mo reel of a waterfall in some new-agey video about finding yourself or something. The whales roar.

I have time to think, *What the hell am I doing? What have I done with my life? What am I going to do with my life? Am I going to lust after unattainable, stupid jocks forever? Am I going to go to parties to perv all over the puke potential my whole miserable adulthood?*

Neon-girl's tits come out of her bandeau and jiggle like a platter of watergate salad. Her face changes into a perfect, terrified O, and all the guys' eyes widen. The whales become deafening. I guess this is what an out-of-body experience is like.

What the hell am I doing? I think.

The whale roar answers *absolutely nothing*.

———

At our end of eighth grade class party, Mark tried to kiss me. It was as traumatizing as it was masturbation-worthy.

The party was held at this women's club in one of the dinky, ritzy suburbs nearby. The kind that's basically a beach town with no beach but has stores full of ridiculous spinning lawn decorations and gardening garbage, art galleries, boutiques with toe rings and hemp necklaces, stupidly expensive coffee shops with trendy coffee-pun names. Mark and I walked there wearing the suits we wore last year for my cousin's wedding. Lots of old ladies told us how cute we were, then we pretended to puke in the hedges once they were gone.

The party itself was extremely under-chaperoned, which led to most of the things that made it interesting. Someone, I don't know who, spiked the punch. Mark took this as an opportunity to drink almost all of it. He just stood there, in his too-small suit because he had a growth spurt that year, ladling himself paper cup after paper cup full of spiked punch. A true opportunist.

Naturally, kids started acting stupider than usual. Someone started a cake fight on the lawn by smashing a nice, sugary slice right between Ali McDonell's tits. Ali wasn't the scream-and-run-away type, so she fought back, and pretty soon, half the grade was running around throwing cake at each other. The chaperones were near tears, but there was nothing to be done about it, because inside, they had bigger problems, and they were outnumbered.

Seventh grade was when people first started experimenting with kissing. I remember hearing a lot of whispers about it, *Mary Pat likes Duane, and after school, they're gonna meet at the flagpole and do it.* And do it, in seventh grade, meant kiss. And kiss meant pucker up, peck, and run away giggling. It wasn't much when it started.

But over the course of the last year, the kisses got bigger and wetter and grosser, and pretty soon, after ten p.m. at middle school dances, teachers would have to run around with little flashlights and break up all the couples making out on the dance floor. It was disgusting. I never made a habit of attending middle school dances, but from what I remember, everyone looked like wild dogs fighting over the last scrap of gazelle with their tongues.

By the time the eighth grade end of the year party rolled around, they were all experts in chaperone evasion, and the kissing was just a precursor to the new sheriff in town: handjobs. Everyone was talking about handjobs. Who had given a handjob to whom, whose dick was big, whose hands were soft, and on and on and on. Eight grade became a handjob race. Who could get the most handjobs. Who could get the most girls to give them a handjob.

At the front of this race was Mark, with seven girls and thirteen handjobs, because Natalie Hiddlebrook was a handjob master, and she and Mark sometimes carpooled together, which allowed them precious time in the backseat for her to bestow him with six separate handjobs on six separate occasions.

Everyone else was pissed that Mark was so far ahead of them in the handjob race, so once the cake started, everyone inside the women's center got busy whipping it out. There was the main banquet room with the punch and the empty floor where people were supposed to be dancing, but a few doors led to a promising realm beyond that, bathrooms and hallways and a creepy industrial kitchen with knives hanging from a metal rack on the ceiling.

People scattered once the chaperones ran outside to inflict a cake ceasefire. I stood there, awkwardly, wanting neither a handjob nor a suit smeared with icing. Trying to occupy myself, I poured a cup of punch from the dredges of the bowl Mark had formerly annihilated. I took a sip and wrinkled my nose, because it tasted how I would imagine nail polish remover to taste, only fruitier. After a few minutes of thundering rap music in a mostly empty room and acetone poisoning, Mrs. Dillert rushed in, face red and flustered, usually neat gray bun coming undone in flyaways. There was a little smudge of frosting on her blazer. "Jake," she said, sounding way more panicked than I have ever heard a teacher. "Where did everyone go? Did you see them leave?"

"I don't know, Mrs. Dillert," I lied, not wanting to be responsible for the premature end of the handjob race.

She paused and laid her hand on my shoulder for a moment. "You're a good boy, Jake," she said.

I stared at her, wide-eyed, because she had no idea what I thought about at night or what I got up to on that beach in Hawaii. Then she squeezed me with painted talons and rushed off into the hallways to bust the racers.

In girl-boy pairs, like animals coming off Noah's Ark, kids started emerging, giggling, suits and dresses in various states of disarray. Then, Mark barged onto the dance floor, looking distressed and very alone. He saw me, then grabbed my shoulders. "Dude," he whispered, very seriously. "Come to the bathroom with me."

Of course, I thought he was gonna tell me some sordid details about his latest few handjobs, like he was gonna compare techniques or something. So when he locked the door behind us and then grabbed me and tried to kiss me *on the mouth,* I actually fell down, onto the floor, on my ass. "What are you *do-*

ing?" I sputtered, wiping my lips repeatedly on my suit jacket sleeve to try and get rid of any remaining Mark-taste because who knows what that sensory information would do to my delicate late-night psyche.

He crouched down in front of me. "Duane is one handjob ahead of me," he explained breathlessly. "And the teachers are coming up and breaking the guys and the girls apart. So I gotta stay in the race." He reached for me again, and I shoved him off.

"So you found *me?* What the *fuck*, dude," I panted, sitting on my hands so he wouldn't try and stick his dick into them.

"What's your problem? I thought this would be, like, a dream come true for you or some shit."

"Uh, *no*. Just because I'm gay doesn't mean I want to give you a handjob in a bathroom at the frickin' women's center. There are, like, a hundred people outside probably--"

"Is this because we're best friends? Do you think that makes it weird? Because I think it's less weird that way."

I stared at him, because he clearly had no idea what he was doing to my brain. "Dude. Find someone else, I am *not* gonna jack you off."

Mark sighed a huge, complaining sigh, then sat back on his haunches, rolling his blue eyes. "Jake, you're the prudiest gay guy ever. I'm pretty sure any other guy would already have their hand on my dick," he whined. "I'm gonna lose the race now."

I thought about it, for a second. About what might happen if I caved and jacked Mark off, in this bathroom, at this party with all the smashed cake outside on the lawn, in the rosebushes. Would he freak out later? Probably not. Would I? Maybe. What did it matter if the reason I got to jack Mark off was because he was trying to win a race, rather than he actually wanted me like that? It's not like those unique circumstances would ever arise. This was probably the only chance I would ever have just to touch him like that. I could. I could do it.

Instead, I shoved him. The train blasted right by me, making my hair lash across my face in the residual wind. "Get up. You are such an asshole."

I borrow Evan's car to get home because Mark is way too shitfaced to walk that whole way. I haul him into the front seat, buckle him up because I know he can't do it himself, and then I shut the door, hoping to fucking Baudelaire he doesn't puke in Evan's front seat. "How are you feeling, dude?" I ask him, eyes flicking over to him in time with my left turn signal.

He doesn't answer my question, instead he slurs, "Tiffany is *succhh* a fuckin' cocktease."

"Oh. Maybe you two can start a club," I offer, because I can tell he won't remember this tomorrow.

"Shuddap, I'm not like that. It's not like that," he says.

"Yeah, okay," I say, rolling my eyes. He keeps trying to sit up but keeps not being able to. I know I can't bring him to his own house because his dad will probably break his nose. I think about how much fucking work it would be anyway to drag him up the stairs. So I drive on autopilot to my house.

Pulling into the driveway, I steal glances at Mark's almost-passed out profile. He's breathing weird, heaving like he's run up the stairs, brow creased and lips slack and parted. I hate him for being beautiful, even bathed in streetlamp and smelling like a distillery.

"Mark. Wake up."

"M'wake," he whines.

I park in front of my house, kill the engine, and sit behind the wheel for a few seconds, rubbing my temples, psyching myself up for the task of bearing most of Mark's weight while we stumble up the lawn and through the door.

"Dude. Tiffany--"

"Is such a cocktease. I know. You told me."

He's a mess right now. Totally out of control. Blackout. I could tell him everything. The truth. Versions of it. *Hey, dude. I'm in love with you. Or, I'm not actually in love with you, I've just been sexually obsessed with you for what feels like the last decade, even though you're incredibly shallow and stupid and sleep with even shallower and stupider girls. But yeah. I think about you when I jack off, when I puke, which are so closely related that I don't even know which is which anymore. You. Your face, your dick, the insides of your stomach on my floor. It will probably go away once I leave this fucking suburb, once I get out and meet real guys in the real world. Or maybe it won't. Maybe it is real love. Maybe this is what real love is–your face, your dick, the insides of your stomach on my floor.*

"Hey, Mark," I say, leaning over his body slumped like a corpse in the passenger side and unbuckling his seatbelt with shaking hands. "What if I was in love with you. What would you do?"

Even though he's barely human right now, I still feel a weird pang of terror in my gut as I say it. I watch him rolling his head back and forth over the headrest, eyes shut.

"I *never* cared that you were *gay,* dude. Slike, never. Homphobia...that shit is *shit,* man. Mthrfuckers," Mark says unintelligibly.

I nod, heart slowing. "Yeah, okay. Time to get you inside."

Mark weighs around eight hundred pounds when he's drunk. I buckle under him, then right myself clumsily. He tries to tell me he can walk, and we argue about it for a while, until we agree that he *can* walk, barely, but he still needs help. I stand under his arm, bearing four hundred of his eight hundred pounds while he hobbles up to my front door. I unlock it, and we thunder as quietly as we can (or at least *I* strive for silence) through the hallway and into my room.

Finally, I'm watching Mark collapse onto my bed like an avalanche, my shoulder aching, lungs heaving. He rolls around for a while, trying to kick off his shoes but instead just kicking the air, my desk, my desk chair. He looks like a beetle on its back, legs flailing. "Just stop," I say, grabbing his dirty, tattered chucks and yanking them off. "Don't hurt yourself."

"You're thbest," he slurs as I take his belt off, cringing and trying not to look at his stomach too much, the pale skin and its dusting of dark hair.

"You suck," I tell him. I leave him there lolling around like a slug on the bed and trump to the bathroom, stripping down to boxers and my t-shirt and brushing the sour taste out of my mouth. I splash cold water on my too-warm face, comb my fingers through my hair to smooth it back. I can do this. I think about the futon in the hallway closet, I think about dragging it into my room so I can sleep on the floor and not worry about my body brushing against Mark's all night. But I'm exhausted, and my shoulder still hurts from Mark's eight hundred pounds of drunk. The last thing I want to do is lug that heavy-ass futon in here.

Trying to believe I don't have ulterior motives, I climb into bed next to Mark, who is quiet and sprawled out and radiating heat. I wonder if he's passed out until he turns to me, horrendously boozy breath hitting my face like a sucker punch. I cough so loud I don't hear what he says, but he says something. Then he starts taking off his shirt.

"What are you doing," I say, inching away, alarmed. His eyes are half-lidded, and he's pulling his shirt so far up I can see ribs, then pink, girly nipples. "Do you need help?" I ask, voice miraculously free of panic, even though my insides are knotting up.

He shakes his head, then reaches over with a clumsy, heavy palm, touches the side of my face. I jerk away. "Are you trying to *kiss* me?"

"Dude. Just let me."

"Uh, *no.*" This all seems very familiar. My stomach flips over, and I wiggle away on the narrow bed. "Please don't try and seduce me. You're, like, five minutes away from puking."

"But you're in love with me, you said it," he mumbles, trying in vain to get out of his pants. It's outrageously pathetic. I push him away, easily blocking his half-assed advances with my forearm.

"Seriously dude. Stop. I'm not going to have sex with you," I tell him, very seriously.

He pouts. Like, actually pouts. Pushes his lower lip out like a little kid, making it plump and biteable. I want to smack his face so hard that my whole palm itches for it. "Come on. When's last time you e'en got *laid?*" he mumbles.

I roll my eyes, arms braced out in front of me, blocking his stupid grabbing hands. "It's not gonna happen. Stop trying." He gags a little bit, sputtering and scrunching his face up, swallowing whatever just came up. It's really hot, but he doesn't know I think that.

"See? You're gonna puke. You can't fuck me if you're gonna puke."

"Not gonna puke," he says. He's managed, by some incredible mixture of luck and determination, to get most of his torso out of his shirt and starts in on his pants, fumbling miserably with the button.

"Like hell you're not," I say. I wonder how many times I've busted a nut to the fantasy of Mark puking in my bed. Too many. I run to the kitchen to get a paper bag before the Hoover Dam explodes. When I come back, he's got his flaccid dick out. "Oh, *come on,* Mark*,*" I groan. "You're unbelievable."

"Just look at me naked. I'll feel, like, *so much better,* if you just look at me naked, dude." He coughs, his face red and the whole room smelling like I spilled a beer somewhere. He looks so stupid and uncomfortable and drunk that my dick can't really take it. "Gimme that bag."

"Oh my god." I know I can't just hand Mark the bag because he's not coordinated enough right now to puke in it effectively. I can't deal with cleaning up his puke, the boner will be unbearable, so I opt for the only slightly less sexy version of this scenario where I stand next to my bed, a fist in Mark's hair holding his head were it needs to be so he can hurl up all the beers he drank. He makes the worst, best, most out-of-control animal noise and pukes. It's mostly fluid, tinted a little pink with floating white food and dissolving Adderall bits in it. I run to the bathroom while he's wiping his mouth and apologizing like a fucking idiot so I can grab the trashcan, because this puke is so wet it's gonna soak through the bag.

Everything smells like acid and booze. I can see Mark's dick, Mark's skinny hairy legs and his skinny hairy chest and his blue eyes wide and bloodshot and crying because he's puking so much the tears are just streaming down his red cheeks. I love it when guys cry when they puke. My heart is beating so hard that the whole world can hear it, and my hands shake wherever they're touching Mark on his stupidly naked body.

"I'm so sorry, Jake," he chokes, then alcohol pours out of his mouth and nose like he's a three-spigoted vomit faucet. My erection has a life of its own, painful and throbbing under the pressure of my boxers and jeans.

"There are no words for how much I hate you right now," I tell him, voice scaring me it's so low, so husky. The puke keeps splattering onto my hands. I imagine it leaving little chemical burns, blisters making me remember all the things I want but can't have. Or want but won't let myself have, because maybe things have to be real in order for me to actually want them. But this, this is a fiction. I might be in love with Mark, but he sure as hell is not in love with me. He doesn't even want to fuck me, in spite of his valiant and unending efforts. He's just an answering machine. A wind-up toy.

Mark's hair is greasy in my palm. "I know," he sputters. "I'm sorry." He sits up, shaking and wet and smelly but temporarily done puking. Then he leans in and kisses me with his foul mouth. "M'sorry," he says between kisses that taste like licking the floor of a bar, terrible and perfect. "M'sorry."

I let it happen for as long as it takes me to come in my pants under the pressure of my palm, then I shove him off. "Seriously. You have to stop," I say breathlessly, shoulder buckling under the weight of self-hatred. I remember the whales. *What the hell am I doing? Nothing.*

Mark doubles over, then blows another gallon of puke into my trashcan.

———

Ever since I kind of told Mark I was gay, he's been coming over after school at least once a week to watch gay porn on my computer. I don't even know how it happened. In retrospect, I feel like at some point I should have recognized that his porn watching at *my* house in *my* room on *my* computer and occasionally even in *my bed* was becoming a pattern, but the weirdness of it all didn't hit me until it was too late. It would have seemed unfair to tell him after a whole year of habitual indulgence, "Hey, dude. Can you do that, like, somewhere less confusing for me?"

I had already missed my window of opportunity, as per usual. Mark had established in his stupid, mysterious brain that coming over and watching porn at his gay best friend's was a perfectly acceptable thing to do. And not even the typical stuff with the bottle-blonde girls with tits like someone shoved a pair of basketballs under their skin, the ones who make the gross cat-in-heat noises while they take it up the ass from some huge buff dude. That would have at least made sense, because I assumed Mark was the kind of guy who got off on those types of alien broads and their meows.

Instead, he watched raunchy shit with leather daddies and BDSM. The beefier, brawnier, and hairier the guys were, the more they beat each other up, the longer it held his attention. It was too weird to talk about.

The Tuesday after the whole confessional sleepover, we rode our bikes to the park, like usual. Then once we got bored of spitting drinking fountain water out at each other and trying to seduce the soda machine into giving us its change, we went back to my place. Mark plopped down in front of my computer, like usual. Before the porn thing, he would use my internet to play these dumb flash games on even dumber sites. His favorite was this one called Kitten Cannon or something equally repulsive, where you shoot kittens out of a cannon, and said kittens are further propelled by hitting strategically placed bombs. It's one of those games where nothing changes. Mark could sit there paying it forever, just staring at the screen. He didn't even laugh, just shot flash-animated kitten after flash-animated kitten.

But this time, instead of kittens, he found some free-streaming porno site. I raised my eyebrows but didn't say anything, because it wasn't like I was *opposed* to porn. I still found it fascinating and exciting, even the meowing basketball-tit type, because I was a kid, and sex was still mostly an imagined thing, somehow separate from otter-pop man in that bathroom in Hawaii. I rolled over onto my stomach and slithered to the floor, scooting up so I was sitting at Mark's feet, watching.

There were a bunch of little thumbnails of orange skin and huge, purple cocks. It wasn't sexy, but my eyes were watering anyway. He typed in "gay" to the search engine. My gaze snapped up toward him and his impassive, bored-looking face. My computer thought about it for a few seconds, then presented us with a new set of videos. Same orange skin, same huge dicks. Just the absence of tits this time. It was a bunch of twink-looking guys with really round asses and shaved balls.

"You like this stuff?" Mark asked, looking at me.

I shrugged. "I dunno. Not really." I wasn't sure what I meant, if I was implying I didn't like porn in general, or if I didn't like twinks, or if I didn't like that Mark was looking up twink porn *on my computer while my parents were home.* I also didn't really know what I liked. I liked Abercrombie model type guys but not ones who looked like girls, with the skinny legs and no body hair. And I liked Mark, who didn't look like anyone but himself because unlike most other hot guys, he was a real person. Maybe.

My face was hot and my palms were sweaty. I didn't say anything. He did a new search, and the guys who came up were thicker this time, with beards, tattoos, enormous biceps. Some of them were wearing things that looked like oxen harnesses. I definitely didn't like this any more than I liked the twinks, but Mark snorted, grinning. The videos had titles like, "Straight Jock Takes Bear Daddy Bareback" and "Bryce Brooklyn Gets Pissed In."

Mark didn't ask me if I liked it, he just picked one. "Awesome," he said. There was a kind of chubby dude wearing a black hood on a motel bed and a hairy body-builderish guy behind him with a monster cock and a chest tattoo of a flaming skull. He palmed the hose between his legs and said a bunch of filthy shit about the other guy taking his rod up his little goat hole. Goat hole. *Goat hole.* I was horrified. Mark was delighted. He cracked up.

"This is hilarious," he said. Then he turned to me. "Don't you think this is hilarious?"

I nodded, eyes wide. "Yeah," I said stupidly, because it was obviously what Mark wanted to hear, and if I gave him what he wanted, maybe he would stop, and we could go back to doing something less awkward. Hell, I would have actually *preferred* that he play Kitten Cannon instead of this. *Fuck my hole, daddy*, the dude in the hood said. *Fuck my tight asshole, oh yeah. Make me your little goat boy.*

Goat boy.

"Oh, man," Mark said, kid-at-Christmas smile plastered on his face.

I kept waiting for him to laugh again or make fun of me. Instead, he just sat there, totally into it. I let my eyes skitter down to his lap for a second to see if he was sporting wood, but he wasn't. Or not that I could tell. He was just sitting there, staring at the grainy video of this buff dude fucking this chubby dude, then licking his hairy, gaping, well-fucked asshole. Mark watched with as much investment and interest as he had when he was playing stupid flash games or watching not-porn movies with me. His blue eyes blinked occasionally, but he didn't say anything. Once the movie was over, he just clicked a new one. Two more guys popped up, both ripped dudes with curly hair on their chests. They were making out with so much tongue that some drool was dripping down one's chin.

"Gross," I said. I couldn't help it.

"Yeah," Mark agreed, but he kept watching.

"Um, I'm gonna make some noodles. You want some?" I asked him, trying desperately to derail the porn train.

He shrugged. "Yeah. Just not the shrimp ramen. I hate the shrimp ramen."

"Shrimp-*flavored*," I corrected him. Usually, this got a laugh out of both of us, but he just nodded dismissively. Buff beardo number one was bending buff beardo number two over the arm of this scary-looking metal table contraption, groping his hairy ass so hard that I could see the white, bloodless fingerprints even though the video quality was shitty and pixelated.

One hour and two bowls of cold, uneaten chicken-*flavored* ramen later, Mark was still watching gay porn in a haze of weird, rapt impassivity.

"Dude!" I finally said, exasperated, bored to tears on my bed and nauseous from an hour's worth of grunts and moaning and the word *daddy*. "Can we, like, do something else?"

"Oh, yeah. Sure," Mark said, eyes still fixed on the guys going at it like bunnies in some concrete dungeon. "Whatcha wanna do?"

I don't remember what happened after that. I'm sure I managed to drag him away from the vortex of hairy man-sweat and beard dollops of jizz like mayonnaise, and I'm sure we went to the park or something. I probably thought that the hours of porn was some incidental mishap, and it would never happen again.

But then Friday rolled around, and Mark's dad was always a douche on Fridays, because the next day was Saturday, which he had off, so he could drink himself stupid. Mark usually came over to avoid having to deal with his drunk dad. Typically, we played Wii or stole a few bucks from my (also Friday-drunk) mom's purse for boba tea, which we didn't actually like, but enjoyed shooting out through the straw at our neighbor's windows before running away. I assumed that this would be a Friday like any other Friday, full of petty crime and video games and general despairing preteen boredom.

I was wrong. After school, we came back to my house. I went to take a piss, and when I came back, Mark was already plopped down in front of my computer like Jabba the Hutt, the room filled with deep, guttural moaning.

Thus began the habit. We never really talked about it, and sometimes weeks would go by where he wouldn't do it, and I would wrongly rejoice that it was the end of a strange era. But then he would surprise me again, queue up one of his favorites, "Barker Bison and Marco Macro double team ska8ter boi," or the truly vile, "Stud gets humiliated by busload of DILFs," which featured (to my dismay) a young, hairless teenage twink blindfolded and face-fucked by a bunch of hairy older dudes until he was gagging that thick, clear, pre-puke fluid I knew so well onto their dicks.

The veneer of it being a humorous activity wore off months ago, and Mark stopped asking me if I thought it was funny, but he also stopped laughing. He would just *watch* quietly, for *hours.* I sometimes would leave for a while to do other stuff, finish homework or shoot hoops or frantically scarf up whatever leftovers I could find in shameful clandestine solitude, and when I'd return, he would still be at it. Sometimes in my *bed*, with the covers up to his chin. "Are you jacking off?!" I'd ask, incredulous.

Then he'd look at *me,* like *I* was the crazy one and say, "No. Dude. Why would you think *that?"*

I missed Kitten Cannon. The banality of boyhood, *Newgrounds* and dumb viral videos. I missed understanding my best friend. Because the thing is—maybe the habit meant something about Mark, or maybe it didn't. Maybe it was some huge metaphor for growing up. Maybe metaphor wasn't something that happened in real life. Maybe Mark was secretly somebody's goat boy. Maybe he secretly wanted to be mine. But probably not.

———

When Mark finally passes out half-naked in my bed with booze-puke in his hair, I don't even know who I am anymore. All the things I tell myself every day so that I don't fall into the disgusting loops of human behavior I abhor, eating and fucking and shitting and dying slowly, breath by breath, in love with my best friend I will never let fuck me, are gone from my brain. I can't remember them. I don't remember why I say them, why on earth it's *so important to me* on most days that I don't spiral down into the mess my body is magnetically drawn to if only because it's a body and that is its nature. I don't remember. I don't care. I don't care.

I have an erection again, even though I just shot a big sticky load in my pants already.

Staring at Mark, I zero in on the spot of foam in the corner of his open, kissed mouth, aching and jizz-damp between my legs. Fuck it all. I don't remember. I don't care. There is nothing in the world more important right now than emptying my rapidly filling balls again, and I'm so far past worrying about what kind of animal that makes me, or how shitty I'll feel afterward when I'm just a husk without its hormones and adrenaline and endorphins drowning the disgust and self-pity. I don't care. I don't care. I don't care.

I realize with a stark, aching clarity in this moment that I am *starving.* It's easy to miss the moment you hit rock bottom when your highs are comparatively higher than your lows but are still less than a standard deviation away from the mean or whatever. But here, with my hands shaking and the kitchen with its hollow promises of fleeting glory a few rooms away and everyone in my house dead to sleep, I physically feel myself hit absolute zero. Zero degrees Kelvin. At zero degrees Kelvin, all matter ceases to exist because it's so cold. That's where I'm at, where I've arrived.

Along with all the matter in the world goes my reason. My logic. My self-respect. My handwritten fictions that I am in control, that I'm the master over my own body, that I am *separate* from my own body, that I'm not in love with Mark, that I am somehow alive and beyond my flesh instead of a slave to it. I lose it all, and I don't care.

I stand on shaking legs. My eyes sting, and the whole room smells like a dive bar, acrid and fermenting with bile and beer. I lick my sour lips over and over again, suddenly resenting the vacant burn in my gut, the endless yawning of hunger, of loneliness. Of uselessly attempting to deny my humanity because it sickens me to know I'm not original. I wonder if that means it turns me on to know I am not original, because being sickened is the same as getting hard, for me. And that, even that, isn't original. Isn't me but merely a patchwork of my past, tatters of history and shed selves sewn together and dyed the same color. A shred from the bathroom in Hawaii, a shred from the Little League tournament, a shred from the food court outside the laser tag joint. But I don't care anymore, that I am a patchwork quilt of traumas and memories. I don't care. The temperature drops and drops and drops until matter ceases to exist, and I don't even have the worth left to hate myself as I stumble to the kitchen, mind made up with stoic resolve.

I don't remember how long it's been since I did this, but I'm long overdue. I open the fridge and survey what we have with stinging eyes. Everything feels surreal bathed in the glowing blue light that spills onto the linoleum like a manifestation of the divine. There's the leftover turkey chili. Some congealed oatmeal in a tupperware. The dregs of a potato salad, and although mayonnaise is not my first choice, because puking white things will always remind me of the time last summer I binged on vanilla ice cream and the puke was too cold and smooth to really get me off, it doesn't matter. I don't care. I take the container out, set it on the kitchen table. Then I get the tuna casserole from earlier in the week, some spaghetti, and a bag of wilted spinach for color, even though green things usually turn brown too quickly in the stomach to really keep their greenness, unless it's up as soon as it goes down, but I plan on holding it in for longer than that.

I pour myself a glass of orange juice while I toast a poppyseed bagel and rub my hard dick through my jeans with a sweaty palm, feeling the cooling strings of my last bust nut sticking to my thigh like Gorilla Glue. I don't care. I don't care anymore. My mouth waters in combined hunger and nausea, one and the same, arousal and expulsion, all or nothing. I choose all.

I sit down in front of my feast, sweat on my brow, wondering distantly if Mark has passed out for good, or if he's in danger of aspirating another torrential puke geyser in the near future, and then my wondering turns into whimpering, my dick twitching at the image. I don't care. I don't care. I spear some spaghetti with my fork. Twist until it's wrapped neatly around the prongs, gory red on white like blood on intestinal tubes if I squint, the American flag, someone's head bust open on a ski slope. I think about all this stuff, the shit you scrape off asphalt, America and blood and digestion. And then I start eating.

I'm not sure how long I stay in the kitchen. I'm not sure if anything tastes good, or tastes at all. All I know is that it's going inside of me, fork after fork, mouthful after mouthful, chew swallow chew swallow chew swallow swallow swallow until my throat burns. I demolish the tupperwares of spaghetti, potato salad, chili, the bagel (toasted, with butter), a handful of spinach, the glass of orange juice, and top it all off with a greasy, slice of un-nuked tuna casserole, corpse-cold.

Eating like this feels like jacking off. It has the same rhythmic build up, the same steady increase in intensity with a clear end, a climax, a purging, a storm.

The more I eat, the more it hurts, and the closer I am to this pinnacle. My body changes, twitches and grows and hurts, but I'll end it all soon. Everything will come out of me, the incredible relief, the feeling of losing everything, of getting smaller, of painting the tub tiles in concrete evidence that I am empty. I chew, swallow, chew swallow. Compulsively, desperately, until I can't anymore, stomach drum-tight and aching.

Bloated and stiff and unmoving, paralyzed by the pleasure of disgust, I stand up carefully, gut distended, and stagger to the bathroom. Lock the door. Grab my toothbrush, for old time's and irony's sake. Take off my jeans, my white cotton crew neck, my flannel overshirt. Sticky boxers, socks. Everything until I'm just my skin, loathed and inescapably mine. Pile the clothes on the floor, step over the pile, climb into the bathtub. Sit on my knees, sensitive, heavy erection in one hand, toothbrush in the other.

It's such a familiar ritual that I run on autopilot, images of Mark's watering eyes flashing through my head, his stomach concave and shaking beyond his will as he heaved and heaved. I slide the toothbrush down my throat, close to the tongue, like I'm fitting the final tab into the final slot and completing the model of my own perfection. It hurts. I gag. It echoes through the bathroom, and my mouth fills up with saliva. Sometimes I can puke on the first gag, other times, it takes multiple attempts. I prefer it when it's harder, when my eyes sting and my throat burns, when there's the thick snotty spit at first, streaks of color and food making it impure. I've forced myself to puke so many times before, though, that my body anticipates the action. Over the years, it's gotten harder and harder to prolong the gagging process. I start to purge, and suddenly I'm puking, coming, before I want to. Before I can tease myself and draw it out. It's not as satisfying that way, just like any time you come too fast. But it's been a while since I've purged this much food, so my flesh is confused. Nothing comes up at first, just my body wracked and wrecked and shaking.

I hack, and it feels wonderful. Like scratching the years-old itch in my throat. The one that never goes away. My free hand jerks my twitching dick, and saliva pours out of me in a hot, foaming sludge. Mouthful after mouthful of that thick, salty fluid. More and more, and then. The feeling of something coming *up*, the relief of a substance actually being *produced* from the labor of self-hatred. My eyes stream, and I choke up the beginnings of my binge onto my dick.

Not ready to come yet, I stop, just sitting there with puke, red and chunky and so minimally digested that I can still see the poppyseeds from my bagel dotting the mess like ants, slopped across my stomach, clinging to my pubic hair. Just a little, a half-cup maybe. There's still so much to come. I run my palms through it, pushing them through the hot slimy slickness. I think about Mark. I think about cute guys at parties, their burning eyes and throats as they cough beer into planters. I imagine my toothbrush is one of their dicks, and gag myself with it again. And I lose it.

There is so much food that it lines the bathtub with an inch of vomit, slip-slidey and fire-hot and acidic. I lay in it. Slop it up my arms, onto my thighs, into the rolls of my stomach. I make myself as gloriously disgusting and as untouchable as I feel. I wallow in it, get off on it. I think about how exciting it is that there is so much inside of me still to come out. It smells horrible, like canned tomato soup and old tuna. It steams. I keep coughing, keep crying, close the shower curtain all the way so I'm trapped with my own fumes, drowning in my own baseness. I think of Mark, and Mark, and Mark. Kissing Mark, tasting his recycled beer and bile on his tongue.

If I stop making noise and just sit there, jerking myself off with a palmful of hot, wet slickness, I can hear him snoring in my room. I think about how bored he looks when he watches porn, then gag and cough and spit and finally, as another sheet of puke comes bubbling forth from my lips, I come, shooting so far that it sticks to the opposite wall, below the shower head.

I watch my jizz, white and pearly and excessive, cling to the tile. I'm panting. The storm is over, and here is the calm. Absolute zero. The lowest, the coldest, the calmest, and I don't care. I don't care. I don't care.

But the thing about storms is once they're over, things seem quiet, perfect and peaceful. But then there's the damage. The bills and the insurance claims and the palm fronds and all the uprooted trees, lost pets, trash on the boardwalk. The world is a fucking mess after a huge storm. And then I realize that I'm still sitting in a bathtub full of my puke, and all the magic is gone from the substance. I suddenly *do* care. It comes flooding back into me. My humanity, my shame, my logic, my reason.

My skin cools. My vomit cools. I close my eyes in the pool of things cooling, and imagine getting so cold that I cease to exist.

———

A couple of years ago, I was purging and jacking it at the toilet in the middle of the night when my mom knocked on the door. I almost didn't hear it over the sound of my own moans and gags and stuff; after all, it was just a quiet, cautious rapping of her knuckles. But then, cutting through my fantasies like a fucking buzz saw, my mom's midnight-hoarse voice saying, "Jake? Sweetie, are you sick?"

Of course, I wasn't the kind of sick she thought I was. I was making myself sick, but I wasn't *sick* sick. But I didn't want her to know that. I panicked, spitting the last mouthfuls out and racing over my thoughts, trying to come up with something to say as my boner wilted in my fist like roses in the noonday sun. I was so seriously paranoid that she knew what I was doing, that by some miracle she could *tell* that my puking sounds were different, that it was sex-puking, not flu-puking. "Yeah," I croaked, as pathetically as I could muster.

"Oh, no," she sighed, playing the part of Concerned Mother she occasionally slid into when something especially catastrophic was happening. My mom liked to peace out for most of her motherly duties. Sarah practically lived at daycare and friends' houses, and I had a friend come over and watch porn for hours on my computer when I was in elementary school, and she never even noticed. I was allowed to run wild on a beach where I got molested in a public bathroom. She could win an award in Chronic Inattentiveness with Catastrophic Consequences, if such an award existed.

However, when I got food poisoning or broke a leg or got a D in school or something, she was suddenly Super Parent. Concerned or Firm or Strict in this way that made me want to ask, *Who are you, and where were you when I needed to be picked up from Little League? When I was sucking dick on the beach in Hawaii before my balls even dropped?* It made me wonder, *Why the hell should I ever listen to you?*

My dad, on the other hand, managed to cultivate skills on the opposite end of the spectrum in regards to parenting. He was artificially present for the mundane stuff, saying *hello* and *goodnight* and *don't be late, you'll miss the bus*. He was the one who half-attended back-to-school meetings while my mom drank with her pilates friends. He was the one who helped me with fractions and grounded me when the principal caught me cheating off Zack Anderson's math quizzes. But when something truly awful happened, he faded miraculously into the background, like he had never been there at all, like I had imagined him. He turned his phone off, or casually wandered out the door when one of us was seriously in trouble. The whole year of sixth grade when I was deliberately getting fat and everyone was calling me a child molester, even though I was a child? I don't even remember him living in the house. He went MIA. A ghost. He was a fair-weather parent, someone reading the Parent Script rather than actually parenting in real time.

You'd think that these bizarrely complementary parenting styles would have resulted in me feeling supported both in times of need and in times of not-need, but I don't remember being supported at all. Instead, I just felt abandoned when shit went down, chastised for petty kid-stuff. This was exacerbated by the fact that my mom always ended up playing her Concerned Mother role at particularly inopportune moments. Like when I had vomit drool running down my chin and a wilting boner in my hand.

I scrambled back into my sweats, wiping my mouth with my wrist. "I'm fine, mom," I said, my voice scraping through the air, sounding impossibly big and forbidden for the middle of the night at this private hour, during this private act. "You can go back to bed."

"Is it the flu? Maybe those leftovers were bad. They were from a few days ago…," Her voice trailed off, and for a brief blessed moment, I thought that she was going to leave. I listened hard for the sound of her retreating footsteps, but they never came. Instead, she fucking *opened the door.* This event marked the last time I ever left the door unlocked during one of my purge/masturbation sessions. Even when no one was home and I knew I was promised aloneness for at least a few more hours, I locked it. I never again wanted to see my mom with her sleep-creased face, her dyed blonde hair all messy and unstyled, her eyes swollen and squinty while she hobbled toward me in her sleazy silk bathrobe the color of red wine. It was embarrassing. For both of us.

"Jesus! Mom! I said I was fine," I yelled. I didn't mean for it to, but my voice came out angry. It bounced off the walls, reverberating in the tight tiled bathroom, ricocheting around us like a yoyo or one of those party favor rubber bouncy balls. She winced, and I did, too. "Sorry," I said, quieter this time, my voice hoarse from gagging. "I just. I said I was okay, and I am, can you *please* leave?"

Her eyes welled up, and my heart sank. My mom did this every once in a while, got really weepy and drunk-sentimental about what a bad parent she'd been my whole childhood and started crying about it, thus forcing me to take care of her while she acted like a bad parent yet again. Pat her on the shoulder while she drank and sniffled, said things like, *I tried my best, Jake, I really did, but you were such a difficult child, you pushed me away. You were so* cold, *sweetie.* I really, really did not want tonight to turn into one of those nights, so I stood quickly, washed my hands, rinsed my face without looking at her. "I'm really tired," I said. "You probably are, too. Um. You should go back to bed, in case it's contagious."

She looked at me, reached out and squeezed my shoulders with a shaky hand, standing close enough that I could smell her sleep and vodka breath.

"You're a good boy, Jake," she said after a moment. It didn't sound like a compliment coming out of her lips, it sounded like a dirge. A funeral march. Like she was saying her goodbyes before she tied me to a pyre and torched me like a virgin martyr or a witch of something. It reminded me of Mrs. Dillert, during the eighth grade handjob race. It made me feel like the same sort of invisible, the same sort of dirty underneath.

"Thanks, mom," I mumbled, flushing red, the feel of my dick still fresh on my washed hands, my throat still raw from vomiting. Thankfully, she wrapped her flimsy robe tighter around herself and left after that. No tears tonight. No reminders of how *cold* I was as a child, eating ice cream alone until my stomach hurt, and my teeth chattered, words slurring, numb tongue.

The clean-up process is incredibly laborious. My puke is thick enough there's no washing it down the drain, so before I shower, I need to move all hundred gallons of it from the tub to the toilet. I find an old, trusty plastic cup under the sink that I've employed for this purpose in the past. It's caked in soap scum, toothpaste blobs hardened onto it like barnacles on an undersea wreck, years' worth of plaque buildup. It's got some little Japanese character emblazoned on the side, a friend of Hello Kitty, the manly alternative that's acceptable for little boys to like. He's a black-and-white Snoopy-looking dog with a boombox, and the cup says ROCK!

Poor, pathetic Hello Kitty's friend goes into my puke, again and again. Dip, scoop, dip, scoop, dip, scoop, flush. I dump cup after cup into the toilet, red slop peppered in cooling, undigested spinach noisily splashing into the toilet water. Then, when it starts to mound up, I flush. The short tile pathway from tub to tank gets slippery with puke, footprints of it pooling underneath me, dripping down my naked, fat-scalloped legs. I try not to catch sight of myself in the mirror, a vast naked white whale, Captain Ahab's most favorite boy. Wet, stinking, shining.

After orgasming, everything hot about my vomit evaporates. It becomes gross, heavy, messy, irritatingly copious. Just another substance I have to hurriedly clean up before someone comes to check on me, woken up by countless repeated toilet flushes. At least this time, I have an excuse. If my mom with her stellar timing decides to actually Be a Mom tonight and comes knocking on my door, at least I have Mark as an excuse. Mark laid out in my bed, the trashcan full beside him. I can tell her he ralphed in the tub, too. I tried to stop him, but there's no stopping a volcano before it blows, you just have to let it erupt.

She'd probably get sad and tell me I was a good kid again. A good friend for taking care of Mark, making sure he didn't choke and die in a ditch somewhere. She's always liked Mark but thought he was a fuck up because of his alcoholic dad. It's funny, how alcoholics always hate other alcoholics.

Dip, scoop, dip, scoop, dip, scoop, flush. Puke sloshing in, then spiraling down, disappearing into the u-bend. All matter ceasing to exist. One cup after another after another, the cups plastic rim scraping the sides, Hello Kitty's dog friend's impassively beady black eyes smeared in stomach slime. Eventually, I clear the tub out enough that there's nothing but a red film and a few chunks clinging to the porcelain. I dump Mark's bag and trashcan into the toilet after the last scoops of mine, letting him dilute me, making the thick sludgy mess frothier, broken apart. Then, I flush us both down. Our mingled pukes, swirling down into the pipes, the sewer, washing out eventually into the ocean for fish to eat.

Once the last trace of it is gone, I use the detachable shower head to blast the remnants in the tub down the drain before rinsing myself off. Partially chewed bits of food stick in my pubic hair, between my rolls. One by one, they fall away, washing in rivulets down my legs to circle the grating before either disappearing or catching there. I wish it felt like a baptism. A purifying ritual, cleansing away my sins. But it doesn't. I feel just as dirty as I did before. I get out to mop up the slick pink footprints with wads of toilet paper, polish the floor until it shines.

Back in my room, Mark is snoring. I can still smell the faint whiff of beer even though I flushed his puke, the boozy bite hanging in the air and mixing with the lingering notes of high school party. Cologne, perfume, cigarette smoke, weed.

My body hurts. Every inch of it, inside and out. Stomach wrecked from twisting, throat raw from retching, back and neck sore from leaning over to clean. I spent so long making sure the crime scene was left spotless that the sun is already coming up, leaving the world beyond my window stained blue, chirrupy birdsong and the crash of faraway traffic ebbing and flowing like waves against a shore. I try not to think about what I'm doing as I crawl into bed next to Mark's sleeping body, the hectic heat of him touching me with clammy fingers. I just do it. I don't care, I don't care. I'm too achey to sleep on the floor, too worn out to even pretend I was ever gonna drag that futon in. I burn up in his sleeping heat, instead. Look at his profile in the beginnings of dawn light—big nose, frizzy curls, long eyelashes like a hatchet blade. His lips—the lips I finally let kiss me—are parted around the occasional wheezy snore. I imagine smothering him with a pillow. I imagine him throwing up again, a lazy burble that he would aspirate in, suffocate on. I imagine kissing him again like he's Sleeping Beauty, awakening him from some enchanted slumber. When he comes to, he'll love me back.

Sleep comes fast, after that. Drops like a guillotine blade, heavy blackness on my heavy body. I don't dream.

When I wake up, the world is beautiful. It's night again, somehow, and moonlight is filtering down to the yard in glittering silver rays. Mark stirs beside me, sitting up with a jolt and peering over my shoulder. "Hey, dude," he says, not sounding hungover at all. "Do you, like, want to go dance in the moonlight?"

Which is *crazy,* because it's exactly what I was thinking, too. I woke up with a real hankering to just do a moonlight boogie. Bolt outside and shake my hips and lift my hands up to the bright bounty of sky and thank the universe for being so goddamned *beautiful.* "Hell, yeah, I do," I say, launching out of bed. When my feet hit the floor, they don't slip on puke. They don't even hurt anymore, nothing hurts.

My body is brand new. My body is beautiful, because it's under the moonlight, it's on this Earth, this beautiful beautiful Earth.

Mark follows me, giggling. We're both giggling, giggling like schoolgirls, tittering away, big stupid grins plastered on our faces. I reach out and take Mark's hand for some reason, and he lets me. Or, I let him let me. We touch like it's not the end of the world. I become an opportunist, I won't let this train pass me by. I tug him out the door and into that crazy moonlight where we whoop and holler and crow like roosters, like Peter Pan. "God, the dirt is beautiful," he says, falling to his knees in my yard, ripping up fistfuls of squeaky, dew-damp grass. "I just want to, like. Fucking dig in it."

"Oh, my god, what? Me, too! Like I was just thinking about that," I say, voice too fast, too high. A helium voice, a little-boy voice. I should be self-conscious about that, but I'm not. I'm elated. Nothing can touch me. Not shame, not the memories of shame from when I actually was a little boy. "Let's dig some fucking holes."

"Yes! Yes, Jake, *god,* you're so smart. Let's dig some fucking holes," Mark says, sinking his fingers into the dirt. A cold, crumbly, black clod comes out in his fist, a worm's pink posterior wriggling, half-in, half-out. We laugh at that. We laugh at everything. Everything's funny when the world's so fucking beautiful.

We dig, and dig. Dip, scoop, dip, scoop. Dip hands in, scoop the dirt out. My nails are black half-moons, and so are Mark's. The clean tub and my dirty body seem far away, forgotten. Like a lifetime ago, and I can let them float out to sea easily. Every mortifying thing I've ever done, every mortifying thing that was ever done to me, falling off like fleas jumping ship on a corpse, hurling themselves into the holes we're digging. Dip, scoop, dip, scoop. Mark beside me, sharing a private smile, a dopey happy easy grin, like we understand each other, because we *do*. We're connected, now, bound by our shared realization that the world is so, so beautiful. Above us, UFOs glow and hover and rotate, casting us in their glorious blue light. I don't look up.

Acknowledgments

Massive thank you to my wonderful beautiful wife Blake, for witnessing the births of these stories, as well as their resurrections, and completions. She's seen them as their worst and ugliest, just as she has seen me, and I'm forever grateful for her steadfast and fearless companionship through every stage of my growth as a writer. I also would like to thank her for doing all of the fiddly formatting shit that makes me want to scream, and for loving my writing, and for loving me.

Thank you to Jen Stout, my dear friend and wonderful editor for making these stories legible, screaming in the google docs, and always bringing a bottle of gin when she visits. Thank you to my other guest lecturers as well: Sierra Merrill for walking me through so much of the self publishing process, Lanchi Le for providing a glimpse into the scary traditional publishing world, and Kaylie Allen for her eloquence and wisdom. And lastly, thank you to each and every one of my students who eagerly attended the lectures of BLOOD/INK/BONE and allowed me to share my love and passion for the craft of writing with you. Teaching you all motivated me to finish forgotten projects and put my own advice to good use, and I could not be more grateful for the learning experience we shared. Here's to further necromancy.

About the Author

Phoenix Mendoza lives in the woods where she raises pigeons and buries roadkill and writes. An unashamed enthusiast of the carnal, compostable, and corporeal, she is wholly dedicated to finding and luxuriating in the junction where beauty and disgust meet to rot together.

Printed in Great Britain
by Amazon